Books by Susan Day:

The Roads They Travelled

Who Your Friends Are

The Roads
They Travelled

Susan Day

Leaping Boy Publications

Published by Leaping Boy Publications
partners@neallscott.co.uk
www.leapingboy.com

Printed and distributed by Lightning Source UK Ltd.

A CIP catalogue record for this title is available
from the British Library.

ISBN 978-0-9935947-2-4

Main Characters

Singleton family:
Sadie
Wilf, her father
Ivy, her stepmother
Maurice, her half-brother

Bryce family:
Nell
Agnes, her mother
Edwin, her father
Eddie, her brother

MacNee family:
Marcie
Ronnie, her brother
Her mother
Her aunt

Swallow family:
Ginny
Kath
Maud, their mother
Will, their father
Billy, their brother

Jakimowicz family:
Zygmunt (Jack)
Josef, his father
Maryska, his mother
Blanka, Lena, Lisa, his sisters
John, Carolynne (Carrie), his children
Baba, Maryska's mother

Ted Doughty
His children: Rita, Theresa, Kay, Valerie, Tony

Hamish Farquhar
His children: Heather, Duncan

Gus Treasure
Eric Horns
Bernard Lynch
Roger Smith

Part 1

CHAPTER ONE
IN WHICH MILES ARE COVERED AND STORIES EXCHANGED

Here's Sadie Singleton wheeling her bike out of the alley and into the street. Squinting into the deep shadow on the other side she can see someone – a girl and a bike. Good, she thinks, Kath's out already, no hanging around. But as her eyes adjust to the shadow it's an unknown girl she sees, and she is looking at the door as if unsure whether she's at the right house. They both stand, not looking at each other, waiting for the other to make the first move. Then Sadie – it is her street after all – says, 'Are you looking for Ginny?'

The girl shakes her head. 'Kath?' As if not quite sure of the name.

'Oh Kath,' says Sadie. 'Have you knocked?'

The girl nods, her hair falls in her face and she tucks it back behind her ears.

'I'll knock,' says Sadie, and just then Kath opens the door, with her hair still wrapped up in a scarf.

'Hello Nell,' she says, looking over Sadie's shoulder. 'Won't be long. Looking for hairclips. Wait here.'

The girl moves out of the shade and sits down on the kerb. Sadie makes a face, nose twitching, lips thin. Now Kath's sister Ginny appears in the open doorway. 'Still here? I won't be long.'

'Is *she* coming?' says Sadie. Nell – still as a dog in the sunshine – barely shrugs as Kath reappears, apparently ready.

'Is *she* coming?' says Sadie again.

'I can't help it,' says Kath. Sadie watches her big face crumple up because she can't please everyone.

'Why don't we go?' says Sadie. 'She can catch us up if she wants to.'

Kath cheers up. 'I'll tell her.'

'Don't tell her,' shouts Sadie to her back. 'Let's just go.'

'It will be all right,' says Nell. Sadie makes the face again. It was supposed to be just her and Kath today, but first this Nell has been brought in, and now Ginny, and Kath hasn't even hinted at, Do you mind? or, If it's all right with you. Whose outing is it? Sadie would like to say.

Nell puts her shoes back on and sits on the saddle of her bike, ready to go. Her long brown legs touch the ground easily. Sadie is smaller than Nell but her bike is bigger and she stands next to it, irritably spinning the pedal. But hers is a good bike with all its spokes and two working brakes, even if her feet don't touch the ground. Kath's bike, waiting for her propped up against the wall, somehow could not be anyone else's, such a heavy black unmanoevrable machine it is. You need hands as strong as Kath's to work the brakes on this one.

Ginny has still not caught them up when Marcie MacNee steps off the kerb in front of Nell.

'Where you going?'

Nell shrugs. 'Just for a ride.'

'I'll come,' says Marcie. 'Just let me go for my bike.'

'If she's coming,' says Sadie to Kath, 'then I'm not.'

'What's up?' says Kath.

'She's a big bully. I should know. She *is*. I was at school with her.'

'We're not children now,' says Nell. 'We won't let her do anything.'

Sadie looks at Kath but Kath says nothing. She stands looking back along the road as if she's worrying about Ginny, but Sadie knows she is trying to work out whose side to be on. Kath likes there to be a lot of people, every one of them her friend.

'If she's coming,' says Nell, 'she'll need some sandwiches. I'll go and tell her.' She props her bike up and ambles down the alley, just as Ginny arrives.

'What are we waiting for?'

'Nell and Marcie MacNee.'

'I'm going home,' says Sadie.

'We can't go without you,' says Kath. 'You're the one what knows where we're going.'

'I'll go next week,' says Sadie, feeling the lump of disappointment thicken in her throat.

'She's scared of this girl Marcie,' explains Kath.

'If she's coming I'm going home,' says Sadie again.

'Can I borrow your bike then?' says Ginny. The one she has is a bit like Kath's, a man's, big and black and heavy. 'I'll look after it, and I'll give you something.'

'She won't,' says Kath. 'She says things like that.'

'Can I though?'

'You might as well,' says Sadie sulkily. No one has asked her to stay, she might as well go home. She and Ginny swap bikes, move the contents of the baskets and Sadie is ready to go home, waiting only for some sign of friendship from Kath, when Nell reappears, with Marcie and a bike. Following them a boy of about twelve who is clearly Marcie's brother, same red-brown face, same black lank hair falling in his eyes. He doesn't speak but grabs the handlebars and starts to wrestle the bike from his sister. Marcie holds on. The others – even Sadie – look on, not joining in. The siblings kick each other, unable to use their hands, then Marcie leans forward and bites his hand. Now he does make a noise – a sort of roar – and punches her with the injured hand, sobbing. Then a stout woman appears with a coal shovel.

'Let it go you little cow. It's his bike, not yourn.' She goes to whack Marcie's backside with the shovel but the girl steps off the bike.

'Take it then, I don't want it.'

'I'll see you tomorrow,' says Nell to Marcie as they prepare to ride off.

After a small hesitation, Sadie goes with them, on Ginny's bike. 'I'll have my bike back,' she calls to her, but she is being left behind and Ginny in a rare burst of energy is leading the girls up Nags Head Road towards the High Street. Marcie runs along beside them for a while but has to stop and stands on the kerb watching them go.

'Her brother's a dumbie,' says Sadie when she comes alongside Kath.

'Was that their mum?'

'No, one of their aunties. They're diddikois you know.'

'What's that?'

'I don't know, that's what everyone calls them.'

Two boys, sleeves rolled up to their elbows, wave to them from the pavement and Kath stops.

'Hello Eric.'

'What's going on?'

'We're escaping from the Germans,' says Kath.

'Go on.'

'No, not really. We're going to the country.'

'To stay?'

'Don't talk barmy. We've got to go to work tomorrow.'

'Whose idea was this then?' People said Eric was worse than a girl for wanting to know everyone's business.

Kath indicates Sadie.

'I know her,' says Eric.

'She works with me,' says Kath, making it sound as if she's some sort of boss, thinks Sadie, which she isn't. 'Her brother's been evacuated. We're going to see him.'

'Where is he?'

'Bumbles Green,' says Sadie. She likes the way it sounds, countrified, like something out of a Rupert Bear cartoon.

Eric's friend, leaning against a lamppost, winks at Nell and she looks away.

'Let's go,' she says, but Eric hasn't finished.

'I've seen you before. Don't you work in the bread shop?' Nell nods. 'And that only leaves you,' says Eric to Ginny.

'She's my sister,' says Kath. 'And she's older than you so don't go getting any ideas.'

Eric runs an eye over the bikes. 'Well I hope you make it there and back.' He laughs, meaning he doesn't think they will, and the friend laughs too.

'Who's he?' says Kath.

'Gus.'

Nell and Ginny have simultaneously had enough and push their bikes away from the kerb. Sadie follows and after a moment Kath simpers at the boys and follows too.

'Don't be late for church,' Eric yells after the group, and doubles up with laughter, which they fail to notice.

'What do you think of him?' Kath says to Sadie.

'Nosey.'

'I don't mean Eric,' scorns Kath. 'What about Gus? Handsome isn't he? I didn't know his name before.'

'I know where he lives.'

'Tell me.'

'Just along from me. I'll show you.'

They pause before they reach High Street, to gather and re-establish themselves as a group. Kath and Ginny have a small dispute about who should carry their sandwiches, which Kath wins by threatening to put Ginny's share in the pig bin by the side of the road.

'Do you know the way?' says Ginny to Sadie.

Sadie has a written list of places to go through but she's resentful of Ginny for taking her bike and doesn't want to let her take over the direction of the journey as well. 'My dad's told me how to get there. It's the other side of Nazeing.' She is unaware that her father has not the best grasp of geography.

'You been there before?'

'In a car,' says Sadie, showing off.

'Whose?'

'My step-grandad's.' This appears to silence Ginny's questions.

It's about nine-thirty, too early for the church people, and there's no motor traffic moving. The sky is hazy, it will be hot later. Front gardens, railings sawn off, are still fluffy with blossom. Cats and dogs amble about, the dogs sometimes following the four bikes, barking. One is so insistent that Kath kicks out at it.

'You shouldn't do that,' says Sadie.

'Not yours is it?'

'Course not. But you don't want to hurt it.'

'Who says I don't?'

As they ride over the railway line Nell whispers to Sadie, 'She argues all the time doesn't she.'

Sadie shrugs. She doesn't seem, Nell, to be quite the same sort of person as us. Something different about her. Something different about the way she talks. Sometimes you're not sure what she said, and then it dawns on you. Not that she's said much yet. And she's friendly with Marcie, which doesn't speak in her favour.

There are no houses now on either side of the road. A lorry goes past, with a single soldier sitting on the tailboard, waving to them.

Sadie stops, letting the others go on, and takes the list out of her skirt pocket. 'Stop,' she shouts. Nell hears, calls to the others.

'We've gone wrong,' says Sadie. 'I knew we shouldn't have crossed over the railway. We've missed Waltham Cross.'

'Let's see.' Ginny, of course. 'Waltham Cross, Cheshunt, Broxbourne. Oh it's all right. I know the way from here.'

'How do you?' asks Kath, but Ginny ignores her.

Sadie feels entitled to moan, it being Ginny's fault as she sees it. 'We've missed seeing the Cross. I always like seeing the Cross.'

'We'll see it on the way back,' promises Ginny, leading off again.

Half a mile further she calls, 'Stop.'

Kath, yards in front, applies the difficult brakes. Nell stops her bike with her foot. 'What?'

'I want to show you something.' She turns to Sadie. 'This is better that your old Eleanor Cross.' Ginny turns up a green lane and when the grass gets longer and the going more difficult they leave the bikes and continue on foot.

'Where are we going?'

'It's not far.'

'What?'

'Something. Wait and see.'

Kath, not one for waiting and seeing, grumbles, but keeps up with the others. Here, away from the road, birds are singing as if demented.

'Why do birds sing?' says Sadie to Nell, but Nell only shrugs and smiles as if she knows but there's no point telling someone as stupid as Sadie.

Ginny was right, it wasn't far. Kath has managed to get stung by a nettle and rubs crossly at her leg, but even so is impressed by what she sees. 'Blimey,' she says. 'Will you look at that?'

They all are. It's a white marble archway, ornate, two-storied, one wide arch and a smaller one each side, surrounded by weeds and brambles and barbed wire, like something out of a story book, a fairy story, a fairy war story. Ginny waves an arm, as if it's hers, and waits for questions.

'What is it? How did it get here? What's in there, behind the wire?'

'It's some sort of arch, or gate, or something. This woman who lived in the house -'

'What house?'

'Big house, you can't see it from here, this woman brought it from London, had it put up here. She's gone now, it's Royal Engineers in there now, training.'

'How do you know all this?' asks Kath sharply. 'How did you know it was here?'

'Someone showed me.'

'Someone,' jeers Kath. 'Some Royal Engineers someone I bet.' She throws herself down on the grass among the buttercups and bees and sings, loudly 'Roll me over in the clover, roll me over, lay me down and do it again.' Ginny ignores her, Nell and Sadie giggle. 'I'll tell Mum,' says Kath.

'Suit yourself.' Ginny turns to the other two and says, 'They say that this woman, Lady Someone, entertained Churchill in that room up there.'

'Entertained?' says Sadie. 'What, like, sang him songs?'

Ginny's turn to shrug. 'I don't know. It's just what I've been told.'

'It looks haunted,' says Sadie. 'I want to go now.' She walks back down the lane and Nell runs to catch her up.

'Bees buzz, birds sing,' she says. 'It's just what they do.' Behind them they can hear Kath and Ginny alternately bickering and laughing. It's what they do.

Starting off again, Sadie hoped that she would get her own bike back, but Ginny appears not to hear her when she asks, and sets off in the lead, as official route finder. Sure enough, she leads them into Cheshunt, and by asking a woman sweeping a step, finds the right road to take them to Broxbourne. They begin to feel far from home. Their wheels spin more freely, Kath starts to sing

(I'll Be With You in Apple Blossom Time), the sun comes through the mist, birds fly above the hedges plucking insects out of the air.

'Swallows,' says Nell.

Sadie giggles and Kath and Ginny look sharply. 'What you talking about?'

'Those birds. Swallows.'

'Are they?' Kath is as far into the countryside as she has ever been.

Sadie explains. 'Their name, Kath and Ginny, it's Swallow. Kath Swallow. See? She thought you were talking about her.'

It's nice, it feels like another step nearer to being all friends together. Nell smiles. She has a pleasant face, though her hair is not fashionable, being still cut in a straight bob. Kath and Ginny have theirs permed, they do each other's, at home, the kitchen reeking of ammonia. Sadie's hair is long, rolled and pinned when she's at work but today loose and wavy past her shoulders.

'Let's have a rest.'

They sit together on a wall, feet in the grass.

'Shall we eat something?' Everything they could scrounge from their mothers is in their baskets, along with their gas masks.

'Better not yet.'

'Drink then.' Kath and Ginny have cold tea and offer it round, but the other two prefer water.

'Anyway,' says Ginny, 'what's this about a step-grandad? How do you get one of them?'

'Sadie's family is really – well you won't never believe it,' says Kath.

'Don't be daft,' says Sadie. 'It's easy if you get it in the right order.'

'Go on then.'

'All right. But don't interrupt me cos I'll lose where I am.'

9

'Go on then.'

'First my mum married this man.'

'Your dad?'

'No, this other man, this is back in the other war, the Great War.'

'Was he killed in France?'

'I don't know – no he couldn't have been, he died after my sister was born.'

'Well how old's she?'

'I'm not sure, I don't see her any more, she's about twenty, more than twenty. She's married, they live in Camden Town. So then, my mum got married again to my dad.'

'Your dad, the one that lives in your house?'

'Of course that one, I couldn't have two could I? And then, when I was about five my mother died.'

'What did she die of?'

'I don't know. I don't remember it. No one talks about her.'

'Do you remember her?'

'Well I do, sort of, but only little bits. I remember holding her hand and looking at her shoes walking along and I remember pulling her apron tie, you know, to make it come undone, and running away.'

'Was she in hospital?'

'I think she was. I think they took me to see her. There was this noise all the time, trolleys and things, rattling, and the windows were high up so you couldn't see out.'

'We've been to a hospital,' said Kath. 'Our Uncle Ernie, he got taken to the North Mid when we got bombed. But they wouldn't let us see him. Our mum went in, just to say who he was, and then he died. She said it was just as well.'

'What did she mean?' asked Nell.

'Well he wouldn't have had no legs so what would he have done? And we couldn't look after him with all

10

them stairs. And at least he never knew about Auntie Glad.'

'So,' says Ginny, 'after your mum died, your Dad married again. What's her name?'

'She's called Ivy. I have to call her Stepmother.'

'What a mouthful. What's she like?'

'She's all right. I suppose. She'll be glad when I get married and leave home.'

'Did she say that?'

'Not exactly, but I know it. She's all right, she lets me wear her clothes but she's not properly friendly if you know what I mean. These are hers.' Sadie stretches out her legs to show her brown leather sandals. The other girls nod.

'So your brother, what's his name?'

'Maurice. He's eight, nearly nine.'

'Short work,' says Ginny.

'Is he a nice boy?' asks Nell.

'He's nice. I've always looked after him. I do miss him, but you see, he wasn't going to be evacuated, he didn't want to go and Stepmother didn't want him to, and Dad said if there were bombs they'd fall on the docks, you know, in London, not this far out, but we didn't know what it was going to be like, you see, hearing it wherever it is and sometimes one coming down over here. Maurice was getting nervy. So his grandad – that's my step-grandad – he knew these people out in the country – they had a 'vacuee but he went back home – they said they'd have Maurice.'

'Does he know we're coming?'

'No. How could I tell him?'

'Send a postcard.'

'Oh. I never thought of that.'

'Never mind,' says Kath. 'It's Sunday, he won't be at school, he'll be there. Let's go.'

As they ride past churches now people are coming out of them – posh people says Ginny – with prayer books, the women with hats and handbags, men in suits and trilbies. They stand round in little groups before shaking hands and moving off to their own homes.

'I wonder what they talk about,' says Sadie to Ginny.

'The war,' says Ginny confidently. 'They say prayers that we'll win.'

'Do you think we'll win?'

'Well they don't think so do they? If they thought we could win why would they need to pray about it?'

'But do you think so?'

'I don't, no. They'll starve us out.'

'How do you know?'

'Where I work. That's all I can say, I'm not allowed to talk about it, it would spread alarm and despondency.'

Kath, prompted by the sight of churches, albeit with bells silenced, is singing. (The Bells Are Ringing, for Me and My Gal.) She is in front now and her voice comes back to them, strong and tuneful.

'She gets it from our mum,' says Ginny proudly. 'Me and Billy, we can't hold a tune, but she always has done, from being a baby Mum says.'

Kath brakes at a crossroads. Which way? The others catch her up and stop too, wondering. Kath now – it must be something about being in front – takes a decision and scoots her bike across to a couple sitting on a bench. The others hear her plainly.

''Ere mister, what way is Bumbles Green?'

Mister does not reply, though he looks ready to, but Missis, if that's who she is, stands up and comes over the verge to Kath.

'Just one moment, young woman. Is that any way to ask a question of someone?'

'I only asked.'

'No you did not only ask. You rudely interrupted a conversation, without a please or an excuse me. Bad manners like that will not obtain you an answer.'

'Blimey,' says Kath. 'If that's how you want it.' And cycles on, blushing.

'She's got no manners,' says Ginny, and they all follow Kath as she speeds off down what proves to be the wrong road.

But they are cheerful enough. This is proper countryside, green and breezy, bright with flowers and for the most part tidy with money. There are no destroyed buildings here, no piles of brick rubble. Even the shabbiest of cottages and most tumbledown of outhouses are not as depressing as the sooty and jerry-built back streets with their taped up windows and damp comfortless shelters.

'Of course we're a target,' Sadie's dad would say, disregarding that he'd previously said they wouldn't be. 'There's industry here ain't there, the Small Arms, and the Gunpowder, and the electricals, and the gas works, just think if they hit the gasometer, what a bang that would be.'

'Shut up Wilfred,' said Ivy. 'No need to go on about it. I'm trying not to think about it.'

'That's right,' he said, maybe sarcastically, maybe not, 'you try not to think about it.'

A mile or so down the road Ginny makes a discreet enquiry of an old man walking his dog and is able to get them back on track for Nazeing. And now it really is time to eat so they sit in a row on the grass, tucking up their skirts – except Nell who wears shorts – and getting themselves outside of their sandwiches. They have bread and dripping, or bread and cheese, and Kath and Ginny also have bread and jam for later. Sadie has a piece of cake, another piece of which is wrapped up for

Maurice. Nell has some stale doughnuts, enough for one each.

'Marcie gave them to me,' she says. 'She works at the bakery. It's a shame she couldn't come with us.'

'That's what you think,' said Sadie, quietly.

'We're in the country,' says Kath, 'you'd think there'd be apples or blackberries or gooseberries or something.'

'Not in May,' says Nell.

'What do you know about it?' Kath doesn't mean to be rude, it's just the way it comes out. Nell seems to know this.

'I used to live on a farm.'

'A real farm?'

Nell shrugs – because she doesn't understand the question? Or because she can't be bothered to come up with an answer?

'Look at our legs,' says Sadie. 'Don't they look funny?'

They consider the eight legs in front of them. Ginny's are the longest, but her ankles are very solid, as are Kath's. Nell has long skinny legs without any shape, Sadie's are short but her ankles are so slender as to look breakable. The sandals borrowed from Stepmother are too big and have rubbed red marks on the top of each foot. Nell wears plimsolls and Kath and Ginny stout black shoes, the ones they wear to work.

'What's funny about them?' says Kath.

'I was just thinking, if you cut the legs off us, and mixed them up, would you know which ones went with which body.'

'I'd know which ones were mine,' said Ginny. 'I can see where I cut myself shaving.'

Then they can't be bothered any more, and all together lie back in the grass and look at the sky.

'We had this Auntie,' says Ginny, 'Aunt Em she was called, she used to tell us clouds were angels. Do you remember Kath?'

'No,' says Kath. 'Is she the one who chased Billy with an axe?'

'That's her. But she didn't mean it, she was just doing it to frighten him cos he was giving her cheek.'

'Who's Billy?' says Nell. 'And where did she get an axe?'

'It was always by the back door, for firewood. Billy's our brother.'

'He's my twin,' sighs Kath. 'He's always been awful. He'll say anything, he doesn't care.'

'He never said anything to Aunt Em again,' says Ginny. 'It's years ago now, when she did that but he won't be in the same room with her. If she comes in the front door, he's out the back. But we don't see her any more, it's too far for her to come.'

'I've never seen Billy,' says Sadie, 'even though I live across the road to you.'

'He goes out early,' says Kath. 'He has to be first at the station to unlock the waiting room. And anyway, he don't use the front door, he climbs over the back wall.'

'What for?'

'Just what he likes to do. He likes climbing. He's joining the army soon. October.'

They go quiet, thinking of people they know, watching the angelic clouds drifting pacifically overhead.

'Well,' says Sadie, 'shall we go?' So near now to Maurice, she feels entitled to chivvy them a little bit.

So they ride through Nazeing in the sunshine, the air filled, you might think, with the smell of roast – such little roasts nowadays – and gravy, though actually, all that has been available has been eaten and is now getting washed up.

'Where now?'

Poor Sadie looks helpless. This is not how she remembers it. How can she find the right house when the landmarks she remembers – hedge with an arch cut in it, blue-painted gate, horse trough across the road, telephone box on corner – are not to be seen? 'There must be another road.'

'What's their name?'

'I don't know.' She does know but she's not telling Kath for fear of her indiscreet mouth.

They ride around for a bit, the street is deserted in the Sunday heat, it's the sort of place where children aren't allowed to play out on a Sunday. Or any day? Presently though, a boy of about twelve appears, with a tennis racquet. Ginny does the job this time.

'Excuse me.' Looking at Kath to show her how it's done. 'Do you happen to know a boy called Maurice – Maurice what?' to Sadie.

'Singleton.'

'Yes.'

'Could you direct us to his house, you know, where he's staying?'

'Who are you?' he says.

'German spies,' says Kath. 'What do you think?'

'I'm his sister,' says Sadie.

'I'm not sure of the exact house,' says the boy. 'But I know who you mean. If you go down there, past the school, there are three houses in a row. I think – well I'm pretty sure – it's one of those.'

'Thank you,' says Ginny graciously, ignoring the face that Kath is pulling at her.

They stop. The grass verge has been cut recently and the smell of grass fills their noses. Blue front gate, front garden given over to potatoes, not that the girls, Nell excepted, would recognise a potato plant. Full of butterflies of excitement and anxiety, Sadie knocks at the door. And Maurice opens it. Sees Sadie, looks

16

behind her, hopeful, then disappointed, then realistic. 'Hello.'

'Who is it?' calls a woman's voice.

'It's my sister.'

Sadie is welcomed in. Mr and Mrs Pottinger – yes that's their name, Sadie thinks it's like something out of a book of nursery rhymes – are a couple in their fifties. Their son is in the RAF, their daughter lives along the road with her children, her husband away in the army. They have taken to Maurice who is, truly, a likeable and biddable boy.

'Have you come all this way on your own?'

'I came with my friends. They're outside.'

Mr Pottinger makes a special journey to the front window to look. Kath and Nell are chasing Ginny along the road throwing grass in her hair. There is shrieking.

'We don't let Maurice play out on a Sunday,' says Mrs Pottinger. 'He's been to Sunday school this morning and he'll take the dog for a walk later, won't you Mo.'

'We could take the dog out now,' offers Sadie, but the Pottingers are firm. Gypsy has a walk at half past five and anyway, would be too excited by girls on bikes.

'But if you want some time with your brother – why don't you take your sister to look at the garden? You can show her what you did this morning. I'll be putting the kettle on, though it's a bit early.'

It's the best they are going to get. Sadie and Maurice go out through the back door. The lawn is immaculate, the apple blossom blooms. Maurice shows Sadie all the daffodils whose dying foliage he carefully knotted that morning after Sunday school.

'Why?'

'So they don't all flop down and look untidy.' Already, in a couple of months, Maurice's voice has changed. There are consonants at the end of his words, sometimes aitches at the beginnings. His sentences have a beginning, middle and end. But he is still her little brother. She loves his prominent new front teeth, his slightly too big ears, the way his left eyelid has always drooped more than his right, so he looks as if he is just going to wink.

'Did Dad say you could come?'

'He said I could if I had someone with me, so Kath said she would.'

'Do I know her?'

'No, you'd already come here when they moved in. They got bombed out – second time too – and they're upstairs in number sixty-four across the road.'

'Who are the others then?'

'Kath's big sister Gin, and Nell.'

The dog – a daft black spaniel – has joined them and Maurice shows Sadie how he is training it to jump over a stick. Training has some way to go.

'Do you like your school?'

'It's all right. Better than Alma Road anyway.'

'What's your teacher like?'

'A man. Mr Fogg. We call him Foggy.'

'Is he old?' It sounded like an old man's name.

'I suppose so. He's got a beard like pirate. He takes us all into the woods to do nature study.'

'What's that?'

'We just run around, and hide, and that. He doesn't mind.'

'You been slippered yet?'

'No. No one has.' Surprise in his voice as if he's only just realised.

Mrs Pottinger calls them in from the garden. 'Are you hungry dear?'

Sadie knows the proper answer is No, but she can't bring herself to turn down food, and anyway it would be a lie, so she gets through two slices of bread and butter (real butter) and two cups of tea.

Ginny and Kath and Nell, meanwhile, have stopped chasing around and are sitting on yet another grass verge.

'The first time wasn't so bad,' Kath's saying.

'It was worse,' says Ginny. 'We didn't know it was going to happen. We weren't in the shelter or anything.'

It was when we were living in Shoreditch.'

'I'd just got home from work, it didn't take me long then, I could walk it if I wanted, just from the City. We was all in the kitchen -'

'– if we'd been in the front room we'd have been sliced to pieces by glass –'

'– but we never used the front room -'

'– but say we had –'

'Anyway this bomb's dropped in the street outside. You never heard such a noise in all your life.'

'We ran out the back but we didn't have no shelter cos our yard was just concrete.'

'There was me and her and Mum just standing in the yard, shivering.'

'And we didn't dare go back in.'

'Anyway they shifted us out of there in case the foundations gave way.'

'And they did, I went past only a few days later and the front wall was gone.'

'And we moved to Tottenham.'

'Seven Sisters Road.'

'There about three weeks and what do you know? Direct hit.'

'Were you in the house?'

'Do I look dead? Nah, we were all out. Just Uncle Ernie and Auntie Glad were in.'

'Where were you?'

'About ten o'clock in the evening. Friday night. We was all out with our mates. Billy in the park. Mum and Dad down the pub. Someone comes in, goes, Willy your house just copped it.'

'Nothing left.'

'All our stuff.'

'Auntie Glad in pieces.'

'Dug Uncle Ernie out but he died.'

'So we come down here.'

'It's quieter.'

'And you still go to work in the city?' says Nell. 'What job do you do?'

'Typing. Shipping firm. Been there since I left school.'

'But what do you type?'

'Lists,' she says. Lists of cargoes in and out of the port. Ginny knows more than most people how many ships are being sunk and their cargoes lost. Occasionally she has felt alarm and despondency herself, less on account of the lost loads of wheat and corned beef than of the lost sailors, who would no longer be available to dance with her at the Tottenham Royal or Charlie Brown's, and possibly, in the future, marry. 'It's good pay, better than what I'd get round here. I don't mind getting up early.'

'We all get up early,' says Kath. 'I start at half past seven and me dad does shifts on the buses and me Mum goes early to clean them and Billy goes round the station and he has to be the first one there.'

'It's bad luck,' says Nell, 'being bombed out twice.'

'Twice in a month,' says Kath, gleefully morbid, 'and the second time all we had was what we stood up in.'

'Well we got a few things out. That bike of Kath's, it was Uncle Ernie's, it was out the back, but everything else, if it wasn't smashed to smithereens it was covered in soot and brick dust. You don't know how much soot is up a chimney till one falls down.'

'Your poor Auntie Glad.'

Ginny shrugs. 'We didn't like her much, she was always on at us, but she didn't deserve being blown to bits. She should have gone down the shelter but she wouldn't, she was afraid of rats, she used to sit under the table.'

'Is that where she was?'

'No one knows, they never found her really, only her shoes.'

'Ernie was with her we think, but he never said, he wasn't saying nothing by the time they got him out, so that was that.'

'We're bad luck,' says Kath. 'If there's a raid, stay away from us.'

'Are you scared?'

'Only when there's a raid on. The rest of the time, who cares?'

They all go quiet. Then Ginny says, 'She has nightmares. She beats me black and blue in her sleep.'

'No I don't.'

'And you scream.'

'I'm going to get Sadie,' says Kath. 'I'm bored waiting here. They might have asked us in.'

'I'll go,' says Ginny. 'We don't want a repeat of bad manners.'

Ginny rings the bell and waits. 'Oh hello Mrs Um. We were wanting to speak to Sadie because we really should be leaving soon, if we're going to get home in time.'

Sadie has been trying to forget that she has people waiting for her, or that she has to leave this comfortable armchair and the prospect of more tea, and maybe cake, later. And Maurice. She's sad to leave him, though she'll be able to tell Dad and Stepmother that he's well and happy.

'I've got something for you.' She goes outside to the basket of her bike. A piece of cake, some new socks that Stepmother has knitted, and a letter. When she goes back in, he is seated at the table taking the lid off a large biscuit tin.

Mrs Pottinger explains. 'Maurice is going to sort out my buttons for me. Aren't you?' Sadie looks at the tin brimming with buttons, mostly black, from coats and jackets, or white, from shirts, but with odd flashes of red and blue.

'Never throw away buttons,' says Mrs Pottinger. 'I've had some of these forty years but you never know when you'll want them again. Maurice is going to string them so that the all the same sorts are together and I know how many we've got.'

'Last Sunday I went through magazines,' says Maurice. 'I cut out all them puzzles and all them poems and all them knitting patterns and all them handy hints and put them in different piles.'

Sadie doesn't know what to say. She has never known Maurice sit down and be usefully busy at something for someone else. What about running round the street with a gang of boys, hiding in coal-holes and getting covered in black dust, or knocking on doors and running away? What about climbing on people's fences or hanging on the back of lorries or getting injured in stick fights?

'You tell your mum and dad that Maurice is a good boy,' says Mr Pottinger kindly. 'We're very pleased to have him.' He gives Sadie sixpence. 'Now you came the long way round to get here – make sure you go back through Waltham Abbey. You know how to do that?'

Sadie thinks she doesn't but feels unwilling to say so.

'Make sure you go straight home, you and your friends.'

Ginny is still at the door. 'Could we fill our water bottles please?' No problem as water is free, and they fill the lemonade bottles at the kitchen sink.

Sadie and Maurice rub noses, which is something they have done since he was a baby. 'Cheerio then Mo,' she says. 'See you soon.'

'Not if I see you first,' he responds, and then laughs and hugs her round the waist.

They go back to the road to find Kath, fuming and Nell, contentedly poking a stick into an ants' nest.

They are tired now. They have reached their destination, seen Mo, given him his cake and socks, it has all been a bit of an anti-climax, and now they have to go all the way back. They ride along quietly, Kath and Sadie in front, then Nell, Ginny some way back.

Ginny shouts to them to stop and turn round. 'Here, we need to go down here. It's a short cut.'

'What?' Although the road signs have been taken down she is looking at an old milestone which points to Waltham Abbey.

'But the road goes to it anyway.'

'This will be shorter. If we cut through here I bet we'll get home quicker.'

'How do you know?' says Sadie. Of all of them she is the most deflated, the most in need of being home again.

'You've never been to Waltham Abbey,' says Kath.

'You don't know where I've been.'

Nell peers along the path. 'It's a bit stony.'

'Remember, Mr P said Waltham Abbey,' says Ginny. 'So I'm going this way.'

'Don't,' says Sadie. 'We ought to keep together.'

'Well come with me then.' Ginny has already lifted her bike – Sadie's bike – over the stile. 'Tell you what,' she says, 'I'll just go to that bend and see what it looks like. You wait here and if I call you, you come. If it seems to go the wrong way I'll come back.'

They can't turn her so they wait, watching as she cycles off. At the bend she stops and looks, then waves them to come.

'Shall we?' says Nell.

'She's got my bike,' says Sadie.

'She's my sister,' says Kath. She begins to haul her bike over the stile.

'Wait a minute. She's coming back.'

She is, and she's wheeling the bike.

'What's up?'

'Puncture.'

'What?'

'Your bike,' she says to Sadie. 'It's got a puncture.'

'Well it's not my fault.'

'You didn't ought to have gone down that path,' says Kath.

'It was a good idea,' says Ginny. 'It could cut miles off.'

'Well what do we do now?'

'Anyone got a puncture repair kit?'

No, nobody has.

'What a shower you are,' says Ginny. 'You'd think one of you would have thought of it.'

'Well why didn't you?'

'I was in a hurry. You lot had all day yesterday to think of it.'

'Well too bad,' says Kath. 'You'll just have to walk.'

They set off, along the road, riding slowly while Ginny pushes the bike along. After half a mile or so she says, 'What about someone else having a turn pushing? What about you Sadie? It's your bike after all.'

'You wanted to ride it.'

'No I didn't, I was doing you a favour.'

'Oh of course. And I suppose I didn't ask for it back, did I?'

'Come on, fair's fair. Just push it for a little way and then I'll do it again.'

'No,' says Sadie firmly, but watches Ginny then mount the bike and ride along on its flat front wheel. 'You can't do that.'

'Well I can't walk all the way home. It's hot. My feet hurt.'

'All right,' says Sadie, 'just a little way.'

Ginny jumps on her own bike and sails away, overtaking the others.

'Wait for Sadie,' yells Kath, but Ginny calls back, 'Just navigating. Back in a mo.'

Nell rides slowly alongside Sadie. 'That wasn't nice of her,' she says solemnly.

Sadie shrugs. 'That's Swallows for you. And take my advice, don't ever lend em money.'

The next few miles are miserable. The day is still hot but clouds are building, a big bank of dark grey rain cloud that blots out the sun in the west. 'It better not rain,' says Kath.

Kath is pushing the bike now, Nell's already had a go, when she saw Sadie's feet getting blisters from Stepmother's sandals.

Ginny calls from up ahead. 'Look, come and see. We're saved.' Kath is the last to get there. She sees a small petrol filling station.

'It's shut.'

'But look, a house next door. I bet that's where the bloke lives.'

'We'll have to pay.'

'Then we'll pay,' says Ginny.

'Have you got any money?'

'I haven't, no, but one of you must have some.'

'You never have any money,' shouts Kath. 'I'm always paying for you. You owe me at least fifteen bob, don't think I'm not counting.'

'Look,' says Sadie, 'let's just pay up. I've got some.'

'So have I,' says Nell. 'After all, it's slowing all of us down, this puncture.'

Ginny goes off to the tumbledown bungalow and after a bit comes back with a lad younger than them. He's pointing down the road and clearly telling Ginny which way they should go home. 'We're paying one-and-six,' she says. 'This is Freddy.'

And he quickly and neatly deals with the puncture, casting looks all the time at their ankles, and blushing. The girls wait while he goes through getting the tyre off, fetching a bucket of water, finding the hole, holding up the thorn to show them, drying it, applying a patch, putting the tube back in and the tyre back on. Pumps it up. Pockets the money.

'Thank you,' says Sadie.

'Thank you,' says Nell.

'Give him a kiss then,' says Ginny.

'No.'

'I'll do it,' says Kath and kisses him loudly on the cheek, holding a handful of hair so that he can't get away. He bolts for the house.

Sadie claims her bike and Ginny doesn't even argue. They set off as the rain begins. Big drops splat on the road, sending dust up to splash on their legs.

They shelter in a bus stop.

'We'll never get home,' moans Sadie.

'The rain will pass,' says Nell. 'Look, you can see sunlight coming out over there.'

Sadie gazes westward, amazed. 'I've never noticed that before.'

'What?'

'Clouds moving. Rain coming and then moving. Sun behind clouds. I thought rain turned on and off, like a tap.'

Nell shakes her head silently.

'How do you know about things?' says Sadie.

'What things?'

'What birds are called, and weather, and things like that.'

'Just because – where I used to live, it wasn't as built on, there was more space and – '

'Where was it?'

'Yes where?' says Kath.

'Guernsey.'

'Where's that?'

'In the English Channel. Near France.'

Ginny says, 'It's occupied isn't it? Nazis are there.'

'Yes,' says Nell. 'We came here because the Germans were coming.'

'Everyone?'

'What do you mean?'

'Everyone from Guernsey, did they come to England?'

'No, we could choose. My dad stayed behind, to look after the animals.'

'What animals?'

'The farm animals. Not many. Just three cows. But they're quite valuable. To us anyway. And some chickens.'

'Hold on,' says Sadie. 'Tell me again, I don't get it. It's a farm, it's a seaside, it's near France. I'm all confused.'

'Guernsey,' says Nell, 'is an island. Sea all around it. Near France. Some people speak English, some people speak French.'

'You speak English.'

'I speak French too.'

'Say something.'

Nell says something. Kath and Sadie look stunned, Ginny tries to look as if she could do it too if she only wanted to. She says, 'So your family have a farm.'

'We did,' says Nell. 'I don't know what we have now. It was only a little one. My dad worked on a big farm – tomatoes – '

'Oh,' cries Kath, 'Guernsey tomatoes. You used to get them in shops.'

'They grow in Guernsey,' says Nell. 'I expect the Germans eat them all now.'

'You're doing it again,' complains Sadie. 'Big farm, little farm.'

'My dad worked on a big farm, for the farmer,' says Nell. She's very patient. 'But we had some land of our own. It belonged to my grandad and when he died it came to my mum. So that's where we keep our cows. My dad would milk them before he went to work, and my brother did the evening milking.'

'Can you do it?'

'What, milk a cow? Of course.'

'What were they called?'

She smiles. 'Lucille, Marianne and Sybil.'

'Not Buttercup?'

This makes Nell laugh, maybe for the first time today. 'Guernsey cows are not called Buttercup.'

'How old's your brother?'

'Eighteen. Just.'

'What's his name?'

'Eddie.'

'Did he stay? To help with the milking?'

'My dad wanted him to, but no. He came to England with us and he's in the army.'

'So how does your dad manage?'

'We don't know. We don't know what's happened. We haven't heard any news of my dad.'

She isn't crying, thinks Sadie, I'd be crying if it was my dad.

'Tell us it from the beginning,' says Kath. 'While it's raining.'

'There used to be soldiers, English soldiers, on the island. They were called the Garrison. Then your government took them away, after Dunkirk. They needed them to make up for all the ones that got killed and captured. They knew the Germans would come but they didn't want to fight them, so they sent round all the houses – if you want to go to England, be on the harbour, with a suitcase and we'll take you to England.

My parents argued all night because my mum wanted us all to go.'

'Stick together,' said Ginny.

Nell went on as if Ginny hadn't spoken. 'She said, Never mind the cows, but my dad wouldn't leave everything behind. She said, You weren't even born on the island, but he said he wasn't leaving. Then my brother – he said he would go to France in a boat and join the French army and my dad told him the French army was finished and he'd do better, if he wanted to join up to join the British army, but why did he want to get killed when he could stay and keep his head down and not have to fight. And I wanted to stay with my dad but Mum said no, she needed me with her – '

'Anyway,' says Kath. 'You wouldn't want to stay and get raped by Germans.'

'Maybe my mum thought of that,' says Nell. 'But she didn't say it to me.'

'When the war finishes,' says Sadie, 'you can go back.'

Nell shrugs.

'It's not like a shower of rain,' says Ginny. 'It doesn't just blow over. Someone has to win it.'

The rain lessens, slows, drips, stops. The sun slants through leaves and shines on the wet road.

'My old man said follow the van,' sings Kath. 'And don't dilly dally on the way.'

They have four working bikes again. They eat a doughnut each and drink water. Ginny has a cigarette. They set off together, four abreast. They are warm in the sun, it's a long evening and a short night, less darkness for the bombers to come in, and maybe it will cloud over again later so there's no moonlight for them.

Up and down Britain, soldiers and airmen move between camps and barracks, carry out training exercises, clean and maintain their machines of war, miss their families and wonder what will happen. The length and breadth of Europe people starve and worry, winning or losing it's not a comfortable time. Unbeknown to Kath and Ginny, Sadie and Nell, trainloads of prisoners are carried across borders. Somewhere to the east prisoners of war sit out the war in prison camps. Somewhere much closer an as yet small number of Italian prisoners do the same. Nell wonders if her brother is an ordinary soldier, or will he, because of his French, be dropped into France as a spy, as her mother thinks he will. Kath is already thinking of Billy's birthday in October and what it will mean.

But now, at this moment, a blackbird singing in the hedge, the tyres swishing through the wet, Kath humming quietly, the pedals of the bikes clicking and whirring, the sun shining on their bare legs, their hands on the handlebars, now it is peaceful, now it is all right.

They cross the river and having stopped briefly to look at the Eleanor Cross in the last of the light, they are bowling along, nearly home, when a man waves from the pavement at Nell and Ginny. 'Hello girlies,' they hear him call.

'It's me dad,' says Sadie from the rear.

'Hello duck,' he calls, 'I thought it might be you.'

'Where's your bike Dad?'

'Oh,' he says, 'I was just out for a little walk and a smoke. You know what Ivy's like about smoke. Tell you what though –' he looks at Ginny 'that looks a nice strong bike. How about you sit on the crossbar and I'll carry you home? How about it?'

'Tell you what,' says Ginny quickly. 'I'll swap with Sadie and she can have the ride.'

It's done before he can argue. Sadie leans into him and smells the cheap tobacco and the cheap brilliantine and strong soap that make up his proper smell. Kath is singing again – 'You'll look sweet upon the seat.' Ginny shoves her so that she wobbles into the kerb and they both laugh.

Nell's house on Nags Head Road is the first to be reached. Her mum is looking out of the upstairs window and waves to her.

'Bye then,' says Nell.

'Bye,' says Sadie from the crossbar.

'See you in the shop,' says Kath.

Ginny gets off her bike and hugs Nell. 'I hope you hear from your dad soon,' she says.

At the next corner Marcie is standing in the shadows and waves as they pass but none of them notices her.

The Swallows' house is in darkness but Billy is sitting on the step. 'Mum and Dad are in the pub,' he says. 'I'm locked out.'

Sadie waves again as she pushes her own bike across the road and down the alley to the rear of the house. She will tell Stepmother about Maurice, she will have a cup of tea and go to bed. It's been a laugh and an adventure, time off from work and the war, something to remember.

CHAPTER TWO
IN WHICH A DISAPPEARANCE IS
WIDELY DISCUSSED

It was three years later, early in the summer of 1944 that Marcie MacNee disappeared.

She missed going to work one Saturday and when she failed to turn up at the bakery on Monday morning the baker sent the newest little girl, so pale and pigtailed she could have been still at school, to the baker's shop, to ask Nell if she knew anything.

Nell was wrapping loaves in paper and when she lifted her head the little girl could see that her eyes were swollen and red. But she said she hadn't seen Marcie since last Thursday when she spoke to her in the street. Then she ducked her head again and would not speak.

Then the little girl was sent round to the house to ask if she was ill. She returned to tell them that Marcie's auntie said they hadn't seen her since dinnertime on Saturday, or maybe teatime Friday and that she had probably run off with a soldier.

Certainly at that time there were plenty of soldiers about, on weekend leave, there being nothing for them to do in camp but wait for the invasion that everyone knew was going to happen. Sadie's Jack had been on leave so that they could get married, and he'd returned to his unit on Friday, just as Nell's Gus came home for two nights.

Ginny and Kath discussed it at home. 'Why would she say that, Run off with a soldier? Where would she go? They're all on their way to France.'

'That auntie don't know much,' said Kath. 'She just says the first thing that comes into her head.'

'Do you think Marcie would run away?' said Ginny.

'Maybe. If – you know.' They looked to see if their mother was listening, and she seemed not to be, being preoccupied with the business of moving to another house.

For more than three years now they had lived in the same block of dwellings as the MacNees, a three storey block, sooty on the outside and confusingly divided on the inside, dark and dank with no front garden or area. The Swallows had three rooms on the top floor and it seemed to Kath and Ginny that they spent more time hauling water from the tap on the landing, or coal from the shed out the back, or taking rubbish downstairs or washing to hang out than they spent living in the place. Billy had been home on leave too, and so once again they'd had to put out his camp bed every night and put it away every morning, and rediscovered what a bind it was. Kath and Ginny were glad he'd gone away again – they suspected him of going in their room while they were at work and they had not forgotten that once, a couple of years ago, Kath found him trying on her camiknicker. And what was worse he hadn't taken off his boots and in his hurry to get it off managed to put his foot through the gusset.

'Now, where has your father got to? He's got to go and see about a cart.' Then, 'That Marcie,' she said, 'she's not such a bad girl, but she don't think neither, same as that auntie. They better hope she has run away because if not something worse has happened to her. Kath, run acrost and see is there things in there want chucking out.'

They had managed to get a house on the other side of the road, in the same row as Sadie and next door to Gus. 'Blimey,' said Mrs Swallow as Kath got up and willingly went as instructed, 'never see her move so fast.'

'It's Gus,' said Ginny, 'she'll be in heaven just living in the house next door.'

Her mother stopped what she was doing – which was turning pots out of a cupboard and on to the table – and considered. 'Three things,' she said. 'He ain't there.

He's back down on Salisbury Plain or somewhere like it. He's got a girl, his mum's told me, nice girl, she says. And I thought Kath had got a bloke. Hasn't she?'

'Ted,' agreed Ginny. Their eyes met and they said no more.

The following Saturday some boys, of whom Sadie's brother Maurice was one, found a shoe in the bushes and took it home. A black shoe, buckle fastening, heel and sole worn uneven, toes scuffed. Maurice's mother took it straight across to the MacNees, and the auntie agreed that it did look like one of Marcie's. 'Then what you want to do,' said Ivy firmly, 'is take it up the police station and report her missing. Should have done it a week ago.'

She went home and told Sadie what she had said. Sadie said Marcie was no loss to anyone and no one liked her anyway. But she was feeling sick and miserably pregnant and if Ivy had known about the pregnancy she might have excused her sourness.

Two policemen – one young with a limp, one past retirement age – came and asked questions of everyone in the street. When had they last seen Marcie? How did she seem? What did she say? Which way was she going? Did she have a boyfriend? Had she recently broken up with a boyfriend? They didn't mention the word murder but by then they didn't need to as everyone knew that she would not have run away with only one shoe, a shoe which she had lost, apparently, not a hundred yards from home.

From her auntie, the police learned that Marcie was a good worker but an obstreperous young madam, that she had no steady boyfriend as far as the family knew, that she seemed to know everyone in the neighbourhood and there were those who liked her and those who didn't, but that no one had threatened her, as far as they knew, and that Marcie knew how to take care of herself.

They noted, the police, that she had a brother, a strong looking boy, but deaf and dumb; that he stayed silent – naturally – while auntie answered the questions but did not look in the least upset at the lack of his sister. Where were Marcie's parents? Her mum was upstairs in bed, had been for all the years since the boy was born, nearly sixteen that was, and their father had not been seen for nearly all that time. 'Gone,' said auntie. Why hadn't she reported that Marcie was gone? 'I thought she'd come back,' she said.

The police talked to the little group of boys who had found the shoe but though they were eager to say something of consequence, there was nothing they could say. It was not clear which of them had first spotted the shoe in the long grass under a bush beside the path; three of them claimed to be the one. The police searched the area but did not find the other shoe, or anything else of any use to them.

They talked to the girls who knew Marcie. Sadie said she always avoided her if she could, Marcie had bullied her through their schooldays and she didn't like her or want anything to do with her. She couldn't remember when she last saw her, maybe a week, maybe more before she disappeared, but whenever it was she didn't speak to her, but crossed the road to avoid her. Around the time Marcie disappeared Sadie was busy getting married and saying goodbye to her soldier husband – she frowned – and she hadn't heard about it until Kath Swallow came and told her probably on the Monday or Tuesday. Her husband's name was Jakimowicz – yes of course she could spell it, he was with the Canadian forces waiting to go to France, she wasn't expecting to see him again until after the war – tears filled her eyes and the older policeman would have felt sorry for her if she hadn't looked so mean with her pinched little mouth and screwed up eyes.

Kath said she had known Marcie ever since she moved to the area after they were bombed out in 1941. Marcie was all right, but she didn't see much of her because of the bad feeling between her and Sadie, who was Kath's best friend. Marcie didn't have a particular boyfriend, though Eric was thought to be quite keen on her. Yes, she had seen Marcie and her brother come to blows when they were younger, it used to happen all the time. The last time Kath saw her was on the Friday evening, the day after Sadie's wedding, about six o'clock. She was standing by the level crossing gates as if waiting for someone to be coming out of the factories, she was dressed in an ordinary way, no, Kath didn't think she had a coat on and she didn't know what her shoes were like. She seemed normal and they passed a few words, not about anything particular. Kath didn't ask her who she was waiting for. It didn't seem unusual for her to be there – because Marcie started work very early at the bakery she finished work before most people and quite often would wait for a friend at that time. Marcie said, Cheerio see you tomorrow.

Ginny could not remember seeing Marcie around the time of her disappearance, unless, and she wasn't sure whether to say this or not, unless Marcie was the girl she saw in the entry late on Friday night, when Ginny was coming home from dancing. She only saw a shadow, or two shadows in the dark of the passage as she was going by, and it wasn't even the entry to Marcie's home, but the next one along, and she assumed the other shadow was a man but she couldn't swear to it. She said she knew nothing about how she got on with her brother, it was very rare that he was seen out.

The younger policeman was called away to deal with something else –'We're a bit stretched at the station' – and it was the older one on his own who knocked on the door of the house where Nell and her mother occupied the upstairs rooms. The policeman, bald and lined and overdue for retirement, first went in downstairs and spoke to Mr Page, who said that he knew no young girls, and anyway, he never went out. Then he shouted up the stairs and the policeman, wheezing softly, climbed them to speak to Nell.

Nell and her mother had two rooms and a bathroom. The policeman was first taken into the front room, dark because the curtains were drawn against the sun and half filled with two beds, but when he became used to the dimness, very tidy. Then the woman took him into Nell's room, where there was another double bed and a single, and Nell sitting on the edge of it, crying, in a way that looked set to become a habit. Her mother looked at her with a sort of resigned pity, and sat down on the bed next to her. The policeman remained standing, though he would have loved to take the weight off his feet.

Nell punctuated her answers with sniffs and gulps. Yes she had known Marcie ever since she started work in the bakers, because Marcie not only lived close by, but brought trays of bread from the bakery over to the shop. 'Don't cry Miss,' said the policeman, 'we'll find her.' But Nell's mother assured him that she wasn't crying for Marcie, but about her boyfriend, who had been home on leave and gone back on bad terms with Nell, after a row – another row – over whether they should get married. 'She thinks she won't see him ever again,' said her mother sadly. Nell said Marcie was her best friend, in a way. No she didn't seem to have a boyfriend, no she hadn't heard her talk of going away with anyone. She hadn't seen her since Friday, at work as usual, spoke to her only briefly as there were customers in the shop. Mrs Bryce watched her daughter carefully through the interview but said nothing herself about Marcie, beyond that she knew her by sight.

The younger policeman who had seen Marcie's brother and spoken to the aunt thought there might be bad feeling in the family and that the brother might have injured Marcie in a fight. But they had searched the house, even the room where the mother lay in bed, motionless except for her eyes, and found no evidence of violence. Back at the station, he started to make a list of men and boys in the area who would know Marcie: Her brother Ronnie MacNee; the father and brother of Kath and Ginny, both called William Swallow, son known as Billy; Wilfred Singleton, the father of Sadie; Mr Page; Gus Treasure, Nell's boyfriend; Eric Horns, Gus' friend, and said to be sweet on Marcie; Jack Jakimowicz, new husband of Sadie.

Then he stopped writing because there was any number of men and youths in the area, both living and passing through. Countless people worked in the factories, rode their bikes to and from work, could have stopped and talked to Marcie, met her after work on Friday night, or Saturday midday. Any number of servicemen might have visited the area, or Marcie might have gone out of the area, to a dance somewhere. The shoe might be hers or it might not. She might have been last seen Friday six o'clock, or Friday midnight or even, according to auntie Saturday dinnertime. She could have run away. It wasn't that there was nothing to go on but there was too much to go on and if, as he said, what we're most likely looking for is a drunk soldier who's got out of hand and gone too far and strangled her to keep her quiet, well, we shall be looking for ever because he's not around here any longer and never likely to be again. And unless, or until, she turns up, one way or another, we might as well get on with something useful.

CHAPTER THREE
IN WHICH THERE IS A BIRTH AND A DEATH –
NOT IN THAT ORDER

It was Kath who was the second person to know that Gus had been killed.

It had been Christmas Eve, a Sunday morning and Kath was dusting the front room on the orders of her mother, so that it could be used for Christmas Day. As she was making sure the corners of the window frames were free of any dirt – her mother would check – she saw Mrs Treasure going past, telegram in hand.

'I just knew,' said Kath to Sadie. 'You could tell, the way she was walking, like she was on strings.' Kath blew her nose and wiped her eyes. 'My poor little Gus.'

'Don't say that to Nell,' said Sadie. 'He wasn't your Gus at all.'

'Have you seen her?'

'I went round,' said Sadie, 'and I saw her but I didn't stop. I just said I'm sorry and come away. She looked rough.'

'Do you know what Gus said to me?' said Kath.

'When?'

'Back in the summer, before he went off to the invasion.'

'Yes, but I didn't know you ever talked to Gus. When was this?'

'Oh, just one evening,' said Kath. 'I think he was coming home from seeing Nell and I was just standing out by the front gate.'

'Just standing,' said Sadie sceptically.

'Anyway,' said Kath. 'He told me that he asked Nell to get married – oh, ages ago, and she won't, and she won't let him touch her or anything – you know, and sometimes he feels like chucking it all in.'

'Poor Gus,' said Sadie. Jack came briefly into her mind – what if he was killed and she became a widow?

– but he didn't seem really real and she let the thought go.

Ginny came into the room where they were sitting by the fire. 'Where's Mum and Dad?'

'Down the Falcon.' It was Boxing Day, it was raining, everything had a flat, finished feel.

'Well this has been a happy Christmas for one and all,' Ginny said. 'How are you keeping Sadie? Not long to go now.'

'About six weeks,' said Sadie, smoothing her front.

'Have you heard from Jack?'

'Somewhere in Holland. That's all I know. The weather's wet. He don't say much.'

'Well, they're not allowed to,' said Ginny and Kath gave her opinion that it was a good excuse for those that didn't like writing. 'Like Ted,' she added.

'I've just been to see Nell,' said Ginny. 'Her and her mum, they're in a terrible state, not just Gus you know, but Eddie. He's missing.'

'Sometimes they turn up,' said Kath.

'Sometimes. I think that could be worse though, while you're waiting, just not knowing, thinking about it all the time.'

'Well what about you Gin?' said Sadie. 'Kath's got Ted, and my Jack's in Holland and Nell's brother in France. Who have you got to think about?'

'Oh I've got dozens,' said Ginny. 'I spread my worry around and they all get a little bit.'

'No one special then?'

'No not me. Ding dong wedding bells, always ring for other gels.'

'Oh you'll get married one day.'

'I might not want to.'

This was not a position Sadie understood so she said nothing, just sat on the bed feeling the baby stretch slowly under her hands, under the print cotton smock that she had made herself out of an old frock of

40

Stepmother's, and tried to remember what Jack looked like.

'She only says that,' said Kath, 'cos no one's ever asked her.'

'I'll be off.' Sadie got off the bed and pushed her swollen feet into her shoes. 'Stepmother's mum and dad are coming for the evening.' She sighed. 'I'm supposed to stay awake.' She stood up and something seemed to ping inside her and when the liquid ran down her legs she looked in amazement, wondering where it had come from.

'Oh Lord,' said Ginny.

'Does it hurt?' said Kath.

The three of them stood for what seemed like minutes, as if waiting to see what would happen. Then, 'We'd better get you home,' said Ginny.

'Stepmother's not going to like this,' moaned Sadie.

'Sod Stepmother,' said Kath. 'Come on, we'll take you home, it's only along the road.'

'Can you walk?' said Ginny anxiously but Sadie seemed no different from normal. Out in the cold air though she began shivering as the water turned chill on her legs. 'I hope my shoes ain't ruined,' she said.

'Here's your dad,' said Kath.

They hadn't seen him through the blackout until he was close and he seemed rather unsteady, though everyone knew he was teetotal.

'Hello Mr Singleton,' called Ginny, she said afterwards because he looked as if he was in another world. 'We're bringing Sadie home.'

'She's having a baby,' said Kath.

He peered at them in the dark. There was no smell of drink, but as Ginny said later, 'I could swear he'd had some, and no one can say we don't know the signs, can they Kath?'

Then he seemed to recognise them. 'Three little maids is it?' he said in his usual way. 'Hello my love.'

This to Ginny as he put his arm round her neck. 'Coming inside for a piece of cake?'

Kath was already knocking on the door.

'Not now Mr Singleton,' said Ginny. 'You'll need to look after Sadie.'

He made a weak attempt to kiss Ginny but only managed to put his nose in her ear. Stepmother was at the door now, with Maurice behind her and Sadie was being hurried inside.

'Ta ta,' called Kath. 'We'll see you tomorrow.' As if nothing special was going to happen in between.

They went back to mop the floor. 'Honeymoon baby,' said Ginny, and they laughed.

To Sadie, meeting her dad outside the house merged into the dreamlike sequence of events. At first there was confusion, even hilarity. Stepmother, though cross – 'Couldn't you have waited till after Christmas' – bustled efficiently and got out the rubber sheet and all the newspapers they'd been stockpiling, and the box of sheets and towels. 'Trust you to be awkward. We weren't looking for this to happen for at least another month.' Sadie thought of saying 'Honeymoon baby' but suddenly couldn't be bothered. Stepmother continued to scold but her eyes were shining with excitement.

Later when the pains really started and each one was worse than the one before, like being pushed higher and higher on a swing, all the while thinking Slow down, slow down, let me get off; holding on tight – what was she holding on to? the rails of the bedstead, but then it was the swing again – holding on so she didn't fall off and die, Stop it, stop it, no more; then she didn't know that when her father was sent for the midwife he came back with the news that she couldn't be found and may have gone to visit her sister in Barnet. And was sent out again – Stepmother panicking by now – and came back with someone else, someone roused from their bed in the early hours, and then when it was morning and the baby was finally born and the pain stopped as if by magic, there was Nell's mother in the room, with a sponge and a bowl of warm water and Stepmother with a clean nightdress, and the baby was wrapped up and pronounced a fine big boy. And her father coming in before he went to work, all tearful, with cups of tea, extra sugary, for them, and Maurice putting his head round the door and being shooed away.

In the evening Kath and Ginny came after work.

'Did it hurt?' said Kath.

'Not half.'

'Does it still hurt?'

'Not so bad. I feel as if I've gone a few rounds with Joe Louis.'

'Well you're looking all right.' It was true. Sadie looked tired but she was smiling and sparkling in an unusual way.

'What are you calling him?'

'John. And Jack wanted him called Joseph after *his* father, but that's so old-fashioned, he can have it as a middle name.'

'His initials will be JJJ,' said Ginny.

As they were leaving, Kath turned and said 'Oh – I meant to tell you – they've found a body, they think it's Marcie.'

'Kath!' said Ginny. 'Give Sadie a bit of time.'

'What?' said Kath. 'She'll get to know soon enough.'

But Sadie didn't seem to care.

Nobody much seemed to care about Marcie. There were too many other things to care about at that time, too many other deaths to hear of, too many other people in danger, somewhere. Marcie's body was found, wrapped roughly in a piece of old tarpaulin, as the cold wind blew away the last of the leaves from the ditch that ran beside the hedge bottom, not very far from where her shoe was found. But how could it have not been noticed, lying and rotting and smelling so close to the path all summer long? It was boys who found it, boys on their way to the railway bridge to look at the trains, quite little boys of an age to scuffle about in hedge bottoms looking for conkers or whatever else boys looked for. Little boys for whom probably a hedge would be for ever something to shudder away from. The police came and took it away.

Ginny went to see Nell to tell her about Sadie's baby, and found to her surprise that she already knew, in a great deal of detail.

'I didn't know you were a midwife,' said Ginny to Nell's mother.

'Death and birth,' said Mrs Bryce, 'I can deal with them both.' Which Ginny thought was a strange thing to say, but maybe she just meant that Gus was dead and probably Eddie too, and that a new baby was compensation, of some sort.

When her mother left the room Nell said, 'So I'll never have a baby now.'

Ginny tried to decide what to say. Never say die? Never mind? Never is a long time? 'You never know,' she finally said.

'Gus will never have a baby now,' said Nell, and Ginny had to agree with that.

'Neither will Marcie,' said Nell.

'Oh. You've heard about Marcie? I wasn't going to say anything.'

'Why not? It's old news now isn't it.'

'So why did you say that? About her never having a baby?'

Nell – she was sitting up on her bed, leaning against the headboard and she stopped pleating the sheet with her fingers – looked directly at Ginny. 'Marcie was going to have a baby,' she said.

'You didn't tell the police,' said Ginny.

'What could they do?'

'How do you know?'

'What?'

'She was having a baby.'

'She came to my mother,' said Nell, still looking at Ginny, carefully, to see what she would say.

'Your mother. Because she's a midwife?'

'No. Yes, she is. And she gets rid of babies for people.'

Ginny was quiet, looking down at the floor. When she looked up again, Nell was pleating the sheet, without looking at it.

'Why are you telling me?' asked Ginny.

'I thought you might know already. But anyway, you might want to know one day. You or Kath.'

Ginny laughed, surprising both of them. 'I suppose I might, if I'm not careful,' she said.

Nell smiled a small smile, probably the first one in months. 'Better to be careful,' she said.

'I'm sure,' said Ginny. And they said no more.

The police went to Marcie's aunt with some scraps of a summer dress and a heavy gold necklace. She wasn't so sure about the dress, it was so weathered and faded. The necklace, that was a different thing.

'How have you got that?' she said. It was supposed by her to be kept upstairs, in a locked box, guarded by the never still eyes of Marcie's mother.

'When did you last see it?' asked the policeman.

'Not for years. It stays in its box. It belonged to my grandmother' – and truly it did look old-fashioned – 'Marcie never knew it was there, how could she get it?'

She checked the box. No necklace. Called Ronnie, asked him, by signs, had he seen Marcie with it? He nodded.

'Just once? Or lots of times?'

He flickered his fingers. Lots.

'You'd think whoever did it would have taken the necklace,' said Kath to Ginny.

Ginny shrugged. 'Poor Marcie.'

'Who do you think did it?' said Kath.

Ginny didn't answer. She had her thoughts but Kath was too tactless and blundering to be allowed to share them, and anyway, Kath would only have more nightmares. She kept her thoughts to herself.

CHAPTER FOUR
IN WHICH PEOPLE FIND THEY HAVE
TO LIVE TOGETHER

When it was all well and safe into the past, Sadie would tell her daughter about coming to Canada.

'I didn't know nothing,' she said. 'Canada was just a word. I never dreamed of anything like it in real life. Your father never even told me a quarter of it.'

Jack met her in Montreal, barely demobbed, unfamiliar without his uniform, and they took the train to Kingston. Then the ferry, and then they stood on frozen feet listening for the truck that Jack's father would be driving to meet them. Jack carried their three kitbags and Sadie carried John and they waited in the churned up sullen light of the half-dark and the snow, without speaking.

When he came he greeted Jack in Polish, crying, standing back to look, hugging him again. Then with a tentative gesture to Sadie, took John from her arms and hugged him too, then held him away to look at his face. His face that was by now red and crumpled and getting ready to cry. He gave him back to Sadie and shook her hand, then hugged Jack again and threw the bags into the truck.

'Look John, we're going in a lorry.' Sadie was almost too tired to make the effort to be cheerful, what she wanted more than anything was to be warm and asleep. She sat between Jack and the door with John on her knee, rubbing his feet to keep them warm.

Jack suddenly said to her in English, 'There it is.' She looked and could see a little light, still far off. Home, she thought. There was a question mark after the word. John, having been awake most of the night, became heavy and went to sleep.

The truck had barely stopped when the door next to Sadie was flung open and she saw Jack's mother. The woman looked past her to her son, then back. Sadie did not feel welcomed by her expression. I hoped *you* wouldn't come after all, said the expression. Sadie struggled to get down the high step, on her frozen feet with a sleeping child in her arms. The woman waited – only just – for her to be out of the way, then swarmed up the step, pulling at Jack, sobbing and chattering in loud Polish.

Two girls stood by, waiting. The older one smiled at Sadie. 'Sorry about mom,' she said. 'She's been waiting for this since the day he left. Come into the house and get warm.' This was Lena. She turned to her sister. 'Help with them bags,' she said.

Sadie sat in a chair by the stove and it was some moments before she took in that there was an old lady in the kitchen and that she was pointing and complaining. It was Sadie's shoes, it seemed that were concerning her, that were muddy from the yard and should have been left at the door instead of tracking mud across the floor. Lena, Lena again, with quick tidy movements whipped Sadie's shoes off and wrapped a blanket round her feet ('It's the dog's blanket,' she whispered, 'but it will warm you up.') and began to produce hot drinks, and food.

'Lisa,' she yelled out of the door, 'get yourself in here and help.'

It was strange, being in a bed that didn't rock. There'd been the ship, and the trains, and it had come to feel that was the way it had to be, that was the way of the whole world, rocking, sometimes more, sometimes less. Sometimes regular, sometimes scarily sudden. Sadie closed her eyes and it seemed to bring back the rocking feeling, faintly, and when Jack reached past John to touch her she was already asleep.

John was in this bed too for the family had not organised anywhere else for him to go, and Sadie, through her tiredness, was grateful for his familiar solid warm body and the way it lay between her and her husband. The number of nights she had ever spent with Jack, in a bed, from bedtime till morning, was precisely one. Their wedding night. He had been sick in the chamber pot, from drinking after the ceremony, and she had been feeling sick, from a pregnancy begun two months before. It was not a pleasant night, nothing like the brief spring afternoons when he was stationed nearby and could visit most weekends and they could sneak into her bedroom while Stepmother went out visiting and Maurice was out playing till dark.

Morning came. Sadie couldn't tell what time it might be when John woke up, as their room had no window. It wasn't even a room, as she understood the word. When Jack sat up in bed, as he did, trying to get John to come to him, his head touched the roof. Apart from the bedstead there was no furniture, and no room for any, and the mattress, that she had slept so well on was not a sprung one, not even a flock one like she was used to, and certainly not a feather one, but a straw one. Sadie was silent. All the time on the ship, sitting listening to the other women with John on her knee; all the time on the train, looking out at trees and trees and trees, under a last light covering of snow, she had imagined that the end of the journey would be something like home. Now she would like to be back on the ship.

'Sadie,' said Jack. 'I have to tell you, here they call me by my proper name. Ma won't like it if you call me Jack.' She said nothing. 'Zygmunt. Zyg if you like, my sisters call me Zyg.' She nodded slowly.

That first morning they were allowed to stay in bed long after the rest of the family was up, but on all the other mornings Sadie was wakened by her mother-in-law banging on the door. Often Zyg had already slid out of bed and was dressed and in the cowshed. Sadie would dress herself and John – which amounted to putting some more clothes over the ones they had slept in, and go through the room where the sisters slept, past the cupboard where the grandmother slept, warmed by the stove pipe going through it, and down to the kitchen where the parents slept.

'I always slept in the kitchen too,' said Zyg. 'I never had a room of my own.'

If Sadie had been able to see the family before Zyg's return, she would have understood what a relief it was to have him back. Relief that he had not been killed was only a part of it. He was needed on the farm – 'We missed him so much,' Lena told Sadie, 'we didn't know how much we needed him till he was gone. So many jobs you need two tall men for and we only had one.' Zyg was not a naturally practical person but the years in the army had given him new strength and confidence, and he was happy, even joyful, to be back on his father's farm. They all called it Pop's farm but it was courtesy only. The farm was in the hands of Maryska.

Sadie soon got to know how the family worked. Joe was useless. Nice but useless. Lisa was friendly but lazy. Baba was old and cross, cross and demanding. She had looked after the hens for years but even that was now getting beyond her, in the winter at least. 'When the better weather comes,' said Lena, 'she'll be able to go outside again.' Lena did the work, organised the others, directed them, made decisions, monitored their work, redid it often, sat under the lamp with her mother to do the paperwork in the evenings. Maryska held the power. The money, what there was of it, all went through the hands, and into the hiding places, of Maryska.

Only the old lady, her mother, called her Maryska. Neighbours, though few and far between, called her husband Joe, and handed out friendly claps on the shoulder or – the women – smiled and held out a hand to be shaken. But they straightened their faces if Maryska came into the yard and called her Mrs

Jakimowicz. Sadie did the same and no one ever invited her to do different. But she also kept her eyes open and her tongue quiet, as she had learned to do with Stepmother and she soon knew that Maryska had secret money stashes round the place. The flour bin had an inner sleeve against the mice but it didn't reach to the bottom and under it was a packet of dollar bills. There was a treacle tin at the back of the cupboard that contained coins, another packet of bills slid between sheets of newspaper under a pile of sheets – these were just the ones that Sadie discovered in her first few weeks.

Sadie had no money of her own – none of them did. Poor Lisa went to school in her sister's cast-offs, Maryska herself wore her mother's old clothes, black long skirts, flannel petticoats. Sadie's own clothes were useless for winter and she had to submit to sharing things with Lisa, never mind how much shorter she was. Still – this was her first breakthrough with the family – she was handy with a needle and thread (the only thing, she thought, that she ever got from Stepmother) and when they saw her letting out the waist of Zyg's best trousers – he had put on weight while in the army though he looked set to lose it again on the farm – they began to bring her little mending jobs on their own clothes. She turned the collar of Joe's best shirt, relieving the family of having to buy him a new one, she reshaped a blouse for Lisa so that it fitted instead of being full. She offered, but was turned down, to put a fur collar on Maryska's coat. She knitted fingerless mittens for all of them out of scraps of wool, keeping the best wool to make clothes for John. Even Maryska softened towards him at last as he ran about the yard in a white knitted vest, before he fell in the mud which never entirely hardened even in the summer.

That was in the evenings, by lamplight. They had no electricity – well, plenty of people in England had no electricity but most of them, Sadie believed, had gas. Here, Lena didn't even understand the word; gas, she said, was for trucks.

Words. What a problem words were. The grandmother – Baba – had hardly a word that she could use to Sadie. Here, she would say, No, Go – that was what got her through the day with Sadie, and with Lisa who pretended she didn't understand Polish. Maryska could read and write but only in Polish and her spoken English was so strange, so unlike any English Sadie had ever heard –unlike Zyg's, who spoke to her ears like a character in a film. (They called a film a movie – not that they ever went to one, hardly.) Helping Maryska round the house, which was all Sadie could do to begin with, was a nightmare, the sort where everything you say or do leads you down a wrong road, further and further from where you wanted to be. 'Souse,' said Maryska, and then louder, 'Souse!' wanting Sadie to pass something to her, and finally fetching it herself and poking it in Sadie's face. 'Souse.'

'Saucepan,' said Sadie, but she could tell her mother-in-law did not believe her. Her own language which she had never in her life had to give any thought to, was no longer her own. Between the members of the family there were linguistic misunderstandings all the time, even without Sadie being involved, but she added another dimension with her cockney voice, her lack of aitches and her use of obscure slang which she didn't even know was slang.

'Taters out there,' she would say, and when questioned could only say it was a word for cold. Lena began to disbelieve her and suspect that she was making fun of them. Lisa laughed at her but stored her words away, in case of some future need. 'Love a duck,' said Sadie. This was how her father spoke and even people like Stepmother who didn't, could understand him. 'Where's your titfer?' she asked John when he was being dressed to go out, and he knew what she meant, he was on the way to being trilingual in Canadian English, Polish-Canadian English and London English as no one else was or even knew it was possible to be.

They had not the smallest idea of where Sadie came from. They perceived England only from a very rare trip to the movies – English people lived in castles, or else country cottages, they were poor and humble or haughty and rich. Sadie, who had never seen a servant in her life – unless you counted Kath's mum who swept out the buses – who had never lived more than a hundred yards from a corner shop, who had never seen the sea until she arrived at Portsmouth to board the ship for Canada, who was pale and thin from six years of war and rationing, who wanted now that the war was over, nylons and permanent waves and an inside toilet, Sadie in turn had no idea of the pioneering thrust that had brought these people out of rural Poland and across Europe and an ocean, collecting stamps on their documents in every new country, in search of, or hoping for, something they didn't have. What that thing was, Sadie never learned. She had never known the feeling of needing space.

So much space. So far from the house to the track, from the track to the road, from there to the store. So far to the cowshed to fetch milk for the kitchen, so far to the gate to look in the box to see if there was a letter from England. So few letters. A scrambled scrawl from her father, barely readable, with a brisk note at the bottom from Stepmother and sometimes – well, hardly ever – a note from Maurice too (Dear Sadie, I have not time to write much, I have to do my homework.) Kath – no more than a card at Christmas (From Kath and Ted and Family, no more than that, not even the children's names.) Sadie herself never had time to write to them more than once or twice a year and Ginny seemed to understand this because she didn't wait for a letter before sending one, about once a month, on a Sunday night when she was at home washing her hair. She would fill an airmail sheet – not hard for she had big expansive handwriting – and tell Sadie some bits of gossip and news. Billy's Joyce was expecting again, sweets had come off ration and gone straight back on again, there were new houses being built at the side of the park.

Nell wrote more often because she didn't go out like Ginny did, but she had less to say. She was well but her mother was not well. The weather was cold. Not as cold as it is here, retorted Sadie in her head. She felt that she had never in her life had so much to complain about. Life was too hard, the work was too hard, the difference between Canada and England, between being Polish and being English, was too hard. The shock of the surrounding space, the forest, the snow, the smell and heat and size of the animals, the unending feeding of them, tending them, moving them from place to place with their malicious hooves and their loud breathing, the unending clearing up of shit.

The unending work to repair fences and gates, machinery and tools, and the house itself, the battle to keep everyone warm and fed. She didn't feel secure enough to complain. They would just look at her, she knew, wondering why it should be any different for her than it was for them. In bed at nights she sometimes complained to Zyg, in a roundabout sort of way. You should have married Nell, not me, she moaned. Zyg – and in the dark she couldn't see his face – did not argue, but gave her a quick hug and turned away. John by now was sleeping with his aunts. It was summer and the heat under the roof stuffed her mouth and seemed almost to stop her breath. 'Blanka never complained,' Zyg told her when she huffed and thrashed about trying to find a cool place in the bed. Blanka was the oldest sister, older than Zyg. When she heard he was coming home with a wife she took the opportunity to marry a postman with only one eye, and went to live in Kingston.

'My grandmother,' said Lisa to Sadie, 'is an illegal.'

'What does that mean?'

Sadie, having no grandparents of her own, had little experience of old people. Her chief feeling about Baba was fear – that she might speak to her, might need help that required touching, might cough uncontrollably, might – sooner or later *would* – spit into the stove and miss so that someone (and all three girls tried to pretend they hadn't seen) had to scoop it up on the shovel and slide it into the stove to hiss.

This was early on in her time on the farm and she was still getting to know her sisters-in-law. Lisa's eyes sparked with delighted malice. She loved nothing better than gossip about sins and crimes, and stories about crooks and outlaws and rascals, especially local ones.

'If they knew she was here, they'd send her back where she came from. Listen, I'll tell you, and then you can tell me a bad story.

'After Mom came here, and Blanka and Zyg were born and before Lena and me, Baba was still in Poland and she wanted to see Mom so she saved up some money, or stole it maybe, and walked out of Poland with a cardboard box –'

'What about her husband?'

'Oh, dead. Anyway, she gets across Europe and she gets a place on a ship and she doesn't have to pay because she gets a job as a maid to this rich woman, but it's only as long as they're on the ship because this rich woman has her own maids in New York. And the ship isn't going to Canada but Baba figures it's OK because Canada and the USA they're next to each other and she's already walked across most of Europe. So all the time they're on the ship – Pop told me this and it's a secret – Baba is taking this rich woman's clothes out of her trunk and putting them in her own cardboard box, but then it gets too full and so she takes her own things out and exchanges them and even then she had to steal a bag from somewhere to put some in, and when it's time to get off the ship she hides, with her box and her bag full of all this stuff, and sneaks ashore – don't ask me how because those immigration officers, they're on to you like bugs, but maybe she looks innocent, like little old lady –'

'How old was she then?'

'Well I guess, around fifty, sixty. She's nearly eighty now, we think, she's forgotten exactly. Anyway she got here from New York, across the border and everything, we don't know how, with all this rich woman's stuff and turned up on the farm one day and has never been off it since.'

'Never?' Sadie was more horrified by this detail than any other. Trudging across a continent or two, sleeping in barns, being chased by dogs, being wet, cold, hungry, lost, these were things she couldn't imagine. Being stranded on the farm, never to leave, that was something that struck her in the heart.

'Never,' said Lisa. She sat back, satisfied, on her bed. 'Now you can tell me something.'

But Maryska called them down at that moment – Lisa was to go and call the men in, Sadie was to keep John away from the stove, and it was a week later, on another Saturday, before Lisa reminded Sadie.

Sadie had no talent for story telling. 'Well,' she said, reluctantly, 'there was this girl got murdered.'

'Did you know her?'

'Oh yes. She lived across the road to me and she was in my class at school.'

'Did you like her?'

'No.'

'Why?'

'She used to hit me. She used to sit behind me and pull my hair and when we went out in the yard at playtime she was always pushing and shoving.'

'Is that all?'

'She was dirty. My stepmother said they had fleas in their house and I mustn't play with her.'

'So how did she get murdered?'

'No one knows.'

'Did they find her body?'

'In the end they did.' Sadie did not want to tell Lisa it was on the very day that John was born, it always seemed like an unlucky omen. 'She was in this sort of field, under the hedge, in a sort of ditch.'

'What was her name?'

'Marcie.'

'Who do you think did it?'

'I don't know.'

'Make a guess. You must have someone you suspect.'

Sadie closed her mind to any thought but the most comfortable one. 'I think her brother did it. They were always fighting, he wasn't quite right in the head, you know, I think he went too far, not meaning to, if you know what I mean, and then he had to hide her. That's what I think.'

'Did they arrest him?'

'They never arrested no one. Not enough evidence.'

This was not the last time Lisa asked about Marcie's murder. Sadie became sorry she had ever told her. She did not want to remember, it brought back too much, it made her homesick in a strange and uncomfortable way, it made her slightly ashamed, and she felt that she couldn't look down on the Jakimowizces when she had such happenings on the street where she'd lived. But she liked talking to Lisa. Lisa was lazy and charming, cleverer than the others, prettier than Lena, rosy and flirtatious. She was interested in the details of Sadie's life in England. Even the idea of living in a street with houses on both sides, with shops and pubs on the corners, with railway lines and buses and dustbins and streetlights – though they had all these things in Kingston, to Lisa they were foreign and exciting, and she could use them to show off at school about her English sister-in-law.

The story of Baba's stolen clothes took root in Sadie's head. She imagined the clothes, silk dresses, fringed scarves, linen underskirts, a fur coat even. She imagined the colours, ivory and eau de nil, peach and midnight blue. Scarlet. At last, one day, she asked Lisa. 'What happened to them?'

'Oh,' said Lisa casually. 'They're under her bed.'

Winter came again. To open the door took your breath away and roused Baba to shriek from her nest by the stove. For John to go out he had to be wrapped in so many layers that he could hardly walk for fabric. He pulled off his mittens and immediately cried to have them put on again.

Then, at last, spring and the ice melted to slush in the day and froze into slippery ridges at night. Then, suddenly, fiercely, it was summer and insects had to be kept out of the house. At least the washing could be hung outside to dry and John could run about in the yard. Sadie was pregnant.

CHAPTER FIVE
IN WHICH A PROBLEM IS SOLVED,
OR MAYBE CAUSED

Kath was pregnant. It was a bit soon after the first one, people seemed to think, but Ted was back in civvies, he was home, they were together every night, what did people expect. Ginny was the worst disapprover. 'Crikey Kath, give us a break, where you going to put another one?'

'We'll get a council house,' said Kath. 'You watch, they'll give us one of them prefabs.'

Ginny, now, was working in the council's Housing department, and she had told Kath this herself, and it was just like Kath to say it back to her as if it was her own idea.

'I know they will, but not till after the baby's born. How are we going to manage for space?'

Ginny slept in the tiny bedroom that used to be Billy's. Ted and Kath and baby Rita had the front bedroom and the use of the downstairs front room as well. Mr and Mrs Swallow slept in the back bedroom, rocked by the trains going past at the bottom of the garden. Already there were too many adults in the house. Too many people queuing for the outside toilet, wanting a bath on Sunday night, trying to get to sleep through the baby's teething, getting up early for work and waking the baby. The bath, for Ginny, was the worst. Filling it by means of saucepans and kettles was bad enough, getting her parents out of the room and making sure Ted didn't come barging in – accidentally on purpose she said to herself, and she would say something to Kath if it happened again. And then going up to her room in a dressing gown and sitting there on the bed trying to get dry and warm, and put her hair in curlers with a mirror not big enough to see your earhole in.

She envied Nell because she and her mother had an indoor bathroom to themselves. In theory they shared it with Mr Page, but in practice he never came upstairs, maybe because he was old and his legs, or his heart, weren't up to it, maybe out of delicacy, maybe it was simply that he felt no need to be very fussy about being clean. He used the outside toilet always, and washed in the kitchen, occasionally.

'If you want,' said Nell, 'you can come and have a bath here.'

'Won't your mum mind?'

'You can give her something for the gas. She won't mind, she likes you.'

It became a custom with Ginny, then, to take a bag with her clean clothes and towel, and her curlers and cold cream along to Nell's on a Sunday and spend the whole evening there. The bathroom was fitted with a vast water heater, a temperamental and explosive gadget that Mrs Bryce went in and lit with a spill while Nell and Ginny stood at the door, ready to rescue her if it blew up.

So Ginny lay in the big iron bath one summer evening. It was past eight o'clock and warm enough for the window to be open. She could see blue sky outside, and though most of the children playing had been taken indoors she could still hear one or two urchins calling to each other down the street. She worried. How long since she'd seen Bernie? Stupid question, she knew exactly, to the minute, when she'd said goodbye to him, lingering kiss, pressing herself against him, breathless with lust, in a doorway by the bus stop, hoping the bus would not come and he would be too late to catch his train and they could go back to bed. Seven weeks and two days and she had not come on. She knew she was expecting, she was not a fool.

She had been a fool. It was her own fault, it wasn't anyone else who made her go with the Irishman. It wasn't even his fault, she had to say to herself, he had hesitated, he had held himself back and she had said, Do it, do it, it's all right, and he, eager and relieved of responsibility had plunged into her, there in the workmen's caravan where he lived on the building site.

She did not expect to see him again. She had no address for him. She knew his name, his marital status – married – the county in Ireland which he had come from – Cork – and which he had gone back to. Her thoughts skipped and skimmed, they refused to settle on the problem of the moment. She thought of his eyes, dark as a Spaniard's, she thought of the sight of him unexpectedly waiting for her after work, because the rain had stopped the job they were on. She remembered the scuffed brown of his battered work boots and the cheese sandwiches they ate sitting by the river one day in her lunch hour when he was supposed to be somewhere else and how he screwed up the greaseproof paper and threw it into the river and it bobbed away among the ducks. She thought of the weight of his body on hers and she felt how much she missed him. The water was going cold although she'd had it as hot as she could bear from some vaguely hopeful idea that it might help.

Sitting on Nell's bed with her hair wrapped in a towel, and thinking she ought to write to Sadie but it seemed too much trouble, she remembered – not that she had ever forgotten – what Nell told her all that time ago when they had been talking about Marcie. The memory of Marcie always made Ginny shudder inside. She tried never to think of the body lying there, but the picture would come into her mind in spite of trying. She always imagined her lying on her back, looking up at the sky, eyes open. She tried not to wonder about flesh, its colour, its touch, its smell. She tried not to think about rats and maggots. The ditch was gone now, and the hedge. The land was set aside for building houses on sometime soon, and most of the people who would live in them would never know that there was once a dead body found lying in the brown scrubby winter grass.

All right then, she said to herself, it's got to be done. And while Nell was having her bath Ginny went into her mother's room.

Mrs Bryce kept her room very tidy, unlike Nell who tended to be casual and disorganised, always losing stockings and putting on her jumpers inside out. Like Nell, her mother was tall and thin, and since her son had been killed and she'd found out that her husband had been worked to death in a German internment camp she'd seemed thinner and sadder. She sat in her chair by the window, looking out at the fading sky.

Ginny was not good at working carefully up to what she had to say. 'I'm in trouble,' she said.

Mrs Bryce did not move. 'What sort of trouble?'

Ginny laughed, though she didn't mean to. 'The usual sort,' she said. She kept her eyes on the other woman's feet, big and bare and planted firmly on the cool lino, and didn't see her look up or the expression on her face.

'What do you want me to do?'

'Well, you know,' said Ginny. Now she was beating about the bush, but it was because she felt that she didn't know the right words.

'You have to say it,' said Mrs Bryce. 'I can't guess at what you mean, you have to tell me straight out.'

'I want rid of it,' said Ginny, and to her own ears it sounded like a sentence she never thought she would say. 'I want you to get rid of it.'

'How far on?'

'Seven weeks, maybe eight.'

'Sure?'

'I'm sure.'

'I'll do it for you,' said Mrs Bryce. 'I don't do many these days, I don't take the risks, I'm too old to be worrying about the risks. But I'll do it because I know you. And it's not too far on. The further on, the more difficult it is, you know that. But you do know, don't you, that you'll be sorry.'

'I won't be sorry,' said Ginny. She had expected to have to explain all sorts of circumstances and plead and beg, and she felt a bit let down that it was so easy. Did it really not matter so much?

'Come Wednesday after work. You'll have two days off work, should be all right by Monday. Tell your mother you're sleeping here. Does she know?'

'No.'

So it was easy. Ginny thought of that word easy when she lay awake, feeling the blood flowing out of her, wondering would it ever stop, how much was to be expected as normal, would she die, if she went to sleep would that be her last action in this world? Could you die in your sleep, or would you wake up at the critical moment? She would rather wake up and know, she thought, and then she thought she wouldn't.

The pain was coming on again and she groaned this time, because it was too much effort not to, and Nell woke up – or maybe had been awake all along – and turned towards her and whispered, 'Do you want anything?'

I want to die, thought Ginny but she said, 'Help me across the landing Nell,' and thought, Thank God for indoor lavs. Mrs Bryce came out of the other room and took charge. So she should, thought Ginny, it's all her fault, this.

But next day, when it was over, and the baby was gone, and the bleeding was less and she was sleepy in bed and Nell had gone to work, Ginny knew, as an honest person, that it wasn't Nell's mum's fault at all. It had been horrible, from the disgusting tasting stuff she'd been given to drink, to the poking and stretching and the sudden deep far away pain, to the cramps and the bleeding. But it was her own fault and all she felt towards Mrs Bryce was gratitude, and a little embarrassment. She had not asked for any payment and had seemed, if anything, sadder than Ginny that it had to be done.

It seemed natural, after that, for her to move in with Nell and her mother. The bathroom was part of the attraction, it's true, but as well, the move got her away from Kath and especially Ted, and she liked sharing a room again, and Nell was more comfortable as a room mate in many ways, than Kath had been. Better at listening, didn't have nightmares, less inclined to argue, and much less inclined, as they were different sizes, to borrow her clothes. And grateful for the company. Nell didn't go dancing as Ginny did, she didn't go to the pictures with men and had probably never in her life been in a pub, and Ginny couldn't persuade to do any of these things. But there were still several evenings every week when it was a pleasure to be at home with a friend reading magazines, mending clothes, talking, talking most of all.

Nell talked about her job, about hose joints that came apart and flooded the greenhouses, about workmen who broke panes in the glasshouses and pretended the wind had done it, of seedlings that had been knocked out of the trays and replanted and managed to survive. She had stopped working at the baker's before the end of the war. That had been a job for a child, a school-leaver. Or maybe it was a good enough job for someone who would marry their sweetheart when the war was over, but not for someone who had no sweetheart to wait for. Now she worked in one of the nursery gardens along the Cambridge Road, looking after the greenhouses, telling the men what to do. The men were Italians, ex-prisoners of war who did not want to go back to a country laid waste, little men, dried up before they should have been, who failed to learn much English, who chewed matchsticks and spat and spoke Italian to each other interspersed with short, bitter barks of laughter. They saved their money and sent for their sweethearts and set up home. They never bothered Nell. She told them what to do quietly, assuming they would do it. She never came too close, or became too familiar. Nell knew her tomatoes, and it was only tomatoes she was concerned with. She was taller than every one of the men; they called her, behind her back, La Torre.

Ginny told stories of the girls in her office, what they looked like, what they wore, who they were going out with, who might even be secretly engaged, who thought more of her boyfriend than he did of her. Nell looked forward to hearing every new instalment of the stories of Stella, and Moira, who both thought themselves a cut above Ginny, and of Ruby the junior who was always losing files. There was the office manager and her pernickety ways and unreasonable demands, and the site managers and clerks of the works who brought their reports in and flirted with the girls.

Not only work. They discussed Kath and her children and agreed that they would not have wanted to be stuck married to someone as sly and lazy as Ted. They speculated about Sadie and wondered whether she was really as happy as she said in her infrequent letters. They worried about Nell's mother, and whether she was working too hard and eating too little. They talked about the weather, and how the buses were so full it was sometimes better to walk, and about the smell from the chemical factory, and whether meat would ever come off ration, and about the new National Health Service, and whether they could get Mrs Bryce to see a doctor. And about fashions and hairstyles, naturally, and how on earth you were meant to make a new longer length skirt out of a skimpy wartime one, and wished Sadie was there to do it for them. So they talked, late into the night sometimes, but there were things they never talked about.

Ginny's abortion was never mentioned, and in a way she was grateful, but it made her feel as if she was forbidden to mention it, so that it became like a dream, unfathomable and even boring to other people, and fading in detail even to herself. She did not tell Nell (or Kath, or anyone) about Bernie. What was the point, when he had gone and she would never see him again, ever. She would have liked to talk about him though, it would have brought back the memory of him more vividly, she would have enjoyed it, though it would leave her sad. And because she couldn't tell Nell about Bernie, she never asked Nell about Gus. Or maybe Nell in some subtle way stopped her asking about Gus, and that in turn prevented Ginny confiding about Bernie. Either way, they both held on to their most important feelings and never let them out.

Autumn came, and winter. In the new year Kath had her baby, another girl, and Ginny was surprised at how shaky it made her feel. Baby, the word baby, was one she could hardly say, not out loud, not even to herself. But she had to hear it all the time.

Kath and Ted got their prefab, nearby so that Kath still visited her mother most afternoons, and Billy and his wife Joyce moved in with the Swallows, expecting their first child. Ginny was glad to be out of it.

CHAPTER SIX
IN WHICH MORE SOLUTIONS ARE SOUGHT

'Don't cry,' said Zyg, and his own nose began to run and Sadie heard him sniffing and rubbing his hand across his face.

'What have you got to cry about?' said Sadie.

Zyg reached out a hand in the dark and tried to touch her hair, or her face, but only managed to poke her in the eye – they were in bed – and she elbowed him away and he lay still, sniffing. Sadie knew he was sorry, she knew he was upset about the baby, but the knowledge was pointless beside what she felt. She had never been so totally miserable. Living here, on this horrible island, sleeping on a straw mattress, getting up at dawn, the caterpillars dropping from the trees in spring, the sweaty airless summer days – these things were nothing beside the fact of the dead baby girl, and yet these things made it worse. She knew – she knew all sorts of things that didn't help – she knew that even if she'd been at home, warm, familiar, even if her own mother was miraculously alive, she would still be more miserable than anyone had ever been, but even so these things, the heat, the dirt, the wind, the cow shit, the smell of cow shit, these things added to how miserable she was.

Zyg – she called him Zyg now, he'd forgotten to answer to Jack – was unable to be any comfort or any use. If he cried she was irritated, if he showed no feeling she hated him. If he tried to talk about the baby she felt violated, if he talked about other things she knew he'd forgotten all about it and had never cared anyway. She hated his mother even more. The baby had been buried on the farm – this is the twentieth century, she wanted to say, haven't you got cemeteries? – next to the two little stones that marked two little brothers of Zyg's that had been born between Lena and Lisa and failed to live.

Zyg's mother cried a lot, reminded by this new death of her own loss. Sadie was impatient. What right did she have to join in on her grief? Not just join in, take over, outdo her even in sobs and moans, making an exhibition of herself. Sadie would not make an exhibition of herself. She forced herself through the days and looked forward to taking her misery to bed and being alone with it. Now Zyg was back in her bed and now he was wanting to be part of her grief. Get out, get out, she thought. Leave me alone. She waited, she stopped sobbing, two tears ran silently in the dark down her face and into her ears, tickling, and she waited until she thought she could speak in her normal voice.

'I want to go and live in the town,' she said.

Zyg could not understand. She did not explain or elaborate, not then, but it was said, for the first time, it was there, between them.

Not for the last time. She always knew how the conversation would go.

'There was nothing a doctor could have done.'

'You don't know that.'

'The baby was dead before she was born.'

'She might have been saved.'

'She was early, she was too small.'

'In the hospital they have incubators.'

'But she was dead.'

'I could have had an operation.'

'You don't want that.'

'I didn't want my baby to die.'

'If it's meant to be, you can't do anything about it.'

That's what they would get back to, the futility of trying to change what could not be changed. Though Zyg said it had never happened, Sadie's nightmares were full of the apparition of Baba invading the room with the priest – in her dreams sometimes with dozens of priests, multiplying like jackdaws – Baba looking on silently as the priest ignored Sadie and blessed the poor dead daughter. The farm oppressed her more and more.

'We could live in the city. Why won't you?'

The summer days wound themselves up. There was harvest, and pumpkins and Thanksgiving. The baby's proper time to be born passed and Sadie pushed her pain down inside and went about the house and farm quiet, hiding all her feelings from everyone, and determined to hold on to her bitterness as if it was something that sustained her.

She went out into the fields one day with John. At the edge of the farm, where the last surviving horse mooched about in a bit of meadow, a pair of legs stuck out from behind a leaky tank that served the horse as a drinking trough, and there was the sound of sobbing. Someone's hurt, thought Sadie, and she had a sudden unwanted vision of dead Marcie under the hedge, and she dropped the pail – they had been going to look for blackberries, she and John – and ran to the person on the ground.

It was Lena, and Lena was furious at being found. 'Go away.'

'Be like that then.' Sadie turned to go but John ran to his aunt and she grabbed him and sobbed still louder, great painful shrieking sobs that frightened the little boy so that Sadie could not go and leave him with her.

'Come on John. Leave her alone.' But he stayed, looking bewildered but not pulling free, looking at Sadie as if expecting her to do something.

'What's the matter?' she said at last.

Lena looked up. Her face was smeared with dirt and tears, like a child's, and red, and angry. 'Paul,' she yelled.

'Oh,' said Sadie.

'I'm older than you,' shouted Lena. 'I want to be married too.'

'Why can't you?'

'There's no room.'

It was true. 'Well,' said Sadie, 'if Lisa –.' But she knew Lisa would never consent to moving out of the bed she shared with Lena, to sleep on the kitchen floor beside her parents.

'She's still at school,' said Lena, 'and no she can't go and live with Blanka, they don't get on and there isn't room.'

'If Baba –' Baba's room was a windowless cupboard where she slept on a shelf, with a crucifix above her head and a chamber pot on the floor underneath.

'Even if Baba died –' Lena crossed herself.

'Then Lisa -'

'Why should she? Anyway she won't. And anyway, I don't want to live like this. Paul doesn't. His family have a proper house, with hot pipes all through.'

'Can't you –?'

'Live there? What about the farm? I would be too far away. They need me to work here. Just one bedroom and I could get married, one bedroom with a floor and a window and room for a press, like we used to have.' She meant, before they had to have John sharing their room, in their bed in winter, taking up floor space with his mattress in summer. She was calm again, calm and bitter.

'If,' said Sadie, 'if Zyg and me went to Kingston you could have our room. Or Lisa could.'

'Paul would work on the farm,' said Lena, pretending she was thinking this for the first time. 'But how would you pay for lodgings?'

'Zyg would have to get a job in Kingston. He'd have to.'

'Would you mind though?'

Sadie pretended to think about it. 'John would miss the farm,' she said, 'but he'll be going to school soon, and he can still visit. I think we could manage.' She thought things might work out her way, with Lena on her side.

It was Lena and Sadie against the rest of them. The rest of them said they could not do without Zyg. Paul was a good strong boy but they could not do without Zyg. They could not do without Sadie. She had learned to deal with the hens and make cheese – they did not know how much she hated that cheese, sweating and dripping all over the kitchen, hung up in muslin bags. And she helped look after Baba. Round and round they went. What when Lena had a baby? Who would do her work?

'So I can't have a baby,' said Lena, so quietly that no one heard. 'Ever.'

Josef said he would build more rooms on the back of the house. He would save up and hire a machine to move the pile of muck, and make a nice flat foundation and he would build a little annexe – he said it again, annexe, he liked the sound of it – just as soon as he had saved the money to get started. But they all knew he would never do it. Lena's temper, now that she had once lost it, was never again under control. She and Paul quarrelled weekly, she took to slapping John when he got in her way, and once slapped Sadie when she cut her a piece of rope that was too short to tie round the gate post.

Then the winter, breaking the ice in the wash bowl, brushing the snow off the wood pile, and everything was put off until the spring. 'When the spring comes,' said Josef, 'we'll build.' Regardless that there was no money for it, or there was, but he didn't know it, and if he did, he didn't know where it was hidden. Maryska would, Sadie knew, do everything she could to stop Zyg leaving the farm ever again.

Baba had entirely given up going out into the yard to see to the hens. Even in the most pleasant autumn days she had stayed by the fire, welded to her chair and her stick and swaddled in layers of black. At night Maryska carried her up to her shelf in her cupboard, and the time in the morning when she carried her down again became later and later. She would bang on the floor with her stick, and Sadie would be sent up to see what she wanted, help her out of bed, hold her on the pot, clean her up, after a fashion and put her back into bed. She lay there exhausted, mouth open, black with teeth, breath clattering. Sadie took the pot and emptied it on the midden, then brought it back and pushed it under the bed. Each time, she could touch the box, could feel that it was tied with string. She looked at Baba in the bed. Was she listening, could she stop her just having a look, would she mind? (Yes, she would.) Did she dare? Maybe tomorrow.

Spring again. Sadie fell pregnant, though she hadn't wanted to. All winter she had battled to keep Zyg off her, pretending to be asleep, or too tired, or provoking an argument to put him off, or just pushing him away, roughly. But sometimes, only very occasionally, he got round her, and every time she reminded him. 'I'm not having another baby here, don't forget.'

She was determined. She was leaving the farm, she was going to live where there were ambulances and doctors and hospitals, and, come to think of it, apartments with bathrooms. Zyg could come with her, or he could pay the rent for her. She was going, she was certain, so certain that she began, now that Baba slept for longer and longer in every day, to remove things from the box under the bed, and put them with her own things. She hardly looked at them, for fear that someone would come in the room and see what she was doing, but she got braver each time, and within a few days Baba's box was empty. Unlike the Polish peasant who had stolen the clothes to begin with, Sadie felt no need to exchange her own things for them. When the box was empty, there was one more item. On the little shelf with the crucifix was Baba's button tin.

'Oh yeah,' Lisa had said. 'Baba collects buttons. Best thing you can do if you want to get on her good side, give her a button. Not new ones, mind, she likes old ones, shiny is best if you can.'

She was past even looking at them but Sadie was scared to take the tin away. Maryska would be certain to notice, though no one, she was fairly sure, ever picked it up or looked inside. Sadie had her own button collection, in a bag made of a piece of sacking, and one day she crept to her room with Baba's tin and tipped the buttons into her bag. She loved the sound of them rattling in, a soft, clackety noise. A couple of days later, when no one was in the kitchen, she slipped through with the tin and put some old nails and nuts and bolts in it, from the outhouse. She took the empty box from under the bed and broke it up and hid it at the back of the cowshed in the untidy pile of old and broken bits and pieces that Zyg was forever going to sort out. Then she walked to the store to buy a newspaper so that she and Zyg could read it together and find a job for him.

CHAPTER SEVEN
IN WHICH THERE ARE HOPEFUL SIGNS

They knew now that Nell's father was dead. There was a time during the war when they thought he must be, but he wasn't, and then a long time when he was and they didn't know it. Some people who had been thought dead returned from work camps, and Nell said to her mother that he might have survived, but then lists were published and letters from old neighbours exchanged and it became clear that Edwin Bryce, born in Wales and therefore a British citizen, had been sent in 1942 by the Germans to a work camp in reprisal for the British expulsion of German nationals from Iran. There in the camp, reported another who had been sent with him, he died, of overwork, or undernourishment, or both.

Nell was not sure what she felt. Sad, but why sadder than before when she only believed he must be dead? She did not understand, either, why she felt annoyed. Stupid man, she thought to herself, often. She never thought that way about Eddie, who you could argue had been stupider. When she thought about her father she was not sure whether the moody, changeable man she remembered, who could sing, or swear, or cry, or swing you round laughing was really how he had been. She wondered, if she had ever seen him again, would she have known him?

They had all parted on bad terms, her mother, her father, Nell and Eddie, each of them wanting a different way forward. Her father didn't care who was in charge of the island, he would carry on doing his work as he always did, what difference would it make? Nell wanted to stay too, in the only place she knew, milking their cows, working in the café, seeing her friends, girls she'd been at the school with, boys she could one day marry. Eddie was all for leaving, but that was because he wanted to join the army. Even at the start of the war he would have run away to France to fight except that he was young enough that his father could stop him. Guns and tanks and fighting had always filled his mind. Nell was on his side, and she thought he was brave and noble to leave the island and join up when he didn't have to. His mother wanted him to stay with his father, keep his head down, wait it out, stay out of fights, not get killed, but she wouldn't have Nell stay in an island full of enemy soldiers.

There was a long night of shouting and some weeping.

'We should all stay.

We should all go.

The men should stay, but they need the women or the work won't get done.

Nell must leave, you know what soldiers are, she won't be safe.

Eddie mustn't leave, he'll be put into the army if he's in England.

He wants to be in the army.

He's too young.

He'll be old enough next year.

We should all go.

What about the cows?

Nell will have to go on her own.

Who would look after her? Nell doesn't want to go.

Nell and Eddie can go, Eddie will look after her.'

No one got the whole of what they wanted. In fact, not one of them got anything they wanted, in the long run.

But now, Nell wished more than anything to go back to Guernsey and live there, or at least to go and see it again.

'You just think,' said Ginny 'that it will be like it was when you were a nipper. It won't you know.'

Nell's mother agreed, dolefully. 'Whatever there will be, it won't be nice. Go if you want. All I want is to forget it all, everything.'

This was how she was now, as if she believed it was all her fault, for insisting on leaving for England. She should have sent Nell by herself, and stayed behind with her husband, to keep him fed and looked after so that he would have been better able to withstand the harshness of the camp. She would have kept Eddie safe too, she fooled herself into thinking. He would have stayed on the island – other boys did and stayed safe. He would be alive now instead of blown to bits in Alsace. Who cared about Alsace?

'The thing is,' Nell said, 'she wasn't happy with my dad. She wanted to get away from him. That's why she feels guilty now. It *is* her fault, not all of it, but some of it. And she's not really ill, she's just making out.'

Ginny sighed and wished people could just be happy and normal, like she was. 'I'll go with you,' she said. 'It will be a laugh.'

It was typical of Agnes Bryce that after Nell and Ginny had saved up and bought their tickets she changed her mind and said she would go with them after all.

'I told you she wasn't really ill. She just needs a bit of fresh air and a good meal inside her.'

'And a bit of cheering up.'

The war was five years in the past. Children in British cities still played on bomb sites and in air raid shelters and gun emplacements. Tea, sugar, meat and butter were still rationed. But Nell and Ginny wore new dresses, big full skirts and tiny bodices. Nell's was pink, which she had chosen in the hope it would make her look feminine, but it was too bright a pink, too optimistic, too busy a print and her figure was as flat ever so that she looked like a boy wearing his mother's clothes. The clothes her mother wore, in fact, were her old black suit – long straight skirt and long fitted jacket – that she had travelled to England in ten years before. It smelled of mothballs and fitted so badly that it looked no different to when it was hung on a hanger. Ginny's dress, which had sounded so dull when she described it – mostly white with a grey and purple pattern of little triangles – now looked elegant and modern. She would never have a pretty face, Ginny, but she had a curvy figure, a big toothy smile and brown eyes like toffees. People liked her, especially men.

The three of them sat near the back of the boat and watched the wake folding out behind them under a grey sky. Ginny had never been at sea before. She thought that Nell and her mother must be remembering their journey in the opposite direction, but didn't want to remind them of it. She was feeling nervous. The memory of the goodness knows how many manifests she had typed out during the war came back to her, and the recording of goodness knows how many losses.

'Well I hope they've cleared all the mines,' she said cheerfully. 'It would be too bad if they'd left one behind for us.'

Nell shrugged. Ginny sometimes found the shrugging infuriating but that was just how Nell was. Ginny had grown up combative, that was the thing – arguing with Kath, and their mother, at every turn, and a person – Nell – who dealt with conflict with a twitch of her shoulders left her feeling high and dry, let down and cheated out of a good discussion. What was the point of being provocative if a person could not be provoked? But then, Nell was easy to get along with, undemanding, tolerant, willing to go along with whatever Ginny wanted. What was a bit of shrugging, then?

'Gus came this way,' said Nell.

'I suppose he must have.'

'He looked at these waves.'

Well, thought Ginny, not these actual waves. Time and tide you know. But did not say it.

'He was thinking of me.'

'Of course he was. Probably.'

'No, I mean I *know* he was. Because I'm thinking of him now, here, so when he was here he was thinking of me.'

So if I think of Irish Bernard when I walk past a building site, thought Ginny, I suppose that means he's thinking of me. Very likely. And if I say anything she'll just do that shrug again. But she said, 'It's about time you got over him.'

'I can't.'

'You could get another boyfriend. I'll find you one. What about Eric?'

Nell shuddered, and Ginny, bringing Eric properly to mind, laughed to show that she hadn't really been serious. 'Tell you what, let's have a walk round and eye up the sailors. I remember a time when you had a soft spot for French sailors. Sadie told me.'

'No it wasn't like that. It was just speaking French again. I've forgotten it all now, it's so long ago.'

The island when they got there was both a delight and a horror. Nell and her mother walked round the island and revisited all the places they had known. In the evenings in the boarding house they described to Ginny how this house or that looked just the same, how that house or this had become derelict or been rebuilt. Their own home still had a roof but the inside was gutted and it was used as a calving shed now.

'I don't mind though,' said Mrs Bryce. 'He wouldn't have minded, cows were the things he thought most of.'

What distressed them the most were the fortifications, excrescences of concrete all round the cliffs, gun emplacements and pillboxes, tank traps still there on the beaches, and all made more obscene by the softening green of the spring grass and flowers.

'It looks like it's ready for another war,' said Nell. 'It looks like they could come back and do it again.'

'Don't talk daft,' said Ginny.

'But bad things happen.'

'Bad things happen,' said Ginny, 'but that ain't going to be one of them.'

Ginny met a man one day when she was alone looking from the harbour wall at the sea. He stopped beside her and leaned his elbows on the wall, like a reflection of hers, and when she looked at him he smiled. He was shortish, sandy-haired, tweed jacket, the sort of man who might smoke a pipe. About thirty, she judged. She smiled back.

Nell and her mother were walking around on the island, visiting old neighbours, catching up on ten years of news. Ginny was happy to be left. Conversations about the sad things that had happened to people she didn't know made her impatient and set off a feeling in her of wanting to tell them about the bombing of Ernie and Glad – Ernie and Glad only for a start, there were plenty more people she could mention. But she knew she had no business joining in, so she wandered about on her own, amazed at the spaciousness of the world. She had never been south of the Thames before in her life, strange to say. She had seen the sea, before the war, at Southend, on day trips. Of course I've seen the sea before, she said to herself, but it didn't look like this. And the harbour and the boats and the busyness and the people who knew what it was all about and were in their own element while she was like a fish gasping for her own element (which was what though?), gasping in astonishment too at the scenery and the waves and the beauty of it all.

'Nice view,' said the man.

Ginny had thought she might try being silent and mysterious but as soon as he spoke she changed her mind. 'Look over there,' she said. 'Him painting on that boat there. He's only got one arm. Look, standing on a bucket with a big pot of paint and he's only got one arm.'

'Well, he's not holding the paint,' said the man reasonably. 'See, it's wedged in.'

'But he can't hold on to anything,' said Ginny. 'Look at it rocking.'

'He'll do just fine,' said the man.

Ginny detected an accent but was unsure.

'Are you here on your holiday?' he asked.

'Jimmy Shand,' she said. 'Your accent.'

He smiled. 'Near enough,' he said. 'Scottish anyway.'

'Are you on holiday?' It seemed unlikely that he would come on holiday on his own. She immediately surmised a wife back at the hotel, maybe waiting until the baby woke up until she could join him.

'I'm here with my parents,' he said, and there was a slight grimace which made her think perhaps he hadn't chosen to come, or hadn't enjoyed the trip very much. 'We're leaving tomorrow.'

'Back to Scotland?' Somewhere else she had never been.

'My parents are. I'll see them as far as London, put them on the train, then I'll be back at work.'

They went into the harbour café and drank tea. He had an expressive face, pale brown eyes that squeezed almost shut when he smiled, crooked teeth. He was a doctor, worked as a medical orderly through the war, then resumed medical school, now, recently qualified, worked at the North Middlesex.

'I know it,' said Ginny. 'It's not far from us.'

She told Nell and her mother about him that evening. He had offered to take her out when they were both back home, they had exchanged addresses, he would send her a postcard. Even as she tried to build up the small event into a bigger one that was worth telling,

Ginny knew it was no good. She could go out with him, he was a good catch, a hospital doctor, good-natured as far as she knew, not good-looking but nothing to object to, nothing like a squint, she hated squints. They could have a nice time together and one day he would mention getting engaged, or getting into bed, one or the other, and she would say no. She knew she would say no to him as she had to others (mostly about getting into bed) because he wasn't, and they weren't, the Irishman. Me and you Nell, we're as bad as each other.

She did though engineer that she and Nell would be at the dock when he might be boarding his boat. She could see a couple of older people – he settling the suitcase tidily against the wall, she taking a last look at the bay – and guessed they might be the parents.

'What's his name?'

'Don't laugh will you? Hamish. He's Scottish.'

They both laughed and at that moment he came out of the shop with yesterday's newspaper under his arm.

'This is my friend Nell,' she said. 'The one I told you about.'

Nell was looking her best. She wore slacks and she wore them easily, not self-consciously, and her feet didn't look so big as when they were poking out of a long full skirt. Her smooth brown face was even browner and she had lost the tense burdened look she had had since Gus and her brother had died. She really is quite pretty, thought Ginny, and she's had a lot to put up with. Maybe, it came to her, maybe she could go out with Hamish.

He noticed her, politely, but was more taken with Ginny. He introduced his parents – a neat grey man, also a doctor, and a simpering woman wearing the sort of hat you might wear to a wedding.

Then a hooter sounded and the parental couple gathered their belongings and hurried aboard to get the best places. Hamish lingered, reminding Ginny to get in touch and out of politeness, including Nell in a rather vague invitation. 'Do you like to cycle?'

'Oh yes,' said Nell, which covered the fact that Ginny only said 'Um.'

'We'll have a day in the country,' he said eagerly – did he think it was Ginny who had responded? – and then he had to go because his father had been dispatched to hurry him up and stood at the top of the gang plank, waving.

Nell and Ginny laughed. They threw a cursory wave in the direction of the ship and wandered off arm in arm. The sun shone, the sea sparkled, it was spring, the century was halfway through, men would soon be dying in Korea.

'What did you say that for?'

'What?'

'About cycling. You know I hate it. Still,' she added, 'I'm not interested anyway.'

'You looked as if you were.'

'Did I? Only because he's the only man I've met here. Nah, you can have him if you want.'

'It's time Nell was married,' said her mother to Ginny. They were sitting on the sea wall in the sunshine and Nell had gone to do some shopping.

'What about me though?' said Ginny. 'I'm older than Nell and I'm not married.'

'She needs someone to look after her,' said her mother. 'I won't always be here.'

'I'll always keep an eye on her. She knows that.'

'Not the same.'

'She never got over Gus, though.'

'She never tried,' said her mother. 'So long ago, six years now since she last saw him, and even then she was cold to him, he told me himself – She's gone off me, he said. But before, when he went away first, to join the army, then she was far from cold. I looked out of my

window and saw them, so close there was not even air
between them, just holding each other, not even kissing.
I watched them for so long, and they didn't even move.
Then I was tired and went to lie down.'

CHAPTER EIGHT
IN WHICH SISTERS DO OR DO NOT
EXAMINE THEIR HEARTS

The new houses were being built on Marcie's field. It wasn't called that, really, it wasn't called anything, only in people's heads it remained connected with Marcie. It was just an acre or so of waste ground that presumably belonged to someone, that had once, probably, been part of a farm before the land around was bought and built on. Now this last bit, where children used to play and build dens, but did not any more, on account of Marcie's ghost, would be filled in. There would be even less to remind people of Marcie.

Kath and Ted had three children by now, all girls. 'And that'll do,' said Kath. The prefab could hardly hold them. Their belongings had to be stored under beds and noise of three children shook the walls. Kath heard about the new houses from Ginny, who knew these things from her work at the Council, and went to the office herself, with all three children, and put her name down.

'Poor Ginny,' Kath sometimes said. 'You'd think she'd be married by now.' Other times she envied her sister because she didn't have to wash and cook and clean and shop for five people, and had her own money to spend. Now that clothing was off ration Ginny turned up even more often with a new dress, or blouse, or pair of shoes. When Ginny and Nell went to Guernsey, though it was only for a week, Kath surprised herself by how bitter and resentful she felt. She and Ted managed to take the children for a day out at Clacton but a whole week was beyond them. 'It's all right for some,' Kath said, often.

'Do you love Ted?' asked Ginny. They had taken two kitchen chairs into Kath's back garden to sit in the sun. Ted was at the bottom of the garden out of earshot, pottering about, smoking and tying some late runner beans to poles. The little girls were washing their dolls in a tin bath, squabbling mildly.

'What?' said Kath. She was not one who indulged in conversations that might reveal her feelings.

'You heard.'

'I don't know,' she said eventually.

'Don't know or don't want to say?'

'Both.'

'Well then, did you love him? When you got married? Were you in love?'

'Well you were there, what do you think?'

'I'm asking you.'

'*I* don't know,' Kath said again, as if she of all people could not possibly be expected to have the answer.

'All right, put it this way. If you could have married Gus – if he hadn't been killed, and Nell – let's say Nell didn't want him, and you had to choose between Gus and Ted, which would you choose? I don't mean now, I mean when you were single.' Ginny was leaning forward in her chair and her new dress fell away a little to show her cleavage. Kath glanced towards Ted to make sure he wasn't looking.

'That does seem a long time ago.'

'Don't change the subject. Come on, you're twenty years old, it's 1945, you've got two offers, which one would you choose?'

Kath looked down the garden at her children, in case the little one might be falling down, or the older two fighting over the best doll, but they were behaving themselves, there was no hope of avoiding an answer that way.

'I don't know,' she said again, at last.

'That means Gus,' said Ginny laughing. 'If it was Ted, you'd say.'

'Why do you want to know anyway?'

'I've had an offer.'

'An offer?'

'A proposal. Of marriage, not the other sort. The best one I'm ever likely to get.'

'Who?'

'No one you know. He's a doctor, a hospital doctor. He's very nice.'

'Nice?' Kath sounded doubtful. 'What sort of nice?'

'Kind, thoughtful. Educated. Wants to settle down, wants a family. Earns enough to buy a house.'

'What's his name?'

'Well . . . he's Scottish so he's got a Scottish name.' Kath waited. 'He's called Hamish Farquhar.'

'Farker.'

'That's what I said.'

'Ginny Farker.' Kath sounded even more doubtful.

'I haven't said yes.'

'Why not?'

'I don't love him.'

'That's why you was asking.'

'I wasn't just being nosy. I was thinking, when you married Ted, you still had feelings for Gus, didn't you. I know he was dead, and I know he was Nell's but it was Gus you loved wasn't it?'

'I don't know about loved.' Kath could not honestly use that word. 'I never got near enough, truth be told, to know if I loved him. But I did want Nell out of the way, I wanted him to be my boy. But whenever I got to talk to him all he would talk about was Nell. If there was any loving going on it was Gus loving Nell. I'm blowed if I know why.'

'But what I'm asking you,' said Ginny earnestly, 'is – you married Ted without being in love with him and you're still married to him and you've got three children so, did things change, did you learn to love him as time went on, so to speak?'

Kath thought. 'No not really,' she said.

'Ever wish you hadn't married him?'

86

'Every wash day.'

'Is that all?' But Kath had come to the end of confidences, she could go no further, she called to her two older children to stop splashing the youngest one, then ran down the path to stop the youngest one getting into the bath with the dolls.

But she thought of the day she first saw Gus, when she and Ginny and Sadie and Nell rode on their bikes past him and Eric. She could still see him, leaning on the lamppost in the sunshine, smiling quietly to himself, it seemed, while Eric harassed them with questions. And that soft, excited feeling she'd had then, and every time she saw him. She hauled little Kay back up the path by her arm and proceeded to take off her wet socks. It was time to start thinking about getting some tea on the table. Ginny was sitting with her eyes closed and her face turned to the sun. All right for some.

CHAPTER NINE
IN WHICH THERE IS A BEGINNING, AND
THE BEGINNING OF AN END

Nell ran down the stairs to answer the knocking at the front door. Hamish stood on the step. He carried a rolled umbrella though there was no threat of rain. He smiled an awkward sort of smile.

'So this is the right house? Is Ginny in? You do remember me?'

'She's out.' Nell saw him glance up the stairs behind her, hoping she was wrong, suspecting her of lying.

'I could wait for her, perhaps?'

'I can't ask you in,' she said. 'We've only got two rooms and my mother's ill in bed.'

'I'd like to see Ginny. Don't you know when she'll be back?'

'I'm sorry,' she said. She looked down at him from the top step and noticed that his forehead was chequered by both vertical and horizontal worry lines and she smiled at him.

He said, 'Could you come for a walk with me? I mean, to talk about Ginny.'

'Wait there.' She left the door open and ran up the stairs. He heard her speak and then go from room to room, calling, 'No it's not here' and then 'I'll top up your water' before she came down, looking just the same. She was not, and would never be, concerned about how she looked. She had no vanity.

They walked. During the time Hamish had known Ginny he had never met her near her house. These outer suburbs where London dribbled away into something that wasn't all built on but wasn't countryside either, were new to him. Nell took him across the railway line and along the River Lea. It was neither a proper river, a proper wide and impressive body of water, nor an attractive rushing stream. It was sluggish and dark grey.

Children – muddy, gypsy-ish children – played along the banks, filling jam jars with murky water, kicking water at each other.

'It doesn't look very clean,' said Hamish.

Nell shrugged. They were near the place where Gus had asked her to marry him, but she had been here so often since, the association was faded and dull, like the mere memory of an injury, the bruises all gone.

'What's wrong with your mother?'

'I don't know, she just can't get up.'

Having nothing else to talk about, except Ginny, Hamish persisted. 'How long has she been unwell?'

'Oh ever so long. I can hardly remember her being well. She's having a bad day today, that's all.' It was true, Nell had become accustomed to her mother's state of health, it was so undramatic, this illness, as to be just part of her personality, a sort of physical depression to match the mental one.

'Can you remember when it started?'

Nell couldn't, not really. Coming to England was part of it, Eddie being killed was a big part, the news of her father's death, not unexpected, had been another step downwards. 'She's not been good since we came back from Guernsey. Just feeling down I think.'

They walked on, under the same sun that was shining down on Ginny in Kath's garden. The grass in the meadows was bleached with the end of summer heat. 'I asked Ginny to marry me,' said Hamish, 'and she said neither yes nor no. I was wondering, do you think she still wants to see me? Or is that it, have we parted for good? What has she said to you?'

'Not very much,' said Nell, which was true.

'But from what she said, what conclusions do you draw? Should I pursue it?'

Nell stopped herself from shrugging and thought hard instead. 'It's no good going on at Ginny,' she said.

'She'll make up her own mind. But she's good-hearted, she wouldn't want you to be hurt.'

'If she says no I will be hurt,' he said. 'I know I haven't known her long but she's – she's changed my life. I look forward so much to seeing her. I think of her all the time, even while I'm thinking of other things she's there in my head. Like a song.' He blushed. 'I don't want you to repeat any confidences,' he said, 'but has she said anything, I mean about – whether there's – anyone else –?'

'I don't -'

'Or in the past? Is there anyone she still –?'

Nell said cautiously, 'She's not a child – Ginny. She's always had boyfriends.'

'But I mean – was there anyone – in the war maybe?'

'We knew plenty of boys in the war and some of them' – she was going to say, Didn't come back, but it sounded dishonest – 'were killed.'

'Did she –?'

'I did. But I don't think Ginny did.' Nell jumped over a muddy piece of path, landing lightly.

'But you –?'

'My boyfriend was killed in Belgium in 1944, just before Christmas. He was in an armoured car that was shelled.'

'A long time ago,' murmured Hamish. He appeared to be able to complete a sentence now.

'My brother,' said Nell – having started she was going to get it over with – 'fought with the Free French. He was killed in Alsace. My father was deported from Guernsey and died in a work camp.' It was blank, it was a speech she had rehearsed too often, to herself, in silence. When she spoke the words out loud it sounded as though she didn't care.

Hamish said 'Rotten luck,' and then looked as if he wished he hadn't said anything. Then he said, 'No wonder your mother is down.'

Nell said, 'I should get back to her,' and began to cry quietly.

'Don't,' said Hamish and she obediently stopped, wiping her eyes with her hand, sniffing. 'Sorry,' she said. 'I just worry about her. If she died.'

'People don't die of sadness,' he told her.

'She's so thin. And she seems to have pains.'

'Pains where?'

'I don't know exactly. She never says. But she moans. Quietly. And when anything touches her – ' Nell flinched to show how it was.

'Does she eat?'

'She wants to eat. But it makes her sick. That's why she's so thin.'

'Has she seen her doctor?' It was his day off, and she was not his patient.

'She won't have the doctor.'

'You could call the doctor.'

'She says no.'

'Just do it. Pick up the phone and –'

'We're not on the phone.'

'Go to the surgery. Tell them. What does Ginny say about it?'

'Ginny hasn't seen her lately. My mother doesn't want anyone in her room. Only me. Not even me.'

'Does she cough?'

'No.'

This was stupid, thought Hamish, trying – pretending to try – to diagnose this woman at a distance, and for what purpose, if she had just given up on life, as she was entitled to do, he believed. But Nell's frightened voice – though her expression remained calm – made him feel he could not just leave it there. Also, he thought, if he happened to be in the house when Ginny returned he would be able to speak to her, and demonstrate to her his goodness and his cleverness, both of which he sincerely believed in.

Afternoon sun slanted into one corner of the room. The bed was in the other corner. His examination was brief. He stood up.

'Are you going now?' said Nell. 'What is it?'

'I'll be back,' he said. 'Phone box?'

'At the end.' She pointed.

Nell believed she'd been lonely since Gus died but when, at the end of a long afternoon, her mother had been taken away in an ambulance, and Hamish had patted her on the shoulder, and Ginny still hadn't come home and there was no one to tell her to stop crying, and she hadn't eaten all day, and she sat in her mother's room in the dark, then she knew she was on her own.

Hamish visited Nell several times while her mother was in hospital. Each time he said he was hoping to see Ginny, hadn't seen her lately, how was she, but when she wasn't at home, (or if she stayed hidden in the bedroom) he didn't go away. He and Nell stood on the doorstep talking, sometimes about Ginny, sometimes not, each time for a little longer, getting colder as the winter came on. He asked after Mrs Bryce, but Nell could only say what they had told her. 'It's cancer. There's nothing they can do. It's in her bones. She's looking better. She's sitting up and talking. I think they look after her better than I could. But she may come home, the district nurse would come in – I'm not sure if we could manage, Ginny and me.'

'Ginny and I,' said Hamish and then looked away, pretending he hadn't said it.

One time it was October and the leaves were bright brown against a blue sky. Nell was flapping dust off a duster out of the upstairs window. 'Ginny's not in,' she said. 'Wait, I'll let you in.'

Hamish looked around himself at the room which he had only seen while examining Mrs Bryce and which remained in his memory as smelly and chaotically cluttered with clothes and papers and crockery, blankets and bottles and shoes. Now Nell had evidently just finished cleaning it and fussed around tweaking, bashing a cushion, straightening a pair of shoes, shutting a drawer more precisely. 'It looks nice now don't it? She used to keep it nice, when she was well.'

'How is your mother?'

'She says she's ready to come home.' Nell paused. 'I don't think she will though.' She looked as if she might cry. 'I never thought she was really ill,' she said. 'Sometimes Ginny and me said she was lazy, we'd come home and there'd be no tea for us and she'd been there all day, just doing nothing, and we'd have a grumble at her and she never said.'

Nell, via Ginny, invited Hamish to her mother's funeral but he wasn't able to come because of his work. There were not many people there – Nell, Ginny, Mr Page from downstairs walking with two sticks, Mrs Swallow and Sadie's stepmother and the manager of the butcher's shop where she had worked until she became too ill. Kath would have come, Ginny said, but she couldn't find anyone to look after her children.

Six people, the vicar and a coffin in a cold dark church on a frosty January morning. Afterwards Ginny and Nell sat on their beds.

'What shall we do with the front room?' said Nell. 'Would you like it for a bedroom? Or shall we use it for sitting in?'

She had cleaned the room several times in the last few months, hoping, without any real hope, that her mother might come home. Since her mother died, the previous Saturday, she had not gone into the room at all – Ginny had been in and fetched out clothes for her mother to be buried in. Nell knew that the newly washed curtains and the clean sheets, and tidy pile of old magazines, and the vase on the mantelpiece that stood waiting for the welcoming flowers, would only mock her. She would prefer it, she thought, if Ginny would use it for a bedroom, but sooner or later Ginny would leave, when she finally made up her mind to marry Hamish.

Ginny was thinking about Nell. 'Shall I stay in your room? You might want some company in the night. We can think about the front room later.'

'I suppose so. Anyway there's Mum's things to sort out.'

'You don't have to do it yet. Do it when you feel like it. I'll help you.'

'There weren't many people there.'

'Not many. But not many people knew her. She kept to herself, your mum.' Thinking to herself, Apart from the girls and women she helped out of trouble, and they're not likely to get a day off for her funeral. It was strange, Ginny had often thought, to be on such close terms with her abortionist, but there was no one in the world she could say it to.

'Did you hear?' she said, to divert Nell, 'Ivy Singleton says Sadie's had a little girl. Just before Christmas. And they're not on that farm any more. That's got to be a good thing.'

But Nell, when Ginny looked at her, was asleep, with her shoes on.

CHAPTER TEN
IN WHICH THERE IS ANOTHER END,
AND A REVIVAL

It was February when Ginny met the Irishman again. She was coming out of the office door at five past twelve, going with a girl called Moira, for a look around the shops during their dinner hour, and he was coming in the same door. He stopped when he saw her, he recognised her, he remembered, she could see it in his face. She saw his neck redden and then felt the flush on her own face. Three and a half years had gone by since she'd seen him last, when he had to go back to Ireland where his children were ill, or something, and his wife needed him. She had known that he should, she had understood that he was not, ever, going to be her man, she was going to put him out of her mind. That though was before she knew she'd been caught. All that came back to her and she just nodded to him and turned smartly towards the shops, wondering if Moira had noticed anything, and how she could explain it away. But if she had noticed she wasn't letting on and just went on talking about shoes. The words went past Ginny. Straps, kitten heels, nice shade of brown. She turned to look behind her, expecting him to have gone, and there he was, still at the door, watching her walk away. She stopped. He let go of the door and took one step towards her.

'Go on without me,' she said to Moira. 'I've forgot something.'

It was different this time. Yes his wife was still there, in Ireland, and two children, and they had to be supported. There was no chance of divorce. But this time the wife was not a thing to be suspected, a secret to be discovered, she was acknowledged, almost visible, a real person with a name – Daphne, was that an Irish name, Ginny wondered – and rights, and interests. And she, Ginny, was not an infatuated girl, not a sex-crazed idiot either. She had her Dutch cap (obtained with the disguise of a Woolworths wedding ring), she was clued up, in the know, she could make any decision she wanted. And he – Bernie – oh the long straight lines of his cheeks, the brown eyes, the smile that you would pay good money to see – he was more mature, less panic-stricken by lust.

Then Mr Page died. Nell found him when she went down to the kitchen to boil an egg for her tea. The door was closed, as it was when the old man was washing himself in there, but there were no sounds of water running, or the puffing and blowing he made ducking his head under the tap, which was as near as he came to washing his hair. She knocked but there was no answer. She tried the door but though it was not locked – there was no lock – something seemed to be keeping it shut. She called Ginny, who was getting ready to go out and came downstairs in her slip, with no stockings on. Together they pushed at the door.

'Go and look in his room,' said Ginny.

So Nell looked in the little fusty brown room at the back of the house, and then in the bigger but just as fusty bedroom at the front, and they concluded that Mr Page was behind the door.

'Go and call an ambulance,' said Ginny.

'Can't you?'

'I'm not dressed. Just ring 999.'

So that was that, and before the week was out there were cousins and nephews and nieces coming round sizing up the house, and Nell was given notice to leave.

'Where are we going to go?' wondered Nell. She felt as if she was being somehow shot into the air, with no way of knowing which direction was which. Thank goodness, she thought, for Ginny. She relied on Ginny for sense, and laughter, and gossip and liveliness. Ginny was practical, she knew people, she knew what to do in situations and she did it without making a fuss and bother. Nell had guessed that she had a new boyfriend, from the way she ran out of the door each evening, heels clacking, and returned late, tiptoeing into the room they still shared and whispering apologies as she banged into furniture in the dark.

On Sunday though, she stayed in and they both had a bath and washed their hair and their undies, and then listened to the wireless while they sewed on buttons or gave their shoes a quick shine, promising a proper clean next time.

'Help me,' said Nell. 'I need to clear out my mother's room.'

The clothes were not difficult; there was nothing that would be any use to anyone, just ancient cotton dresses and baggy skirts and jumpers and a thick brown felty wartime overcoat. Her shoes were going thin in the soles, her underwear must have been half a century old. They piled them all together and tied the bundle with string. There was a bag of knitting, navy blue, unfinished. Socks, it seemed, probably meant for Eddie. There were some letters, but nothing personal, only from Mr Geary the butcher, mentioning her outstanding pay and from the Labour Exchange, to say that they understood she was no longer employed and asking her to call in. Ration books. Certificates loose in a biscuit tin. Birth, marriage, and three more births – Edward, Ellen, and Elizabeth, born April 1923.

'Are you really Ellen?' said Ginny and then, 'Who's Elizabeth?'

'Never heard of her.' But it was clear that it was a sister, born between the other two, and at the bottom of the tin, in an envelope, a death certificate – Elizabeth Bryce, died August 1923.

Nell turned away to check under the bed. Here, in a suitcase, her mother kept her medicines.

'We have to throw these out,' she said.

'Too right,' agreed Ginny, looking over her shoulder. There was disinfectant, and cloths and underneath, small bottles. They were briefly labelled, but she saw S. elm and R. leaf and she stopped looking and went to the window and opened it. Inside the suitcase, a canvas bag, which Nell opened and looked inside. It clanked gently like a cutlery drawer. Ginny kept her back turned and said, from the window, 'Straight in the bin. Don't touch, don't even look. Do it now.'

Nell obeyed and Ginny stayed by the window, taking deep breaths until Nell came back.

'I think we're finished,' said Ginny. 'I'll go and put the kettle on, shall I?'

'Make some toast,' said Nell.

CHAPTER ELEVEN
IN WHICH SOMETHING REARS
ITS UGLY HEAD

Nell sat on the floor of Sadie's old bedroom, with her back against the door. She could sit all afternoon like this, she thought, if she had to. She *would* sit like this, anyway, until she heard Ivy Singleton come home. She hated these Sundays, wet Sundays, when there was no one to see and nowhere to go. Hadn't she gone out for a walk, to stay out of his way, and hadn't she been forced back in by the rain. What was she supposed to do? Ginny didn't want her, she was playing at being married to that Bernie; Kath didn't want her, she was busy cooking Sunday dinner, and then she'd be cleaning her oven and having her weekly sit down with the News of the World. Hamish – she'd gone for a bike ride with Hamish yesterday, today he was on duty.

The cycle rides had started with the summer, and become regular. Hamish's bike was much lighter and faster that Nell's so he had to adjust his speed to hers, but she had as much stamina as he did and could cycle all day without seeming tired at the end. They were happy afternoons for Nell. Hedges and fields always cheered her up, she liked stopping at the top of a hill and listening to the birds in the woods, then swooping down the hill, feet off the pedals. She could ride with no hands as well. They took sandwiches, they bought lemonade and drank it out of the bottle, or stopped in tea shops for cups of tea, the sun shone. Nell's mother was still as dead as could be, but it was possible to forget her for a while. Yesterday had been soft warm weather, they cycled out into Epping Forest and went rowing on Connaught Water. It had been quite different, Nell thought now, to be sitting face to face with Hamish as he rowed, quite different from riding side by side. She could see the white vee of his neck where his shirt collar was undone, and the gingery hairs on his arms catching the sunlight as he pulled on the oars, and the hair on his head thinning and receding already. She thought he avoided looking her in the eye, and she began to avoid looking straight at him. Later, back on their bikes, side by side, they stopped being so shy and talked as they usually did. She wished he was here now, and wondered if that meant anything.

Outside her door, stairs creaked.

It was Wilf Singleton who offered her Sadie's room when he found she had nowhere to stay. Maurice was in the RAF now, doing his National Service, there was plenty of room, Ivy was happy with the idea, they would all be snug as bugs, better than looking for somewhere with strangers.

At first it was Ivy that Nell was most afraid of. She was a little, terrier-like woman, with pins and needles stuck through her lapels. She had one manner for her clients, brisk but compliant. 'If you are asking me what I think,' Nell heard her say, 'then I will tell you the organdie will not hang so well as the chiffon, but I can make whichever you choose.' Most people took her advice. Her other manner was for domestic use. 'Where have you been? Where are you going? Why is this drawer open? What are you doing with that? Who asked for your opinion? How long are you going to be in that bathroom?' It was not only people – mostly Wilfred – who infuriated her, but inanimate objects. Plates and cups were bashed and smashed when she was in a temper, saucepans had dents from being thumped against the mangle. When she was cooking she kept up a stream of complaints. 'Nasty useless spud, think I'm eating you? Flamin onion, don't you dare make me cry. Cook, why don't you, do you think I've got all day? Soddin bad egg, wait till I see that grocer.'

But it was Wilf who was the problem. If Nell was coming down the stairs, he would be going up. If she was going up he would be coming down. If she came out of the bathroom he was on the landing, and because the bathroom had no bolt on the door she had to sit on the toilet leaning forwards with her hand on the door, tense. If she went into the kitchen to do the washing up he came too to help. If she sat in her room he knocked on the door and invited her to sit downstairs and listen to the wireless. If she did he sat on the settee and patted the place beside him; if she stayed in her room he invited himself in and sat on her bed, while she sprang to her feet and stood by the door. And he talked all the time, a soft stream of cajoling. 'Now then, it's all right, ain't gonna hurt you, look at you, lovely little girl, come and sit with Uncle Wilf, he won't do anything, more than his life's worth to do anything, you know that don't you, the old trouble and strife she'd have me guts for garters if she knew, but you wouldn't tell her would you Nelly, she wouldn't like it, you know that, come and sit beside me, cuddle up and get warm, blimey there's a bit of a george raft under that door, your tootsies must be frozen, let Uncle Wilf give them a little rub eh, get your circulation back, can't have you going blue now can we.'

Nell thought to herself that Ginny would know what to do but when she saw her, which was rare these days, she couldn't bring herself to admit to what was happening, as if it was her own fault. Maybe it was. She thought now that she should have shouted at him from the very beginning, instead of pretending she hadn't heard and shrinking away from him as they passed through doorways in opposite directions. She had been scared of making herself clear, scared of losing her room and scared of Ivy. Now it had gone on too long for her to appear outraged and innocent. He would say that she hadn't minded all this time – months now – and he hadn't done anything, it was just his way of talking. But today, with Ivy out of the house, it had been more than just brushing past her on the stairs. It had been pressing her into the wall, with the dado rail digging into her back, and all his body leaning on her, and his hands grabbing her behind, and his Sunday stubble and his breath on her neck as she twisted her mouth away from him.

She thought of herself not as an old maid but as a girl still, though twenty-six years old. She had not been kissed since Gus gave her a last despondent brush of the lips more than seven years ago. Hamish sometimes patted her hand, or her shoulder, but that was all. She was sorry to be still a virgin, but then again, her mother had warned her so strongly that it seemed even now a right and sensible way to be. And even, she thought to herself, even if she was going to die tomorrow, better to die a virgin than be interfered with by old Wilf Singleton. Not that he was in person dirty and disgusting, no, he was always tidy and neatly dressed, polished his shoes, shaved every day except Sundays, smelled of peppermint and soap. But he smiled too much, he winked at her behind Ivy's back, as if she was part of his conspiracy, and if Ivy was out of the room, Nell would catch sight of him rubbing the front of his trousers, and when he saw her looking his eyebrows went up in a way that showed her what he was thinking.

And yet there was a bit of her that was excited by it all. She would not admit it, not to herself, not to anyone, she would say that it was nasty, and frightening, and that more than anything she wanted him to stop doing it, and yet she found herself thinking, when she was alone, about her body, and other people's bodies, and when she was with Hamish she would look at him when he was cycling in front of her and consider his backside and his thighs and wonder what he would be like without clothes.

She had no one to talk to about sex. Even Ginny had no words to say on the subject, only nods and sly looks. No better than she should be, she might say, with her eyebrows raised. In the family way, fell for another baby. Took advantage of.

Nell found that the word deflowering kept on coming into her mind. Did it imply that as she was now, she was blossoming? She didn't feel blossoming. But deflowering surely implied something lost, not gained. On the whole, Nell wished she could go back to a state where she never had to think about such things, or if she did only in relation to tomato plants, and cucumbers, whose flowering and fertilisation and fruiting were quiet and calming processes, nobody getting hot and bothered at all.

She survived that Sunday afternoon. Ivy returned, they had some cold meat for tea, left over from Sunday dinner, with a bit of salad, and as it had stopped raining Nell, after washing up, went out for a walk. Wilf did not follow her. She passed by Kath's prefab, hoping that Kath would be in the garden, which she was, picking up the toys that the children had left out in the rain.

'Wait there,' called Kath, and went inside. There was some sort of rule that if Ted was home no one else could come into the house. Nell waited and Kath returned with a letter to show her. It was from the council, offering them one of the new houses, when they were finished.

'That's good,' said Nell.

'I don't know how we're going to furnish it,' said Kath.

'But you want to move, don't you?'

'It's a case of having to,' said Kath. 'I can't have the three of them sleeping in the same bed for ever. But it's more rooms, and bigger rooms and we'll need lino, and curtains and I don't know what else. I don't know how we're going to manage.'

'Maybe Ted will get some overtime.'

'I wish he would. Do you know, I believe, I really do, that sometimes it gets offered and he turns it down. He's lazy you know, he won't do anything without being nagged till I'm blue in the face. It's his mother's fault, she did everything for those boys, they never had to lift a finger, and now they don't know how to.'

'When will you move in?'

'This side of Christmas, all being well.' She sighed. 'That's another thing to pay out for. I'll have to start putting something by every week.'

'Seen Ginny lately?'

'I haven't. Have you?'

'No,' said Nell sadly. 'I miss having someone to talk to.'

'I haven't even been to her new place.'

'Me neither.'

'She hasn't even told me mum where it is. I think there's something funny going on. Do you?'

'I don't know what you mean,' said Nell. She was unsure how much she was supposed to say to anyone about Ginny's new arrangement. 'Keep it quiet,' was the last thing Ginny said to her about it. 'I don't mean you've got to lie, but don't say more than you've got to.' But exactly how that worked out into words and sentences, with Kath looking expectantly at her, Nell did not know.

But here came Kath's littlest girl, shouting – she was a shouter, this one – that there was water all over the floor and Theresa's nightie was all wet. 'Where's your dad got to?' shouted Kath – she was a shouter too – and ran inside. Nell walked on, thinking suddenly and for no reason that she could understand, of Marcie MacNee. It must be that Kath's new house – she would see the building site when she turned the corner – was on the very field. For the first time it occurred to Nell to wonder who had been the father of Marcie's baby, and for the first time, she wondered if it had anything to do with Wilf Singleton. She smothered the thought before she arrived at wondering whether her own mother had anything to do with Marcie's death. That thought had been with her all the years since, she had had plenty of practice at ignoring it. But she felt disgusted all of a sudden at the very idea of having a human body, so insistent and so vulnerable and so traitorous. Air, she thought, air and water, nothing wrong with them, that's all that plants need, I would like to be a plant.

It was in the pictures that Nell started to cry. She and Hamish were watching The Man in the White Suit, and Hamish leaned over and said, indicating Joan Greenwood, 'Eyes like Ginny.' Nell thought he was wrong, but she knew he was still keen on Ginny, though he hadn't seen her for months, so she didn't argue. Her eyes kept on filling and she kept on blinking hard to make the tears go away. It was only near the end – perhaps upset by the sight of Alec Guinness in his underwear – that she began to sob horribly, and Hamish noticed.

It was impossible to wait at the bus stop – there were too many people around – so they set off walking, under Hamish's umbrella.

'What is it?' said Hamish, but Nell thought that he wouldn't really want to know. It was too sordid to talk about.

'I'll take you home then,' he said, but she only cried harder.

'Wilfred and Ivy will look after you,' said Hamish. Nell knew that he thought Wilf was a lovable Cockney character and Ivy was the salt of the earth, which maybe she was.

'Don't say anything to Ivy,' said Nell.

'Someone has to look after you,' said Hamish, and Nell felt unbearably irritated and wanted to say, as Ivy would have, What's wrong with you doing it? but she didn't. As they approached what she supposed must be her home she gathered her strength and said, 'I'll tell you. Don't look at me.' And told him, after a fashion, of how every evening, while Ivy was in the front room, finishing up a big order of bridesmaids' dresses, Wilf had come into Nell's room, or followed her round the house 'with his buttons undone.'

There was a long silence and at last Hamish said, 'Trouser buttons, do you mean?'

'Yes.'

'Is that all? I mean, just buttons undone?'

'Not really,' said Nell. She was not going to able to say the words, was not even sure what words it might be all right to say, and trying to think of the right words was bringing back vividly the sight of the *thing*, lolling out, like a big red tongue, glistening, and Wilf grinning and winking for all he was worth.

'Was he,' said Hamish, rather pompously, she thought, 'exposing himself?' and then she was grateful to him, for knowing how to say it in a way that she could accept, without any undue description. She felt childish and inadequate for not being able to sort it out for herself. Kath, she thought, would have run and got a kitchen knife and threatened to cut it off, Ginny would have laughed him out of it. Sadie might have screamed and run away (but she was his own daughter, surely he wouldn't have?) but Nell was too embarrassed to let him see she had noticed, as if the giant waggling penis was a slight social mishap, like gravy on a chin. And ashamed of herself too. She was in no danger. She was as strong as him and could run faster if it came to it. Ivy was in the house, with a bunch of bridesmaids and all within earshot, so why should Nell feel so besieged, and shaky, and downright frightened.

'I can't go home,' she said. 'I think Ivy might have gone out. I don't know where to go.'

Hamish was quick with a solution. 'We'll go and see Ginny. Maybe she can put you up for the night.'

'I don't think –'

'Or she'll know what to do.'

'But –'

'You know where she lives don't you?'

'Yes but –'

'She's your best friend,' said Hamish. 'She'll want to help you out.'

It was not far to the tiny house, carved out from a much bigger one, that Bernie was working on and he and Ginny were living in. More or less camping in on bare floorboards, while he put in new walls and doors, pipes and fittings. Ginny didn't care about the dust and muck and noise. She helped him in the evenings and every weekend, carrying buckets and mixing mortar and sanding down doorframes. She loved it. She loved him. She was putting distemper on a ceiling, hair hidden under a scarf, when Nell put her head round the door, cautiously, not sure of her welcome and wanting to warn Ginny that Hamish was close behind; Hamish who had been told nothing about Bernie or the new arrangement.

Of course it was immediately obvious that Nell could not stay there, no explanations were needed. When Bernie came into the room, Hamish at first seemed to assume he was a hired workman, until his behaviour – arm round Ginny's waist, blowing teasingly into her ear – forced him to accept what the situation was. It was an awkward situation, no doubt about it, but Ginny – full of remorse at not looking after Nell properly – concentrated on her problem.

'We've got to find you somewhere.' And she concluded that the best thing would be for Nell to stay at Moira's – that Moira who worked with Ginny, and who had a Put-U-Up.

'I'll come with you now,' said Ginny. 'We'll go and see her, then go and get your things. If she can't let you stay we'll find somewhere else, but she will, I know she will, even just for a few days. And then we'll find somewhere. Why didn't you tell me you were there, I would have told you what he's like.'

'I never saw you,' said Nell. She was ashamed of being helpless, embarrassed at being helped, awkward at being in the same room as Hamish and Ginny and Bernie, as if it was her fault. Hamish parted from her outside the door, as she waited for Ginny to set off to Moira's, leaving Bernie to finish the ceiling.

'Thank you,' she said to him.

She could not understand the expression on his face. It seemed as if he was angry with her. 'You could have told me,' he said. 'You have made me look like a fool.'

'No,' she protested.

'You lied,' he said, 'or as good as lied. You kept a secret. You could have told me.'

'I'm sorry,' she said. She might have argued but she had not enough resolve to do it. It was months before she saw him again.

CHAPTER TWELVE
IN WHICH THERE IS MORE WINTER
THAN SPRING

Winter at the nursery garden meant laying off most of the workers. All that remained were two, plus Nell and the owner, Clive Maddox. There was still work to do, washing down all the glasshouses, inside and out, disinfecting, fixing broken benches, checking hoses, ordering seeds and fertilisers, a hundred little jobs to be ready for the spring, when it would start all over again.

Clive was a heavily built young man who looked after the business for his father, who had inherited it, but didn't like farming, or growing vegetables. Clive didn't like the work either. If he could choose, he told Nell one time, he would have a book shop in a nice little town, where he could talk to customers and go home at night without worrying about the weather and the other uncertainties that went with growing things for a living. But he had a young family and couldn't walk away. And his wife was a frail creature who could not manage the children – twins – so Clive was usually seen walking between the rows of glasshouses with one of the children on his shoulders, or sometimes both in his arms.

Just before Christmas he came out of his office to meet Nell as she arrived on her bike. There had been intruders in the night. He wanted her to look for damage. 'Just kids,' he said. 'Boys. I saw a light up in the water tower and when I went out and shouted they came down and ran all over the place in the dark, trying to get away from me. Dropped their torch, couldn't see a thing, crashing everywhere.'

'Are you calling the police?'

'No point,' he said. 'But I will get a dog now. I don't like to keep a dog outside, but it will put them off, barking.'

It was a damp misty day. The cold got into Nell's bones as she walked about, picking up stacks of seed trays and winding up hoses. She noted two broken panes of glass. It was afternoon and nearly dark before she had time to go up into the water tower with a torch. She liked it up there, where you felt far away from the ground and no one could see you. It had a special sort of quietness.

She thought about the gang of boys, trying to find somewhere to go out of the rain, where they could chat and laugh in peace. And smoke. There were some fag ends scattered about, which she swept up, and some names chalked on the wall which she left alone. They would be the names of boys from the council estate that had been built where once her workers were prisoners of war. They would be the boys who when little had swarmed over the streets outside their houses, who later could have been seen throwing sticks at the horse chestnut trees to get the conkers down, and now, too old to play and too young to go in pubs, hung around alternately giddy and sullen.

That was that then, another day over. She was cold in spite of wearing all her jumpers except her best one, underneath a man's coat; she wore wellingtons and two pairs of socks, two pairs of gloves and a scarf. Her head though was bare – unless it rained hard she never covered her head. She headed for the tiny office, to turn out the light and lock the door, and fetch her bike. She would ride home, or rather, not home, but to the place where she lived now, in old Mrs Plant's back bedroom. It was all right. She had been invited to spend Christmas with her, and her widowed daughter, and little Pat. She would visit Ginny and Kath too and after her two days off she would come back to work and gradually the days would lengthen and lighten and she would live through them. It would be all right.

Hamish was standing at the gate, hunched against the cold, almost invisible in the dusk. But she recognised his shape and knew it was him before he saw her.

'I came to bring you this,' he said. It was an envelope.

'You could have posted it,' she said. It looked like a Christmas card.

'I don't know where you live now. I want you to read it, not now, when you get home.'

'All right,' she said, and put it in her pocket. 'Do you want to walk along with me?'

'I have my bicycle right here.'

They rode through the darkening streets, often one behind the other when there was traffic, and unable to speak very much. 'Would you like to come in?' she asked. 'My landlady won't mind.'

He said he would not. 'But you will read my note. Please.'

'Yes of course.'

He patted her hand, though through her glove and his she hardly felt it. Then he went.

It was a weekday evening after work. You could see the days getting longer but this one had been cold and bitter and frosty and as Nell cycled home the gas in the street lamps burned yellow and blue. The arrangement was that she would meet Ginny at Kath's house, to look after the two youngest children for the evening.

'Can't your mum do it?'

'Oh she's going too. I thought Kath would have told you –'

'I haven't seen her –'

'– they're going up town to see the King's coffin.'

'Oh,' said Nell. 'I don't think I'd want to do that.'

'Me neither. I'd do away with the whole lot of them I would. But mum and Kath are going and they're taking Rita so we'll only have the other two.'

'What about Ted?'

'Night shift at the power station. Overtime. Extra shovelling.'

'Well, I might as well,' said Nell.

Kath was in her new house now and the road to it was just a layer of hard core and mud, between two wide verges of more mud and sundry pieces of house-building lumber. Unfinished houses at the end of the street gave the place a kind of wild west look, as if Howard Keel might turn up and raise a roof or two. Nell had never been in Kath's house before. It was a bit short on furniture. In the front room there was nothing except a green chair that Ted's mother had passed on to them, and an ironing board and a pile of clean washing waiting to be ironed. The kitchen had an end for cooking and washing up and an area for the table and chairs, demarcated by a piece of red carpet on top of yellowish brown lino. Above was a pulley airer hung with damp clothes. In the corner of the room was a grey enamelled closed in fire, kept stoked up with coke, and two little armchairs were arranged one on each side. The table was covered with an enamel lid which Kath never took off. She didn't believe in tablecloths she said, they only make more washing.

The little girls – Theresa was four and Kay was three – had spent the day with a neighbour and were tired and beginning to miss their mother. Theresa kept quiet and leaned on Ginny with her thumb in her mouth. Kay was the sort of child who gets excitable, the more tired the more excitable. She rolled on the floor and kicked and only stopped when she banged her head on the table leg and Ginny had to move Theresa to one side to pick up Kay. Then Theresa began to cry, but quietly, and Nell lifted her on to her knee. Nell knew only a little about children. Sometimes Clive Maddox would deposit one or both of his in her office for a few minutes while he did something that needed two hands, but she could barely tell which was the boy and which the girl. She had let them stand on a chair and look out of the window, which shocked Clive because he thought they would fall, but they didn't, they held on seriously tight and watched their father waving the topsoil lorry into the yard. Theresa rested her head against Nell and her eyelids lowered. 'She'll be asleep in a minute,' said Nell.

Ginny opened the front of the fire and undressed her nieces in front of it. She washed their hands and faces and said that would do. Nell held their pyjamas to warm and helped them into them. Theresa was a quiet and skinny child, with vivid blue eyes and dark hair, Kay was as big as her older sister and a lot noisier but did not promise to be as pretty. They drank their milk and Ginny and Nell took them up to bed.

'I've got something to tell you,' said Nell, when they came downstairs. She had been waiting all day to tell someone.

What she had to tell was that she was engaged to Hamish. She could not believe it herself – in the middle of telling she stopped to check with her own memory to make sure she was not making it up.

'Are you happy?' said Ginny.

'I think so,' said Nell. 'I was so surprised. I didn't know what to say.'

'But you said yes.'

'I think I did.'

'Does he think you did?'

'Oh I think so. We're going to go on Saturday and buy a ring.'

'An engagement ring.'

'No, a wedding ring. Hamish says what's the point of an engagement ring. We're getting married as soon as we can. He's got a new job, we'll be moving away from here.'

'I'll miss you.'

'I never see you.'

'We've been busy with the house. You've seen it, you know we couldn't have visitors before. But it's fit for visitors now. And if you don't come to see me I don't know who will.'

'Kath? Your mum and dad?'

'Kath never goes anywhere. And I don't see me mum visiting a house of shame.'

So far, only Kath and Nell knew that Ginny lived with Bernie, in an unmarried state.

'What will you tell your mum and dad?' Nell had asked her.

'I'm going to tell them the truth,' said Ginny in the end. 'I've been all round the houses on this one and I can't think of nothing else to do. If I said we'd been and got married she'd want to see me marriage lines. I'm not ashamed. I'm not one of those girls like Kath and Sadie who just want to get married, never mind who to. I wouldn't care if I stayed single, except I love him.'

'If you have children – ' murmured Nell.

'I don't know if I want any,' said Ginny. 'Well I might. Maybe in a year or two. I know what you're thinking – he's a Catholic – yes he is but he's doing enough sins already, a bit of birth control won't do him no more harm.'

It was late when the royalists returned.

'What was it like?'

'Lovely,' said Mrs Swallow.

'Freezing,' said Kath.

'Were you cold Sweetreet?' asked Ginny.

'Yes,' she said demurely.

'She wet herself,' whispered Kath fiercely.

'She couldn't help it.'

'What did you do?' asked Nell, interested.

'She was in a proper two and eight. Mum had to save our places –'

'There was people there saying she shouldn't have brought a kiddy –'

'– and we had to walk miles to find a lav, she was crying –'

'– well she was cold –'

'– and –'

'Mum gave me her drawers,' said Rita, proudly lifting her skirt and showing a pair of greyish drawers so voluminous on her they looked like a crinoline.

'However did you hold them up?

'Belt of her coat,' said Kath. 'As I say, what a palaver. Still we're back, get that kettle on.'

Mrs Swallow's face was struggling between hilarity and horror. 'You never told me,' she said. 'I never knew you didn't have no drawers on.'

'Well I had to didn't I.' Kath was always sullen when attacked.

Hilarity suddenly won in Mrs Swallow's head. 'You've never been in to see the King with a bare bum. Whatever would he say? Wait till I tell your dad. He'll have a good laugh.'

'Don't Mum, don't tell no one. I'll never speak to you again.'

'Just your dad.'

'Not just me dad. No one, you can't tell anyone. But what else am I supposed to do? She can't stand there freezing her fanny off can she.'

Rita began to cry and Ginny took her on her knee. Nell heard the kettle whistle and went to make tea and at the other end of the room the subject seemed to be resolved – not to Kath's liking however, because within a week there was not a person in the street and beyond who didn't know that Kath Doughty nee Swallow had shuffled past the royal coffin, guarded by guardsmen, with the cold air of Westminster Hall striking unimpeded up her most private parts.

The night was black and windy, and the black ribbons that some people had hung in their front windows, for the king, were invisible in the dark.

Despite the cold, Nell and Ginny walked slowly when they left Kath's, and stood a long time outside Nell's digs, just talking. Nell told Ginny about the letter Hamish had given her, that said he was sorry he had blamed her for keeping Ginny's secret, and asked if she would meet him on New Year's Day, for a cycle ride and a new beginning.

'So I did,' said Nell. 'You don't mind do you?'

'Why should I?' Ginny was genuinely pleased, because she liked both of them, but at the same time aware that she had been Hamish's first choice, so she felt she could be gracious in passing him on, so to speak.

'Another thing,' said Nell. 'Did you ever – when you went out with Hamish – did you ever tell him about my mother?'

'What sort of about?'

'You know, what she did.'

'As if I would,' said Ginny. 'He might ask how I know. No I certainly never mentioned it, honestly, I wouldn't. And you won't ever tell anyone, will you, about me and – your mother.'

'Of course not.'

'Bernie doesn't know, he never knew, and he never will. No one knows do they, only you and me now.'

'Of course not,' said Nell again. She was quiet for a little and then said, 'Do you remember Marcie?'

'Of course I do. Especially tonight. Kath's house must be bang on top of where they found her. It would give me the screaming ab-dabs.'

'No it wouldn't,' said Nell. 'You would get used to it. Think how old your house is, loads of people must have died there.'

'Not people I knew though. And anyway, the bit we live in used to be the outhouses. Still, Kath doesn't seem bothered. Why did you ask?'

'I suppose, just because – thinking of my mother –'

'Being dead, you mean?'

116

'Yes, I suppose that's what I mean.'

'Your mum was lovely to me,' said Ginny. 'That's how I'll remember her, letting me live with you and helping me out – all sorts of ways, not just that one. I thought she'd tell me off you know, but she never did, and never jawed at me about it afterwards, it was as if it never happened.'

'I know.'

'And if she helped Marcie out – well –'

'That's what I mean,' said Nell. 'I don't know if Marcie came to her or not, but do you know she stopped all that after Marcie died? Except for you, you were a special case. If it all went wrong with Marcie –'

'You're jumping to conclusions,' said Ginny. 'And we'll never know for sure. Put it out of your head. You're getting married in a few weeks. That's what you want to be thinking about.'

'All right.'

Nell went to see Mrs Treasure to say goodbye. Mrs Treasure was big in the church now – the Mission Hall – even more committed than before Gus was killed, and Nell had to wait on her doorstep till she came home from her dusting and sweeping of the hall. It was a cold evening, very calm and still, stars just beginning to come out. Nell sat on the wall and waited. She could have gone in next door to see Ginny's mum and dad but she preferred to avoid them, them and their arguments and their intrusive questions. Besides, Mr Swallow was not a well man these days and spent his time sitting by the fire – he had sat by it all winter – making the noise of someone who could not clear breadcrumbs out of their throat.

Mrs Treasure put the kettle on and made tea. She seemed indifferent at first to the fact of the engagement.

'I thought I would let you know,' persisted Nell, 'because I was nearly engaged to your Gus. I wanted you to know that this doesn't mean I never loved Gus.' It was hard to say, the word loved out loud, Gus was the last person she had said it to, she hadn't said it even to her mother, and certainly not to Hamish.

'Don't be silly,' said Mrs Treasure mildly. 'If a nice girl like you can't put it in the past when it *is* past, then what would happen to you, I'd like to know. You and Gus were children, you weren't married, you weren't old enough. Forget Gus.'

Nell felt that she should not be allowed to forget. 'You don't forget,' she said.

'No I don't. But I don't spend my life remembering. You'll have to forget him when you're married.'

'I don't know if I can.' But it seemed, now that she thought about it, that she had.

'I've got other things to think about and so should you have,' said Mrs Treasure. 'It's about time you got married, a few children would get you back to normal, put a smile on your face. You're only young once. You'll see.'

It rushed upon Nell that her future might really be a happy one, she believed for the first time that it might be so, and she smiled at Mrs Treasure, a big transforming smile.

Edmonton Register Office was the venue. Hamish's parents, a best man, Ginny and Kath, though not Ted or Bernie, Sadie's stepmother, and Kath's youngest child lined up for a photograph on the steps outside. Nell stood with her knees bent under her skirt so that she wouldn't look taller than Hamish. Hamish looked worried as usual. His patients must think they're all about to turn their toes up, thought Ginny, not for the first time. Little Kay presented the newly married pair with a silver cardboard ribbony horseshoe for good luck.

They went back to the hotel where Hamish's parents were staying, for tea – fish paste sandwiches and cake and by half past three it was all done and dusted, everyone had gone except the two Dr Farquhars and the two Mrs Doctor Farquhars, full of goodwill but wondering what to say to each other.

CHAPTER THIRTEEN
IN WHICH DISTANCE IS IMPORTANT

'I have to go home.'

'Home?'

'England. There was a telegram.'

Zyg waited.

'I need some money, I need to take an aeroplane. It's my dad. I haven't seen him for years and years. I need to go. I'm going to go.'

Zyg had just come in from work. He had been awake since five that morning, he had been, it seemed, half way across the continent and back and was expecting Sadie to be asleep in bed, not standing in the middle of the room, wound up like a clockwork train, full of demands and plans.

'We don't have that sort of money,' said Zyg.

'We don't,' said Sadie, 'but your mother could put her hands on it if she wanted.'

'Well, ask her,' said Zyg, and then quickly added, 'No don't, it will cause trouble.'

'I'm going to go,' said Sadie. 'I mean, I'm going to go and ask your mother, *and* I'm going to go to England and I'm going to see my dad. You can't stop me.'

'She won't give you anything,' said Zyg. He sat down and took off his boots. He leaned back in the chair and closed his eyes.

'Let me tell you,' said Sadie, 'I have been finding out how much I can put together, all day I've been working it out. With the children's savings accounts, and a little bit I've got, and an advance on my wages, and putting off the rent for a month, or maybe two, I can get home. If you want me to come back again, I'll need more.'

'What about the children?'

'I've thought of that. Carolynne can come with me, she'll travel free, as near as makes no difference, I'll just need to pay to get her on my passport. John will have to go and live at the farm while I'm gone.'

'What about school?'

'Can't be helped,' said Sadie. 'He won't mind a few weeks off school.'

'A few weeks! Did you say what I think you just said? How can you be gone a few weeks?'

'I don't know do I? I don't know what might happen.'

'OK. We'll go and ask Mom for a loan. Only a loan, mind.' Sadie knew they would never pay it back, she at least would never put the smallest effort into paying it back, but she said no more.

Next day she managed to book a transatlantic call to the hospital from the shop and an unnamed nurse who might or might not have known what she was talking about was able to tell her that her dad was believed to be recovering.

'So why go?' said Zyg, on his mother's instructions.

'Wouldn't you?' shouted Sadie. 'If you were in England and Pop might be dying, wouldn't you want to go home?'

'Sure,' said Zyg. 'I'd *want* to but I wouldn't be *able* to.'

They were in the kitchen on the farm, a freezing rain rattling on the windows. Paul was in the warm cowshed, scouring one of the churns – they had had a quantity of milk refused by the factory for being off. Lena was sitting in the best chair nursing her baby. Josef sat near her with Carolynne on his knee. Zyg and Sadie stood in the middle of the room as if they had only just walked in. Maryska had not turned round from the sink since Sadie had made her request.

'Just let me have some money,' said Sadie. 'I haven't got time to be standing here discussing it. I'm going and that's that.'

'Mom,' said Lena, 'is there enough money? If we have it she should go. Seven years, more than seven years she's been here and not seen her family. Remember when Zyg went to the war? That's how Sadie's Pop is feeling, and maybe on his death bed too.'

'She should go,' said Josef, and the money was produced and handed over to a dry-eyed Sadie by a dry-eyed mother-in-law.

For two days Sadie strove to order her life to obey her. Her job, her children, an order for curtains she had promised, a flight, contacting Stepmother, money.

Mrs Munro at the shop sighed sadly. 'This is what happens to us, we move far away, then it's too far to go back.' And said she would keep Sadie's job for her.

She stayed up all night finishing the curtains.

Every afternoon Stepmother went on two buses to the hospital to sit beside Wilfred. In the evenings Sadie did the same journey while Carolynne stayed with her Step-grandmother, tucked into bed in the tiny box room. Afternoons, Sadie mostly visited Kath and they walked, for something to do, to the school gates to meet the three girls. Kath was pregnant again, and grumpy.

'I thought I'd done with all this,' she said. 'Give me pram away and everything. Have to get the whole lot again, from scratch. Lucky I've got some good neighbours.'

She was stout, Kath, at the best of times and this time her pregnancy was making her back ache. Her children were very clean, and well behaved when she was watching them but Sadie noticed that they all nipped and shoved each other when they thought no one was looking.

'How's Ted?'

'*He's* all right.' Kath implied that he led the life of Riley.

'Still working at the same place?'

'He'll never leave. It'd take gumption to leave wouldn't it?'

'It seems to me,' said Sadie, 'that men are just big babies. My Zyg now, he thinks more of his mum than he does of his kids. Or me. You should have seen the work I had, getting him off that farm. But I tell you what, every Sunday we go back and visit, and if she just clicks her fingers, his mother, he's back there like a shot, every time he has a day off work.'

Kath shuddered. 'I don't know how you did it.'

'What?'

'Living on a farm. With animals.'

'Oh I never had much to do with the animals. It was only cows and hens.' Sadie felt superior in her more extensive knowledge of the world.

'I would never of thought you would of done it. You was always quite a timid thing.'

'No I wasn't.'

'Yes you was.'

'Well,' said Sadie not wishing to argue, 'I guess I was never as noisy as you and Gin.'

'You sound like a Yank,' said Kath, 'with your I guess.'

'I can't help it. It's what they say. I work in a shop, I talk to people all day, I have to talk like they do.'

'And your kiddy. It sounds funny coming from a little thing like her.'

Carolynne was walking with Kath's Theresa, holding her hand, and Theresa was looking proud to be the one chosen to look after her, though really there was no choice, Kay being too giddy to be trusted and Rita walking along with her friend, pretending not to be part of the group.

'When am I going to see Ginny?'

'When she's not at work. She'll come round Saturday morning. Ted won't be there, he'll be down the allotment, you can come round.' Kath looked round to make sure the children weren't listening. 'Ginny's not married, you know that don't you. Not properly. I mean, Bernie's like a husband, they live together, but they've never been and got married. Legally.'

Sadie did not know what to think. It sounded exciting and daring, she had not known anyone before who lived openly with a man. And she felt she should disapprove, but somehow didn't. 'No children though?'

'No. Lucky ain't she?'

'Still. But listen, remember that bike ride?' She could tell that Kath remembered.

'That was a laugh wasn't it.'

'She rode my bike nearly all day, I got lumbered with her old crock.'

'She's all right,' said Kath. 'She can be a cow, I know that, but her heart's all right.'

On Saturday Ted was not at the allotment as it turned out, but asleep in bed, after working a ten to six shift. The children were sent to play in the front room and keep the noise down while Kath and Ginny and Sadie sat by the fire in the kitchen. Kath lay back in her little armchair, puffing. Sadie could see her smock – pale green printed with small, hopeful flowers – moving as the baby rolled and stretched. Ginny made a pot of tea. She looked, thought Sadie, younger than she had done eight years ago, certainly younger than Kath. That's what not having children does for you, she thought.

They talked about all the people Sadie knew and some that she didn't. Billy and Joyce, Eric, Mrs Treasure, Moira, Peggy Plant, Eileen whose husband had died. Names and faces she had forgotten to wonder about came floating back to Sadie and she was even interested in them and could join in with the right sort of exclamations.

Ginny saved Nell for a section of her own, accompanied by a fresh pot of tea. While it was left to stand Sadie checked on the children and found an extra child there – Rita's plain little friend had been let in without Kath knowing. Rita had them all sitting in a row counting, playing schools.

'Well then – Nell,' said Ginny.

'Did you go to her wedding?'

'Oh we both went, didn't we Kath. Only a small do, nobody nowadays goes in for these big church carry-ons, nobody like us anyway.'

'His family there?'

'Only his mum and dad. Scottish. Of course I met them before, in Guernsey.' And she told the story of meeting Hamish and going out with him before she passed him over to Nell.

'Why didn't you hang on to him?'

'She met Bernie,' said Kath. It was hard to tell what her tone of voice meant, disapproval, or sarcasm, something like that.

'What my sister should say,' said Ginny, 'is that I didn't want to marry someone I wasn't in love with, unlike some I could mention, and I would rather be with the man I love, married or not.'

'Oh,' said Sadie, and there was a pause while Ginny poured the tea.

'I'm going to see my sister,' said Sadie, to fill the gap. 'I don't even know her really.'

'Could be better that way,' said Ginny, but she grinned at Kath, and Kath made a face back which meant that they were still friends.

'So where does Nell live now?'

'Miles away, out in the sticks. She always was a country girl I know, but honestly, you should see it.'

'Have you been?'

'Only once. It takes you all day to get there, three trains and then a bus unless Nell comes to pick you up. She can drive you know, Hamish taught her, she passed her test first time.'

'I don't know anyone else who can drive,' said Kath.

'I can,' said Sadie. 'Only on the farm tracks mind, I shouldn't go on proper roads, I haven't taken a test. So what's their house like?'

'Well, I wouldn't want to live there,' said Ginny. 'It's quite big, belongs to the hospital, you know, where Hamish works. I say a hospital but it's a loony bin really, people who've had a bang on the head, that sort of thing. Rehabilitation is what they call it, they think that peace and quiet and fresh air is what does them good. I think it would send me up the wall, but what do I know?'

'But she hasn't had any children?'

'No. And yet she wants a baby, I know she does. It's just not happening.'

'She doesn't know when she's well off,' said Kath.

Ginny leaned over and patted her hand. It was the most affectionate thing Sadie had ever seen her do towards Kath. 'Now then,' she said. 'You know you love them when they get here. It's only now you're thinking of dirty nappies and all that.'

'You know what it's like, don't you Sadie,' said Kath.

'Oh I do.' Sadie wondered whether Ginny wanted a baby, and if she did, why she hadn't had one, but the unmarriedness of her and Bernie made it somehow impossible to ask, because that would be treating her as she would a friend who was properly married.

'Anyway,' said Ginny, 'Nell's house. Cold. Draughty. Big though. Could do with cheering up, lick of paint, that sort of thing, but you remember don't you, her mother never had anything nice. I mean we lost ours in the bombing, but my mum always liked something cheerful in the house, like a bunch of flowers or a picture on the wall. I don't mean nothing expensive, but just something nice to look at. But Nell and her mum never seemed to see the point.'

'Nor do I,' muttered Kath.

'Well I do,' said Ginny. 'You must come and see my little house, Sadie. Come tomorrow.'

'She's got it lovely,' admitted Kath.

'But Nell. I think too much happened to her and she can't seem to take it all in. Her whole family dying and then having to live with strangers.'

'She lived with my dad and stepmother,' said Sadie. 'They weren't strangers. I don't know why she didn't stay there.'

Ginny paused in a considering sort of way, but Kath bounced straight in. 'Well, you know what your dad was like. I wouldn't want to be on my own with him, not after what he done to Nell.'

'What?'

Ginny intervened. 'I think he was a bit too friendly, a bit cuddly, you know what I mean. She wasn't used to it.'

'Oh is that all?' said Sadie.

That evening Maurice turned up at the hospital. He sat down across the bed from Sadie and didn't speak to her at first.

'Hello Dad, it's me, Mo.' He waited, watching the grey flaccid face, listening to the heavy breath, then said, 'Hiya Sis. No change then?'

'Hello Mo. Ivy says she thought he opened his eyes this afternoon but the nurse said it's just a twitch, it don't mean anything.'

Sadie and Maurice hadn't met for nearly eight years. He was a boy of twelve then. She had kept a picture of him in her head but he had grown way beyond it. He still had the lazy eyelid and the slightly sticky-out ears, but he was so tall, taller than anyone in the family had ever been. And dressed in a nice suit, Sadie assessed the cloth and the cut. Nice. And so serious. Solemn. Even allowing for being at what might be his father's death bed he looked serious.

'Why didn't you come home before this?'

'Do you know how much it costs?'

'I thought you were well off.'

'How do you figure that?'

'He has a farm doesn't he? He has land, and animals? He's got to be worth a bob or two.'

'Mo, if only you knew. Zyg works on the railway now. His dad farms a few acres. They've only just got electric. He has a few cows, he sells the milk to the cheese factory, for nearly nothing. He grows some potatoes, that's what the family eats, potatoes and cabbage. Six people and two children – three when the baby starts eating – are supposed to live off that farm but me and Zyg get our own money now, they don't give us nothing, except we go and eat there on Sundays with the children.'

'Potatoes and cabbage,' he said.

'More or less. Eggs, when the hens lay, which half the time they don't. Thing is, Mo, I don't know much about it as you can imagine, not being brought up to it, but it seems to me they're not very good farmers, they don't know how to do it.'

'How did they get into it then?'

'What I can gather, what Zyg and Lisa have told me, Josef – Zyg's father that is – came from Poland as a labourer. He had a job for when he arrived but it was for three years, he had to promise to work for three years, for this farmer. So he did, and then he stayed past his three years and then the old bloke died and Josef got the farm.'

'Easy as that.'

'Now, they're crooks – the old folks I mean, not Zyg and Lena – so whether it was above board I don't know, but anyway the farm's his, or at least it's no one else's, but it's not big enough for a family to live off, Paul and Lena work all hours but they still can't make it pay.'

Maurice shook his head. 'I was thinking of coming over there myself,' he said. 'Maybe I'll think of Australia.'

'What about –?'

'Mum. She can come with me if she wants. If –' He did not look at their father in the bed, but Sadie took his meaning. 'So this shop?' She could tell that he hadn't given up the idea of having a ready-made fortune waiting in the colonies.

'Haberdashery. You know, material, thread, buttons, that sort of thing. Only a little concern.'

'Not yours?'

'Not on your life. I only work there till two o'clock so as to be home for Carolynne when she comes out of nursery.' She saw him register the claims of John and Carolynne on any property she might have an interest in. She purposely did not tell him about her curtain-making business, which was doing nicely, more lucrative now than working in the shop, but the shop was a means of getting customers and even, when Mrs Munro was at lunch, of doing some finishing there, on the display machine.

'What about you Mo? What are you doing, are you courting?'

'Not any more,' he said sourly.

'Anyone I know?'

'Name of Irene. You wouldn't know her. Only interested in getting married, girls are. I want to see the world a bit first, make some money, have a good time, that sort of thing.'

'Doing what though?'

'Whatever's required, in an office sense. I do accounts, figures, you know, double entry book-keeping. Dull as ditchwater but it has to be done if a firm wants to know where it stands.'

Sadie thought of Maryska and her envelopes of money hidden around the house, and smiled. 'So when are you coming to say hello to your niece?'

'How old is she?'

'She's not a baby, you don't have to worry, she won't widdle on you or nothing like that. She won't spoil your nice new suit.'

'I could come round Sunday I suppose.'

'Why don't you live at home? Wouldn't it be cheaper?'

'To tell the truth Sis, I fell out with Mum and Dad. I haven't seen them for a while.'

'What was that about then?'

He grimaced. 'Money. What I spend it on. How much I was giving them for board. How many baths I was having. They won't accept I'm grown up now. I did my National Service, I did my two years you know, and a bloke expects to be treated like a man after that.' Sadie thought of Zyg, still treated as a little boy, or a slave, in spite of time in the army, and active service at that.

Maurice glanced again at his father. 'If he gets over this – '

'He won't be himself,' said Sadie. 'He'll want looking after, day and night probably. She won't be able to do it all herself.'

'You'll have to come home.' He sounded quite satisfied with his solution.

'How can I? My family is a thousand miles away. What am I supposed to live on? Why can't you do it? You haven't got any ties have you?'

'You're his daughter.'

'You're his son. I don't see why it always has to be the girls that have to stay home and do the dirty work.'

Although they were keeping their voices to a hiss, there was a perceptible hostility and they were attracting the attention of other visitors in the ward. Neither of them saw their father's face flicker again.

The bell rang for the end of the visiting hour. Sadie, cross and Maurice, sulky, walked out of the rubber doors and along the cold green corridor.

'Excuse me.' They were being pursued by a student nurse, black stocking legs trying to go fast without running. 'Wait.' They stopped at the next door.'

'Singleton?'

'Yes,' said Maurice.

'He's died,' said Sadie.

'Oh I'm sorry,' said the young girl. 'I wasn't supposed to tell you, just bring you back to the ward.'

'You didn't tell us,' said Sadie reasonably. 'I just guessed.' For some reason she felt calm and unemotional, as if this was a small blip in a process, something that would be sorted out in a moment, like a broken thread.

'Sade, we just walked away.'

'He didn't know,' she said. 'He didn't know nothing about it.'

CHAPTER FOURTEEN
IN WHICH A BABY ARRIVES BY AN
UNORTHODOX ROUTE

Ginny was right about the house that Nell and Hamish lived in. It was too big, too cold, too empty, bleak inside and out. There was not enough of them or their possessions to fill it. On moonlit nights the rooms that were still waiting for curtains looked haunted. Draughts blew under doors and left dust on every surface. Nell knew all this but did not know how to put it right.

For the first few months of their marriage, she and Hamish had lived in his one-room bed-sit and were very happy. She went to work each day on the train – it was too far now to cycle – and she was smiling all the way, smiling out loud, you might say, so that people looked at her and wondered what was so good about life.

Well, what it was mostly was making love.

Nell knew that Hamish was keen to have children. He had wanted to specialise in children's medicine, but there was too much demand for rehabilitative medicine and he had evolved into a brain injury specialist. 'Not a surgeon,' he explained, 'more like a parent if you will, telling people what they should and shouldn't do, how they can make the best of things.' It sounded a bit vague to Nell.

She had wondered if he wanted to get married simply to have children, and if his lovemaking would therefore be clinical and official. She knew little herself, only the occasional coy reference from Ginny, and warnings from her mother who of course was used to picking up the pieces from lovemaking that was intended not to produce children. Nell was nervous therefore, about how Hamish would be, and how and whether she would be able to know what to do, and make him happy with her. She was always conscious of being the second choice.

She did want to make him happy, and as it turned out, he wanted to make her happy too. The very act of getting married seemed to click a switch in both of them that hadn't previously been clicked – only quite minimal kisses and clasps had happened before – and their sex life was light-hearted and pleasurable for both of them. Nell was surprised and delighted. She came home looking forward to seeing Hamish and looking forward to bedtime, which sometimes happened quite early in the evening. Living in one room, which she had worried about, actually made intimacy easier; there was nowhere to get away to. And the fact of Hamish being a doctor helped too because she could trust him not to be surprised or alarmed by her periods. She did not tell him however, and knew she would never tell him, about her mother's sideline.

The new house came with Hamish's new job. It was an ugly house from the outside, of liver-coloured brick with stained glass round the top of the windows and in the front door. It had stood empty some time and the inside reminded Nell of Mr Page's house – brown paint and shiny dado rails.

'We'll get someone in to give it a coat of paint,' said Hamish. 'We're very lucky you know. Lots of people haven't got anything near as much space as this.'

'We've never had this much before,' said Nell.

'As I say, we're lucky. And beggars can't be choosers.'

'We're not beggars,' said Nell.

It was only a small town. It ended abruptly at the end of their road, and fields started, growing potatoes and sugar beet, stretching away flatly, to maybe a line of trees, planted as a windbreak near a farmhouse, or all the way to the horizon, to meet the clouds that built and grew far away.

Nell no longer had a job. Hamish earned enough, it wasn't that, but she missed it, missed not only having her own money, but the feeling of knowing things, of having to remember things, of being the one who knew what to do and when. Some days she spoke to no one. She did housework and arranged their small amount of furniture in rooms that seemed too big for it. But what was the point of housework? She and Hamish hardly ruffled the dust, he would never notice if the floors hadn't been washed or the bath taps polished, if he did notice he wouldn't care. She shopped, she cooked, she looked at the garden through the rain-spotted windows and even looked in the phone book in the kiosk to see if there were any market gardens nearby. But all around were farms, busily grubbing out their hedgerows so they could plant peas for the new frozen food company.

And no baby came. After a year she visited a colleague of Hamish's who pronounced her in working order, and told her to relax and enjoy herself, which she had been doing up to then, but being instructed to just caused her to seize up, so to speak.

'You do want a baby don't you?' said Hamish.

'I do now,' she said honestly. 'I never did before I was married. I didn't know much about babies.'

Hamish, who used to say Relax, it will happen in its own good time, began to calculate the best time for conception and ask her to take her temperature to see when she was ovulating.

'I don't even want to do it,' she said sadly. 'I wish they were separate.'

'What?'

'The two things. Making love and making a baby. I wish we could have the one without thinking about the other. Like most people,'

'Not possible,' he said.

'It used to be possible,' she said. 'When we first got married we never thought about a baby.'

'We just assumed we'd have one.'

'That's how I'd like it to be again. I hate all this – measuring – and worrying, and feeling a failure.'

'Do you think?' – Nell believed afterwards that he had been waiting for an opportunity to say this – 'we should think about adopting? Think about it, don't say anything now, just think about it.'

Nell thought. She thought of Ginny's baby that never was, of the girls and women who used to visit her mother with their troubles, of how one of them would instead choose – choose? – to give their baby to come and live with her and Hamish.

'I've thought,' she said. 'I think we should look into it.'

Hamish put his arm round her and she put her head on his naked chest and listened with her other ear to the rain hitting the window in the dark.

Ginny said Nell was lucky – it was one of her least tactful remarks – not to have to use a Dutch cap.

'Don't you want a baby then?' asked Nell. It was the first time Ginny had visited, they were sitting looking out at the flat windswept land, drinking tea. It should have been like the old days when they sat on their beds and gossiped, but it wasn't.

'I wouldn't mind,' said Ginny. 'But I think Bernie might pack up and leave like he did his wife. He likes to be the only baby in the family, I've discovered.'

'But he loves you.'

'Does he? He likes having me to play at being his wife. He doesn't have to do anything. I shop, I cook, I clean, I pay my rent and I go to bed with him.'

'Why do you stay with him?'

'You know why.'

'I know you love him. But it doesn't seem very fair.' Nell, on her own all day with time to think, was surprising even herself with some of the things she thought.

'How is it different from Ted and Kath? She does everything for him, and she doesn't even love him.'

'But he keeps her. She doesn't have to work. And she can have children.' Nell was aware that this was what she was supposed to say, not how she really felt.

Ginny laughed, but there was an edge to the sound of it. 'But I like to work. I like having my own money, I don't have to ask for everything like Kath does. And anyway, she can have children but I don't think she likes them. It's just a job to her. No, I know who's better off out of us two.'

Nell nodded to show she understood and agreed.

'And,' said Ginny, 'if I want to leave I can. No paperwork, no questions asked. I don't belong to him.'

'I think it's quite nice,' said Nell, 'belonging to someone.'

'I'll just belong to me, if you don't mind,' said Ginny stoutly. Does she mean it, Nell wondered.

The house had a front garden which was entirely grass, and a back garden, which was mostly grass. One day – it was still as cold as winter but there was a more lively feeling in the air – Nell went down the garden to investigate what was in the shed. The catch was rusty and she had to force it but it was the sort of job she was good at. Inside the shed there was nothing. Cobwebs, a bucket, an empty sack with a hole in, nothing else, nothing useful. She felt an enormous urge to cry. Her period was due, it was a day late, she did not dare to hope she was pregnant, she would not let herself think about it.

She looked over the fence at the neighbour's garden. It too, as she well knew, was laid down to grass. She thought of Kath's Ted, putting in his potatoes and beans, and even Sadie's dad, picking rhubarb and gooseberries from the back plot. She got out her bike and cycled to the next village, where there was a hardware shop. She bought a spade and a fork, seed potatoes and packets of seeds, tomatoes and runner beans. She laid out the potatoes for chitting on the windowsill of the spare room and spent the rest of the day with her hair covered by a scarf, clearing dust and cobwebs from the shed. My shed, she thought. Her period started.

In the following weeks, whenever the weather was not actually raining, she dug up the turf, starting from the far end of the garden. She noticed the air becoming softer, the birds flying over, the sun a little higher each day. There were no buds to break in the garden because there were no trees, no bushes, no shrubs. But the grass became greener, and grew and one day, unannounced, the gardener from the hospital arrived in a van with a lawnmower and commenced to cut the front garden grass. When he came into the back, where Nell was digging, he approved of what she was doing, in the sort of way her mother would approve of things.

'I don't know what you're doing that for. Going to a lot of trouble that is. What you going to plant?'

'Potatoes,' she said, 'there. And some runner beans. I'll see how I get on.'

'You can buy them down the shop,' he said. 'No need to go to all that trouble.'

'What would you grow?' she asked him.

'Dahlias,' he said firmly. 'Nothing like em for cheering you. Any colour you like as long as it's not blue. You don't want to bother with veg.'

'I'll have some flowers as well,' said Nell, 'nearer the house. Later on.' Maddox's nursery, way before her time, had tried to make money from daffodils, and failed, but the clumps still came up spring after spring, in odd corners and edges, and Nell had loved seeing them, their colour, their intense sunshine. She would have some in her garden. She was conscious of spending money that wasn't hers, on things that only she wanted, but Hamish hadn't objected, not in the least. Though he did say, 'You won't be able to do so much gardening when we've got a baby, you do know that.'

'Of course I know,' she said.

She planted the potatoes, she bought some pots and started the runner beans off, she put the tomatoes to germinate on the windowsill. She bought more seeds, onions, lettuces; for flowers, night-scented stocks. She let herself consider a future that included a greenhouse. She envisaged cucumbers.

On the day that her potatoes first put a little dull green shoot above the earth, Hamish came home early from work, to tell her that the adoption society had approved them as parents. It was very soon after, when the runner beans were beginning to flower, that he hurried home from work between appointments to tell her there was a baby, they could go and see her tomorrow, Nell should start making a list of equipment they would need.

'How soon?' said Nell.

'We need to do three visits, with a week between, that's their rules. Then, if we're sure, we can bring her home.'

'So she's ours already? No one else is going to get in first and take her?'

'She's got our name on her.'

Like setting aside goods in a shop, thought Nell, like knitting wool or a Christmas bird.

CHAPTER FIFTEEN
IN WHICH THERE IS A DRAMATIC EVENT

They could hear the phone ringing in the butcher's shop before dawn but there was no one there to answer it. At 7.30 Mac Hobbs the butcher unlocked his door and let himself in and at 7.37 it rang again. At 7.40 he was scuttling up the fire escape shouting Mr Jakimowicz. Zyg wasn't at home – at that moment he was at Toronto station remonstrating with a man who would not put his dog into the conductor's van – and it was Sadie who answered the door. John – in his underpants – and Carolynne were eating breakfast at the counter, Sadie was standing drinking a cup of coffee and brushing the dirt from John's school trousers.

Having come up the stairs too fast for his fat old body Mac had to pause before getting the strength to knock on the door and it was a few seconds before he could gasp, 'Accident,' and even longer before he could speak properly. Sadie naturally assumed that Zyg had had an accident, and so did John. He began to cry.

'Out here,' beckoned Mac and Sadie went out on to the fire escape, keeping an eye on the children through the window.

'Your sis-in-law on the phone. Accident on the farm. Fire.'

Sadie's first feeling was relief that nothing had happened to Zyg. 'What happened?'

'Didn't get to find out. Sounds bad. They need you over there to help. Come downstairs and call them. They need you.'

John, reassured that Zyg was all right, stayed in the kitchen to watch Carolynne. 'I'll be late for school.'

'Never mind that now.'

Sadie got through to Lisa on the phone. 'Paul and Pop are in hospital. There's only me and Mom here and Mom's hysterical.'

'Where's Lena?'

'Gone to the hospital with Paul. I think he – Sadie, get Zyg and come. We need you.'

'What can I do? I can't milk cows.'

'Just come. Get Zyg off the train and come.'

'Zyg's on his way to Edmonton.'

'Just get him. Come Sadie.'

So Sadie was on the nine o'clock ferry with the children, leaving Mac to call the railway and get Zyg sent back to Kingston. Lisa met them with the truck. Maryska was in the front seat, stiff and silent and apparently calm. Sadie and John and Carolynne squeezed in beside her.

'What happened?'

'Not now,' said Lisa, overtaking the milk tanker.

The farmhouse was black and stinking with smoke, but undamaged. The milking shed was a heap of cinders, beams still smoking, the sick smell of wet ash hanging in the air as if it would never blow away. The day was warm and damp and overcast, as if made by the fire and the water that had been poured upon it.

'Ma,' said Lisa, 'take Carolynne in the house.'

She turned to Sadie and began to let the tears go again. 'They called me from the hospital –'

'Wait – where's Marianne?'

'Oh – at the Macdonalds.'

'Thank goodness. I thought –'

'Oh Sadie –' Lisa fell on her. 'I've been up all night, I called you but you didn't answer.'

'What happened?'

'Pop caught light – they were trying to put it out – Ma and Paul and Lena and Pop, and Pop caught light – I don't know, it must have been a spark I guess – and Paul rushed at him to bat out the flames and he caught light and Lena got blankets and stuff and rolled them on the floor and her hands are burned too and then the firemen came and then the neighbours and they stopped it getting to the house and the ambulance came and they ran a special ferry to get them over, and Ma has just lost her mind and the cows need milking, you can hear them starting now – oh Sadie, I'm so pleased to see you.'

'Oh this smell,' said Sadie. 'It reminds me of the war. Well, we'd better get on with it.' She gathered her wits, as she was the only person who seemed to have any. 'John and me will get the cows in. Can you call the Taylors, or the Frasers, or somebody and see if someone will come and help do the milking. Give Ma some tea – plenty of sugar, see if she can get some sleep. Can you keep Carolynne with you too?'

'Will you really get the cows? I don't feel as if I can leave Ma. When I got to the hospital she was raving, they made me take her away. If you get the cows –' She knew Sadie was scared of the cows.

'John will know how.'

And John did. He loved the farm, John, and he loved to be useful. He knew how to get them from the field without losing them across the road and he could direct his mother as to what she should do. 'Walk behind Mom and don't let them go down the track – they want to go for the long grass – just hoosh at them, then run quick and shut the gate.'

Sadie was proud of him, and of herself. Mr Fraser and his son came over and did the milking right there in the yard and Lisa called the company to say that their milk was ready for collection after all, and waited for the driver and told him all about it, and he put his arm round her and told her it would be all right – which was true in some respects because she married him a year later. But by and large it was not all right. Zyg arrived by four o'clock, in time to leave again to collect Lena from the hospital. Lena came home, bandaged and widowed, and Lisa drove to the MacDonalds to pick up

Marianne, so that Lena could hold her and try to stop crying.

Naturally things on the farm were never the same again. Sadie thought it was like one of those times in the playground when Marcie MacNee had spun her round maliciously hard and when she stopped, everyone and even the buildings seemed to be in a different place. She felt, as she looked around the wrecked farmyard, that same dizziness in the head, the same wishing the feeling would stop, the same panic. The same but worse.

At first neighbours took over the milking, helped by Lisa, but pretty soon Lisa went back to her work in the city, and her bed-sit, and her new boyfriend. Lisa was not Lena. She hated farm work and she had, they all said, her own life to lead. Zyg gave up his job on the railway straight off but Sadie refused to move back to the farm. There was her job to think of, the children's schools, the problem of where everyone could sleep. She thought to herself that Lisa was not the only one who had her own life to lead.

Besides, there was what Lisa had said to Sadie when they were on the ferry together one day. 'Have you ever wondered how that fire started?'

Men from the insurers had been and tramped around, taking notes and photographs, and then paid up, or promised to.

'What do you mean?'

'It's my belief,' said Lisa, 'that Mom or Dad, probably Mom, set that fire on purpose, for the insurance.'

'So why would Paul and your dad try to put it out?'

'Paul because he wasn't in on the secret. Nor would Lena be. They would never do such a thing. They're not so stupid for one thing. Pop would have to help wouldn't he, he couldn't just sit there and let Paul do it all, he had to make it look like it was an accident.'

'But what makes you think it?'

'It just makes sense. It's what they would do. They couldn't make it pay by working. Lena and Paul were talking of leaving, did you know that? And another thing, Lena and Paul weren't at home when it started, they were visiting Paul's folks, they saw the fire from the road. Mom's story that it was something to do with a spark from the truck's engine – did you ever hear such a tale? – and it won't wash anyhow because Lena and Paul were out on the road in the truck, driving home when the fire started.'

'And she's not said anything?'

'How could she? It's too late. It won't bring Paul back. But she won't stay there. You watch, she's just waiting to be well enough, then she'll be out of there, her and Marianne.'

Blanka came to visit when Josef came out of hospital, bringing her youngest child with her 'to cheer you all up.' Blanka was a big stolid unimaginative girl – not a girl at all, but she retained a sort of unworldliness that made you think she would never grow up. She and her one-eyed postman had moved up to Midland and they were never coming back to the farm. She moved about the house fastidiously, wrinkling her face at the smell of smoke which seemed to hang around for ever and ostentatiously cleaning everything her child was about to touch.

Maryska did not seem cheered by the visit, nothing, it appeared would help her out of her deep misery. She sat most of the time in her mother's old place by the fire – she could almost *be* Baba come back to life. Lena had to snap and bully to get her to help with anything and even when Josef came home, shocked and disfigured, she did not put herself out to nurse him. Actually, no one liked caring for Josef, with his head half covered in raw pink hairless shiny scar tissue and his hands useless – worse than Lena's. Little Marianne cried and cowered when he was in the same room, and not many nights went by without her waking and screaming, even though she slept constantly with her mother. Josef could walk all right, his legs were unhurt, but he was slow and old-seeming and took to using Baba's stick to get around the farm. He could do no work and could offer no advice or comfort to Zyg, who himself seemed to age by the day, worn and baffled by the effort of trying to hold it together.

They sold the cows. There was now no income apart from the little brought in by the hens. Zyg rented the fields out as pasture to a woman who kept horses.

Lena and Marianne went to live with Paul's family. When Sadie and her children visited the farm on Sundays the house was so quiet you could hear the dust settling, Zyg out in the yard still clearing away one bit of charred timber at a time. Sadie could look out of the dirty window and see him standing helplessly looking at the rafts of debris. John would be talking to his grandmother, telling her things about school, about ice hockey, about his friends, doing his little best to cheer her up. 'Do you want to go and help your dad?' Sadie would say and he would go eagerly. Whatever it was like, even with its maimed and hopeless people, the farm was where he felt at home. Zyg would rouse himself when John went out to help and they would achieve a little more cleared space, but there it would stay until the next Sunday when John came again. Sadie spent the day cooking and cleaning for the two old people. Sometimes Lisa came over, said a hasty hello, then went off to see Lena, usually, and helpfully, taking a bored and restless Carolynne with her.

Josef got an infection and was taken back to the hospital. Zyg cried when he told Sadie how he'd visited but been prohibited from seeing his father.

'I just looked through the window at him. I don't even think he could see me. I waved to him but I don't think he knew. All connected up to tubes.'

Sadie stroked his hair. She truly felt sorry for the whole family, even the ones she didn't like.

'Come back to the farm, Sadie. It will go a whole lot better if you're there with me.'

She felt truly sorry but she was not going to be dragged into it. For her sake and even more, for John's. She knew he wanted to live there. He felt stifled in the town, he liked the air and the surrounding lake and the smells and the machinery – what little there was – and the work. He talked confidently of when he was old enough to leave school and how he would get the farm back on its feet, rebuild everything, have cows again, make money for his dad. Sadie, though she did not make the mistake of telling him so, thought he should have a proper trade. He was a clever enough boy, he could be a mechanic or an electrician, there was no need for him to waste his life on a patch of useless ground, any more than she had to.

'Zyg,' she said. 'I'm not going to lie to you. I am never coming back to live on the farm. Never. It's not your fault. It's not you. But me and that farm, never again.'

Even when Josef died, as they all knew he was going to, she kept to her resolve. The farm was down to Zyg and Maryska.

CHAPTER SIXTEEN
IN WHICH FRIENDSHIP STRUGGLES
BUT SURVIVES

Ginny got up early enough to catch the first train to Liverpool Street and from there, changing at Cambridge, she went to see Nell. She looked a wreck, she knew she did, eyes and nose red and sore from crying and spots breaking out on her chin. Each time she got off a train she looked to see if Bernie would be there to meet her – though it was impossible; every time someone passed along outside her compartment she looked up hopefully in case it was Bernie, returned from Ireland and come to look for her. She knew it was impossible.

Spring sunshine flooded across the fields of East Anglia. As the train passed, black birds – they were rooks but she didn't know the name – flew up out of trees like burnt paper off a bonfire. She had known it was all going wrong. She and Bernie were pulling each other into a spiral of despondency and bad temper and mistrust, they were too dependent on each other, and too attuned to each other's moods, neither of them could wake up one morning and see the sunshine and feel happy and hopeful – or if they did it would take only one word from the other to dump them back into misery. And she had been thinking about Marcie. She always knew she was in a bad way when Marcie filled her thoughts and stopped her sleeping. Nightmares – nightmares like Kath had – would not be so bad, she thought. She wouldn't at least be feeling that she ought to control them, and at least there'd be some sleep to be had. It was strange, thought Ginny, that whenever anything bad happened, or looked like happening, she remembered Marcie. Arguments with Bernie, her dad's illness and death, even events outside the family, road accidents or distant tragedies, anything troubling brought Marcie into her mind. I'm a happy person, she thought to herself, why should I carry on like this?

She took a bus from the station to near where Nell lived. She bought some sweets for the children and a colouring book for the older one and walked slowly, with her coat unbuttoned and feeling a little better, or if not better, at least diverted from complete despair. Nell's house looked different from the last time she had seen it, which must, she calculated, be about four years ago. Flowers and new green leaves cheered and softened the nasty-coloured bare brick, and the baby slept in his pram by the front door. Ginny resolved that she would show no envy of Nell and her little family – Nell deserved it, she had lost so much and waited so long. Anyway, thought Ginny, if I'd wanted Hamish I could have had him. And made herself stop there because it would only lead her on to think of Bernie, off on one of his visits to Ireland but this time, not promising to come back.

They sat at first in the front room, which anyone could see was hardly ever used. The mantelpiece was empty, except for dust, there was not a book or a magazine or a piece of mending, or a wireless to be seen, just two chairs, and Nell had to bring in some toys for the children. The little girl was all seriousness. She looked at her toys carefully, turning them in all directions and then arranged them on the rug, looked at them, moved a brick or a doll one way or another a little, then sat back and looked again. The little boy – who was not adopted, he was Nell and Hamish's own – crawled across to her and put his hand on a small dog on wheels. The little girl growled at him, growled in a way that shocked Ginny. 'Like a little bear,' she said to Kath later. 'Or a lion.' Duncan was picked up and put in a playpen with his own toys. He pulled himself up on the bars and strained to climb over.

Ginny asked politely how Hamish was. Nell asked politely after Kath and the children, and Mrs Swallow. They knew already, the answers to their kind enquiries, from letters, but they were awkward with each other, nervous, constrained. They spoke of Sadie.

'Do you still write to her?'

'Only sometimes,' admitted Ginny. 'She hardly ever writes back.'

'I haven't heard from her for ages. She must be settled there by now.'

'Have you made friends yet?'

'Not many,' said Nell. 'The woman in the grocer's, she told me you have to live here thirty years before you properly belong. It's better since I had the children. You meet people at the baby clinic.'

Ginny could imagine it – Nell would be shy, and then say something, out of nowhere, unexpected and dogmatic. People wouldn't know what to make of her. She said, 'Nice people?'

'People my age,' said Nell. 'But they don't live near. At this end of town there's no young people, only old ones. They look at me as if I've done something wrong.'

'Miserable old cats,' said Ginny, and Heather looked up from her game and said, 'Where's miserable cats?'

Nell and Ginny laughed and for a moment it felt as if things were normal again, but neither of them could think of the next thing to say, and they sat silent, looking at the children and hoping for some event that would bring them together.

When they went into the back room it was better. It was as big as the front room, but much less tidy. Toys and books and old newspapers, bowls of fruit, shopping bags, piles of children's clothes. Tomato seedlings on the windowsills. The window looked onto the back garden, where washing flapped on the line, toys littered the lawn and yet more daffodils bloomed in the borders down each side.

'I meant to tidy this before you came,' said Nell. 'But never mind. I'm sure you know me well enough, don't you.'

I don't think I know you at all, thought Ginny, but she didn't say it.

'You're not looking too well,' ventured Nell.

'I'm moving back to live with my mum,' said Ginny. 'It's over with me and him.'

'What happened?'

'I don't know. I honestly don't know. It's just – everything's wrong between us. He's gone to Ireland – I know, he's been before, he goes to see his mother, and of course he sees his children and of course he sees *her* but this time I don't see him coming back.'

'Did he say he wouldn't?'

'He did, and then he said he would and then he said he wouldn't, and we parted on bad terms, and that was two weeks ago, and he's not back and I haven't heard from him, and honestly Nell, I think we're better off apart. If he comes back I'll have to move out and go and live with Mum.'

Nell made a face expressing commiseration.

'I know. I don't get on with her either. But she's not been too well since Dad died, she might need some looking after.'

They ate shepherds pie, followed by jelly. Nell was not a very good cook. Then the children were put to bed and to Ginny, having Nell to herself seemed to make conversation easier.

'Did I tell you? We had a proper to-do about Kath's baby's name, you should have heard it. Ted wanted him called Ronald. He's never raised a murmur about what the girls were called, but he got this in his head and he would have it.'

'Kath didn't like it?'

'She was the same as me, no, worse. You know she's always had it for certain it was Marcie's brother that killed her, she said she wasn't going to be shouting her child down the street and thinking of a murderer. I didn't know that she ever even gave a thought to Marcie, but you see, with Kath, she doesn't talk about things like I do, she has nightmares instead.'

'Still?'

'Well, she doesn't talk about that either, but I think she does, from remarks Ted makes.'

'So what's he called then, the baby?'

'Tony. Well, he's Anthony but no one's ever going to say that are they. She let Ted have his way over a middle name, so he's Anthony Ronald, but as she says, she's never going to have to be yelling Ronnie up the stairs. And I tell you what, he's going to be so spoiled. All those sisters treating him like a doll and letting him have his own way.'

'What about you?' said Nell. 'Haven't you ever wanted a baby?'

Ginny felt her face lose its shape and her eyes begin to fill. She smiled, so as not to upset Nell. 'I think it would have happened by now if it was going to. I know we've been trying not to have a baby, but so has Kath and it hasn't worked for her. I wonder if when I went to your mum – you know – whether that did something – I don't know.'

'I don't know either,' said Nell. 'But it's some people isn't it. Some are like Kath, and just have babies one after another, and some are like me, and wait for ages.'

'Still, it happened for you in the end didn't it.'

'I couldn't believe it,' said Nell. 'We were happy with Heather, she was lovely –' (Touch of the tarbrush, thought Ginny, though she knew better than to say such a thing out loud.) – 'and we were thinking we might adopt another when I fell pregnant, and didn't even notice at first, my mind just wasn't on it, where before, every hour I was thinking either am I pregnant? Could I be? Or else I'm not pregnant, it's failed again, I'm a failure.'

Nell looked so joyous, so pretty, so soft, as she said this that Ginny hardly knew whether she wanted to hug her or slap her. 'You're barmy,' she said. She looked out of the window at the back garden. She remembered Nell's house from four years ago, when there was only a barren expanse of grass at the front and back, like a football field. Now there was a garden.

'The front gets the sun in the morning,' said Nell. 'I put Duncan out there in his pram to sleep and Heather plays while I do the garden.'

'So you're happy?'

'Oh yes,' said Nell. 'We're happy. We've got each other. And the children. Of course we're happy.'

'It was the answer to everything, wasn't it, having children, for you?' Ginny hoped she didn't sound bitter, she didn't intend to.

Nell seemed to think for a long time before she answered. 'I always was scared, you know, that the things my mother did – I know this is ridiculous – that I would have to pay for what my mother did. Do you know what I mean? When we took Heather, one of the things I thought was that at least some poor girl had gone ahead and had her, instead of letting someone do horrible things to her.' She looked at Ginny directly again. 'I'm sorry Gin, you're the only person in the world I can say these things to. Hamish doesn't know a thing about it, he would be – I don't know what he would be, I wouldn't dare tell him.'

'I know exactly what you mean,' said Ginny. 'You're the only one that knows what I did. Bernie would have a blue fit if he knew. And I couldn't tell Kath either. She wouldn't say anything, I mean she wouldn't fall out with me but it would be there between us like a – like I don't know what – like a smelly fart that you can't say anything about. I would never know what she thought of me.'

'My mother didn't mean to do evil things,' said Nell. 'She was helping people in her way.'

'She helped me,' said Ginny. 'No, she really did. I suppose, now, that I could have got through it, the baby would be about nine by now, same as Kath's second girl, but at the time, well, I was ready to jump under a train, it seemed like the end of my life, I couldn't see past it. Your mum was so good, I mean like a nurse, very kind and careful, and yet all the time I was thinking about Marcie and I wondered –'

'What?'

'It was you that told me Marcie was pregnant. She came to your mum. People – girls – do sometimes die of abortions – '

Nell nodded. 'My mother never said anything about her. I never saw my mother's – you know, the people that came to her. It was all done in her room, or sometimes at their own houses. It was only that you were living with us, otherwise I would never have known.'

'So there's no one alive who knows what happened to Marcie.'

'Except the person who killed her. If they're still alive.'

When the children woke up they went for a walk around the town. Nell pushed the pram and Heather walked beside them, quietly holding Ginny's hand.

'Does she ever play you up, this one?'

'Never. Hamish says she's too docile. He worries that all the spirit went out of her while she was in the orphanage. He thinks she might have a hard time at school, with the other children you know.'

'I should wait and see,' said Ginny. 'No point worrying about something that might never happen.'

'And I wish she wasn't so jealous of the baby,' said Nell, as if she hadn't heard what Ginny said.

Hamish came home especially early as Ginny was visiting. He was hardly changed, still wiry and quick in his movements, his hair disappearing backwards over his head, his slightly nervous smile showing his crossed front teeth. It could have been me, married to this man, thought Ginny, but it seemed unreal, as if it had never been even a possibility. He asked after her family, and Bernie, and she just said they were all fine, and left it to Nell to tell him later that Bernie had gone. She and Nell walked round the garden while he bathed the children and Nell showed her where the vegetables were going to grow and where the peonies were putting out their red new leaves, and where she was planning to plant an apple tree next winter.

'Who do you think killed Marcie?' said Ginny suddenly. She felt she could not go home without saying it.

'How would I know?' It seemed that Nell had not given much thought to it, though back when they were sharing a room they had talked about it, Ginny was sure, at least once a week.

'Do you think Sadie's dad had anything to do with it?'

'Maybe.' Nell would not look at her.

'But I don't think he was ever violent. Do you?'

'Not exactly –'

'He tried it on with Kath too, you know. She never told me at the time, only told me when he died, never told Ted to this day.'

'Why not?'

'Well, you know Ted. He might get funny.'

'I suppose. So, who do you think?'

'It wasn't Billy,' said Ginny.

'Who said it was?'

'I don't know. People. I know he used to be a bit peculiar but if you saw him now – he goes to work, he behaves hisself.'

'I never heard anyone say anything about Billy.'

'Good. Because it wasn't.'

'It could have been anyone,' said Nell.

'That's what everyone says. But it was *someone*. He might still be living round our way, it might be someone I know.'

'You're not scared.'

Ginny laughed. 'Of course not scared. Just sometimes I can't get her out of my head, like being possessed. You know, she lived next door to us.'

'I know.'

'I might have been the last person who saw her.'

'But you might not. It might not have been her.'

'Every time something bad happens to me, or to anyone around me, I can feel her. Nell, I'm not that sort of person, I don't go in for airy fairy nonsense like ghosts and that, but I can't help it. I wish I could get it out of my system some way instead of going over and over it, and suspecting people.'

'What people?'

'Anyone. Eric –'

'Why Eric? Anyway, he was laid up with his foot.'

'Was he? It's hard to remember who was where. But what if she didn't die till later. He was home by then.'

'Eric used to torment animals. Gus told me. You know, hanging cats from lamp posts, that sort of thing.'

'All boys do that,' said Ginny. 'Billy did. But,' she added firmly, 'it wasn't Billy.'

'Who else?'

'What about Mr Page?'

'He was *old*. Marcie could have run away.'

'*You* could have run away from Wilf Singleton, but you didn't.'

'Yes I did.'

154

They seemed to have lost touch with each other again. Ginny had meant to make a joke, Nell was offended, and hurt that Ginny had forgotten what had happened, Ginny was offended that she was hurt.

Hamish called to them that it was time to take Ginny to the station. Nell drove her there, neither of them speaking very much.

Nell parked in front of the station and they both got out of the car. Nell said, 'Do you suppose Sadie knew what her dad was like?'

'I wonder,' said Ginny. 'Sadie, to me, doesn't seem like someone who sees beyond the end of her nose. But then –'

'You can know something and not know it,' said Nell, and they stood in silence for a little while. 'Come and see me again?'

'Of course. Write to me, won't you.'

'Of course.'

Ginny touched Nell's sleeve. 'Don't worry about me.'

'I will worry. Take care of yourself. Remember me to Kath.'

They looked at each other, the girls that they once were looked at each other, and then Ginny went through the barrier, and looked back, and waved, and disappeared.

CHAPTER SEVENTEEN
IN WHICH THREE MARRIAGES ENDURE

KATH

'Why not?' said Rita.

Kath continued peeling potatoes. 'You girls,' she said. 'Want want want, all the time. When you're bringing in some money, then you can want things, all right?'

'It's not unreasonable,' said Rita. Kath wished she could turn back the clock and have a child who did not pass the 11-plus.

'Everyone else has got one,' said Kay. Rita gave her a look which told her to keep her mouth shut. Theresa was there too, a frail copy of Rita, obediently silent.

'I don't know why you don't ask your father,' said Kath. She tipped the dirty water down the sink and wrapped the peelings in newspaper to put into the dustbin.

'He said ask you,' said Kay. Theresa nudged her.

'You would like it,' said Rita. 'You watch it at Auntie Gin's, and you like it.'

'Gin can afford nine and six a week,' said Kath. 'Where am I going to find that sort of money?'

'Dad will pay it,' said Rita.

'And pigs will fly,' said Kath.

'No listen,' said Rita. 'He goes to the pub doesn't he? How much does he spend there? If we had a telly he would stay at home and watch it. There's westerns and all sorts. Comedies. Variety. He would stay in, I bet. He'll save money.'

'Well you ask him if you want,' said Kath. She would dearly love to have a TV. 'But don't say I told you to.'

'I'll get Kay to work on him,' said Rita. 'She can get round him.'

'All right my lady,' said Kath out loud when they were gone, 'but don't think you can get round me that easy.'

It was the money that was all. As fast as Ted's wages went up – and bloody hell, that wasn't very fast at all – prices went up, and the children got bigger and more expensive to keep. Rita had to have school uniform and was forever moaning that she had to use a school hockey stick when all the other girls – ALL the other girls – had their own. And Valerie wanted a recorder, thank god they couldn't afford it, nobody wanted that squeaking away, and she would soon get tired of it. And Tony now, of course he couldn't wear his sisters' old clothes, it had to be proper boy's things but if it wasn't for a bag of hand-me-downs from Joyce and Billy he would be going to school in a skirt. And they all went through shoes as if they were made of paper, and they were always coming into the kitchen asking for threepence for sweets, or money for one of their stupid magazines and Rita wanted stockings at three and eleven a pair, and if she thought she was wearing them to school to get ruined, she'd have another think coming.

Kath put the potatoes on to boil and started to cut up the cabbage. On the wireless Family Favourites came on and she sang along to the tune. She loved the words, though they were soppy and matched nothing in her experience. Ted did not have an adorable face, never had had, Kath had never been swept away by feelings, even her yearning for Gus had been vague and hopeless and when she thought about it now she could not understand herself. But she knew all the words to all the songs and sometimes sang them as she cleaned and washed and cooked and ironed alone in the kitchen. They kept away some of the worries about where the money went, and cleared the air after a night of bad dreams.

157

If it was not for Ginny the girls would not have such big ideas. Ginny had all the things she wanted. Television, radiogram, fridge, vacuum cleaner, washing machine – why would she want a washing machine, there were only two of them? Bought with her own money too. And clothes. If only Rita and Theresa would grow taller and stouter they could come in for some lovely stuff off Ginny. Always smart, Ginny. Perm, lipstick. Maybe she had to make an effort to keep hold of that Bernie, or maybe all that make-up and smartness was a way of showing everyone she didn't care what they thought. And she didn't care, Kath was sure of that. And why should she? thought Kath. What difference could it make, that someone down the town hall said it was all right for you to go to bed with this person or that person? It just stopped men – some of them at least – from running off and never paying for their kids. Not that Kath ever imagined Ted would run off. Too comfortable here, she thought.

If only he brought a bit more money in. Coke for the fire, the electric bill, the rent. It's not just food and clothes, she said to him in her head, do you know how much soap and washing powder we get through? Bleach, scouring powder. Kath was not house proud in the sense that she needed nice things – matching china or fancy pillow cases – but she was house proud in the sense that she needed things to be clean. She liked to feel she was a little bit better than some of her neighbours who never washed their front step, who you never saw flapping a duster out of an upstairs window from one year to the next, whose children's socks were grey and their collars grubby. It took elbow grease, but it took cash as well.

What she could do with another pound a week. Better not to think about it. 'The rich get rich and the poor get children.' Kath knew the words to all the songs.

NELL

Winter Sundays were slow, rather melancholy days. It might have been nice to have somewhere to go, but they were not a churchgoing family. Hamish, it was true, had grown up in the Church of Scotland, Nell had been taken to church services occasionally by her grandmother when she was small, but now they had left all that behind them. If asked, Hamish would say he was a socialist agnostic, Nell would say that she hadn't thought about it, really.

That Sunday in November mist was rolling in across the fields all the way from the far off sea, wrapping the world in silence, dripping off the leafless bushes in the garden. Nell was glad that Hamish went for a walk in the morning, taking Duncan with him, but they came back sooner than usual, wet and dispirited. Duncan, nearly five years old, with wet feet from stamping in puddles, and fingers numb with cold, was still not chastened enough, not tired enough to want to stay in the warm and play quietly. He was a skinny, ginger-haired, intense, active small boy, with unpredictable sudden changes of mood. Nell's heart sank slightly at their return, because there was still a long time to go until the Sunday lunch was on the table, and she wondered how Duncan would choose to occupy himself indoors. When she put a pair of dry socks on him and told him to go and find his slippers, he set off into the cold hallway, sliding and skidding, making no move to put his slippers on.

'Shut the door,' said Nell, and Heather, sitting on the floor near the fire, bum-shuffled across the room and kicked the door closed. Duncan opened it again. 'Watch me,' he shouted.

That was the start of it. As usual Nell could not grasp how such a big argument could develop from such a small beginning. Heather slammed the door again, Duncan pushed it open while she was still there so that it hit her knee; she kicked it again and he yelled that she had caught his fingers in the door.

'Let me see,' said Hamish, just at that moment coming down the stairs in a pair of dry trousers. 'I can't see any damage.'

'She did, she did,' screamed Duncan, working himself into the certainty that he was hurt. 'Tell her to say sorry.'

'Heather, go and say sorry,' said Nell. But her voice did not carry conviction. She did not believe Heather had hurt him and Heather, though she did not argue, kept her eyes fixed on her long tail of French knitting that she was producing, and her ears apparently closed.

'Just say sorry,' said Hamish, exasperated. 'Just to keep him quiet.' He knew though, and so did Nell, that Heather would be immovable.

'Make her say sorry,' screamed Duncan, and Heather, they could see, smiled quietly to herself and did not lift her head to look at him.

'I need to put the potatoes in,' said Nell. She edged past Hamish, still in the doorway, holding on to his son to stop him hitting his sister, and shut herself in the kitchen, feeling ashamed at leaving it all to Hamish. This kind of scene could go on for half an hour, and there was no way they knew of that could resolve it. In the end something would happen. Heather might give in when she judged that she had won and the noise began to bother her, or Duncan might suddenly recover from his fever of rage and start jumping down the stairs, or doing head-over-heels on the rug. What neither of them would do was to respond to any pleas or suggestions from their parents. Nell and Hamish were helpless.

'What are we doing wrong?' said Nell. This was much later when the children had been put to bed and Sunday was over at last. Nell and Hamish sat either side of the fire, which gave out more heat now that the fireguard had been taken away.

'They'll grow out of it,' said Hamish. 'I expect.'

'But while they're growing out of it,' said Nell.

'It's not so bad in the summer,' said Hamish. 'They can play well together in the garden. It's the space in here, or lack of it. Studies have been done, you know, on rats. They get very aggressive if they are overcrowded.'

'It's a long time until the summer,' said Nell. She was planning her seed sowing for the next year, and filling in an order form. Runner beans, peas, beetroot, lettuce. Rain was still hissing at the windows, but the curtains were closed and the room felt cosy. It was hard to think that in six months time it would still be daylight and she would be able to work in the garden after the children were in bed. Space, she thought, and she thought of the front room, which they never used. For the first time she compared her house to Kath's, all those years ago. Kath also, in those days, had had an empty, cold front room, not even lino on the concrete floor, and the windows running with condensation from the ironing that was the only activity she did in there. The rest of the time the children played in it.

Suppose, thought Nell, suppose Heather and Duncan could have a room to themselves. She had heard of children who used their bedrooms to play in, but in this house they could not be heated; frost formed on the inside of the windows. The front room could have a fire at weekends. The extra work would be worth it. There was a carpet on the floor, curtains at the window – two up on Kath already. They could afford another fire, surely, though they were saving towards buying a house of their own one day. She thought of it as a solution to the biggest problem of their lives. If the children quarrelled it would be much easier to separate them until Duncan calmed down. If they had more space for their toys they would not be under her feet all the time, they would not have to tidy them away before meals, and what a relief that would be, not to have to start the nagging a full hour before Hamish came home from work, and then, usually, to end up doing it herself.

She looked back at her catalogue and thought longingly of flowers. So far her efforts had concentrated on fruit and vegetables, and flowers were acquired, not bought. Her garden was growing like a brain, like a tree, like a map, bit by bit, plant by plant, slowly. She poached things that she happened to spy – a root of lilac pushing under a fence, a tip of a fuchsia that she persuaded to root, seeds from someone else's honesty or marigolds. And she had a talent, which she didn't even need to think about, for putting each one where it would grow strong and agree with its neighbours.

The children were incompatible with a garden. Duncan thrashed footballs and cricket balls into the borders. Heather picked the flowers and pulled them to pieces to see how they were made. Still, Nell looked at the descriptions, the names. Delphinium, phlox, lupin, montbretia. Roses, the names. Etoile de Hollande, Mme Joseph Perraud, Albertine, Zephirine Drouhin – so many French names. Marechal Niel, Gloire de Dijon. She could fill her garden with French roses.

'Do you like roses?' she asked Hamish.

He looked up from his book. 'Of course,' he said. 'Everyone likes roses.'

'So shall I buy one?'

'Buy two,' he said. He smiled at her. He was not usually extravagant. She smiled back. Maybe Duncan was old enough to go and play in the Rec. Maybe Heather would grow out of her destructive habit. Maybe some roses growing over the fence would be able to survive. Plants were easier than children.

Maybe, though, the front room idea would work, if Hamish wouldn't consider it too extravagant. I won't say anything yet, she thought, I'll think it all through first, then I'll mention it. Maybe I can get him to think it's his idea. It's not such a big thing, to have a fire in the front room.

GINNY thought to herself that you could sleep beside someone for years and never know what they looked like as they slept. Bernie, she was sure had never peered down at her as *she* slept, storing up the memory of her, loving the mere fact that she was breathing in and out, looking, in the dim dawn light, at her relaxed face, her tumbled hair, her eyelashes (she was proud of her eyelashes) making tiny shadows on her cheeks.

She knew he was leaving again. She had spent the last four years watching him, asleep and awake, calibrating the chances, waiting for the signs without knowing what they would be. He lay now, on his back, breathing noisily, as men do when they reach middle age and have been on the beer the night before. Ginny lay on her side, well towards her edge of the bed, and looked at the shape of his nose outlined against the pale wall. It was a good-shaped nose, long, thin, straight. His mouth opened slightly and she thought he might wake soon. If he did she would pretend to be asleep, rather than allow him to tell her something she did not want to hear. Outside the room, sparrows on the roof cheeped incessantly.

He did not wake, only rolled away from her, and pulled the blankets up to his neck. Ginny closed her eyes. She had no expectation of going back to sleep.

She thought about Kath. Was Kath happy? With Ted? Ted not only lazy and unappreciative but these days morose as well. 'I don't mind if he does go to the pub,' said Kath. 'I'd sooner have his room than his company. Moaning all the time.' How unhappy would she have to be, to tell him to leave? She didn't sing so much these days, she did a fair share of moaning herself, the fun had gone out of her. Of course she was worried about their mother. So am I, thought Ginny. There was something wrong with Mrs Swallow. Her ankles were swollen, her face was sunken and yellowish, and she refused to see the doctor. 'Old age,' she said. 'That's all it is.'

'Let him look at you, Mum,' said Ginny, 'just to make sure. Maybe you need a tonic.'

'Just leave me be,' said her mother. 'You can't do nothing about old age.'

At least there's this, thought Ginny, if he leaves again I can go and stay with Mum and look after her a bit. Better than living here on my own. Though she loved their little house that Bernie had made out of the old stable block of the doctor's big house. This once was the hay loft; downstairs, the stall for the horse had become the kitchen, with the bathroom opening off it, and their living room was where once upon a time some sort of coach or carriage had been kept, and later, the doctor's big old car. She and Bernie had made the transformation together. She recalled that time as the best time, such fun, camping in the half-built house, making do, sweeping and carrying and plastering and painting every evening after work, till they were dizzy with tiredness, though never too tired to make love.

Would it have been different if they had had a child? She could not tell, she and Bernie never discussed it. If she was a helpless woman, if she did not support herself in all sorts of ways, if she relied on him for money and company and friendship and laughs – would he stay then? When he went back to his wife, as he had done before, did he sleep with her? What did he tell her? What did she know? Ginny did not know what Daphne was like; it was another thing they never discussed, along with his children. Her stepchildren, it might have been possible to say, but she had never met them, hardly seen a photograph even. Katherine and Bernard junior, teenagers now, and their mother – Ginny would like to think of her as a weak woman, whining and demanding attention – now a schoolteacher; they seemed to be getting on all right without Bernie. Is that then, why he's going? Because they don't need him?

I need him, thought Ginny, and almost let herself begin to cry. She pictured to herself a scene where she clutched at him as he went out the door, seizing him round the waist and sliding down to his knees and finally grabbing his ankles as he picked up his bag and freed himself, leaving her sobbing on the kitchen floor. Not on your nelly, she said aloud, softly, and got out of bed to start the day.

It was not yet six o'clock on a summer Saturday, she could have had a lie-in, a morning cuddle, they could have made love, maybe. Instead she drank a cup of instant coffee, dusted the room and swept the kitchen – quiet jobs that wouldn't wake Bernie. She would take him a cup of tea later and maybe it would feel right to get back into bed with him. Meanwhile she would clean the shoes. She lined them up: Bernie's work boots and his good black shoes, her sensible work shoes and her patent leather courts. She put blacking on the two pairs that needed it and left it to soak in while she chipped the clay off the work boots with an old kitchen knife. If he was going away this week he wouldn't need his boots. And if she cleaned his shoes for him, might he not take it as a message that she was telling him to go. She buffed up her good court shoes and then took the polishing brush to his shoes. She would not let him turn up on Daphne's doorstep in shoes that were not shiny; Daphne was not going to think he wasn't looked after here in England. Ginny would make sure his trousers were pressed as well.

She heard the bedroom floorboards creaking and the cistern flushing, and put the kettle back on the gas. But before she could make the tea he appeared in the kitchen, wearing his work clothes. He smiled and kissed her briefly on the cheek. 'I'll have me cuppa,' he said, 'and then I'll be out to look at that new job.'

'It's Saturday,' said Ginny.

'I'm just looking,' he said, 'only to give them a price. I'll be home for dinner. And will we go to the pub tonight?'

'I suppose so.'

When he was gone Ginny sat down and stared foolishly at the line of shoes. Of course I'm relieved she said to herself, but really, if he's going to go why doesn't he get on and go. I can't stand much more of this. It was the smile that told her. He was not a smiler. You had to work hard to make him smile, but when he did it warmed you for a week. But not now, now his smiles were thin, frequent, social things, that only made her shiver.

I will let him go, she said, he can do as he pleases; and it came to her that it would be the only way to keep him. He can go. When he's ready, he can go, and when he's ready, he can come back. It will be all right.

She looked around for something else she could do to pass the time until the rest of the world woke up, and decided she should write to Sadie.

CHAPTER EIGHTEEN
IN WHICH THE FOURTH MARRIAGE
RUNS ITS COURSE

When at last Maryska died, Sadie was excited. A new life would be available to her.

John was sixteen. The cheerful little ways he had as a small boy were gone, along with his clear complexion, but he was still a good boy – hardworking, reliable, solid. He was the sort of boy who would withdraw from whatever was going on, mischief, fun, fights – he would stand back and let it happen without him. Carolynne was more the sort of child who would start mischief, or fights. She was ten – ten going on twenty-one, said Sadie, often – and clever. So sharp you'll cut yourself one of these days, Miss Know-All. She had always been more awkward than John, more self-willed, more demanding. There were times when Sadie wondered why she had wanted a second child so much, and even more times when she said to herself that though she shouldn't love John so much more than Carolynne, she did. John looked like her, in colouring, fair and blue-eyed with skin that went red at the first sunshine of the year, but was tall like his father, skinny like his grandparents – the Polish ones – and with a drooping eyelid like his Uncle Maurice. Carolynne was like a photographic negative of him – tall, but more heavily built, dark of hair and eyes, with pale waxy skin that never changed colour. When they were younger they had seemed to have a closeness that Sadie envied, but it was all gone now. They had nothing in common, they did nothing together, they hardly spoke to one another.

Zyg rang her from the farm to let her know. She said she was sorry, she said the things she thought she should say, but she knew that even Zyg must be relieved it was all over. He had been heroically devoted to his mother, and looked after her better than his sisters would have, for years now, but even he must be relieved, exhausted and relieved. Sadie sat at her sewing machine, sewing Rufflette tape on to a pair of floor-length brocade for a big house near the park, and in her mind planned out what would happen next.

He would need some help to arrange the funeral, then to clear and tidy the house. They should sell the house with its bit of lakeside access – someone would pay a good price to turn it into a summer cottage. The land could be sold separately to one of the neighbouring farmers, maybe that woman Olive who grazed her rescued old horses on it and seemed to have more money than sense. Then Zyg could buy a place in town and he and Sadie and the children could all live together again. John could be apprenticed to a trade instead of persisting with his idea of being a farmer, they could have a nice house with a room set aside for Sadie to sew in, and she would have enough space to do all the projects that crowded her head.

Zyg could get a proper job again. It would be nice to have Zyg back, and be a proper family again, and not have to explain to nosy old women why she and he lived separately. It would be nice to have family weekends, and go to places instead of spending time on the lost cause they called a farm. They would have to sell the truck and buy a proper automobile. Sadie would take her driving test and use the car to deliver her curtains, instead of heaving unwieldy parcels on and off buses to the suburbs. Carolynne would not be embarrassed to bring her friends home when they had a proper house, instead of one that always smelled of the disinfectant used to cover the smell of blood and bone and lard from downstairs. It would be nice.

Over the years since the fire Sadie had visited Zyg at the farm less and less often. John went every weekend, from Friday after school to the last ferry on Sunday, or sometimes the first one on Monday morning. Carolynne went most weekends but rarely stayed overnight, unless it was with Marianne at the MacDonalds. Sadie, also, never stayed over. She could have shared Zyg's bed in their old room, with its claustrophobically low ceiling, but Maryska was now in the next room, that used to be the sisters' room, and it felt too close. John slept on Baba's old shelf. The building that had once slept seven adults and a child was now too small for three people. Before Maryska became really ill, and bed-bound, Zyg had visited Sadie and the children once or twice a month, and stayed over, sleeping in Sadie's bed like a normal husband. Yes, normal. But in the past year and a half it hadn't been possible to leave his mother alone. It will be nice, thought Sadie, to have him back.

After the funeral, she set to on the house. She had always reminded Zyg not to throw anything away without checking it for hidden money, and indeed, under Maryska's mattress there were dollar bills, thirty-seven of them, smelling of urine and old age but dollar bills for all that. Sadie threw the mattress on the pile of things to be burnt. She opened windows and swept floors. The air in the first frosts of autumn sparkled like lemonade, and the sun still shone out of a blue sky. Maryska's clothes followed the mattress, there was nothing in the old black rags to tempt Sadie to keep them, though she did take a minute to cut off the buttons.

'It's good of you Sadie,' said Zyg, when they paused for a rest.

She would have liked to say that she was doing it for him, because she loved him, in a sort of way, and it was something she could do to help them back to being a family again, but the words did not come and instead she said, 'It's no trouble.'

'I appreciate it,' said Zyg.

'It will sell better if it's clean,' she said. 'We could do some repairs too, a bit of paint wouldn't go far wrong.'

Zyg was looking at her and something about his expression frightened her. She rushed forward. 'We could make a thing down by the water, one of those things, what do they call it, where you tie a boat. You and John should clear the gutters as well, they've been left too long. And we need to fence off the land that goes with the house from the fields we can sell, and the front door –' She was plucking random ideas from her grand plan, to head him off because what she saw in his face was pity and she wanted him not to speak. She stood up and picked up the broom. She called to John to ask if he wanted a drink but he failed to hear her. She went into the house and began to heat water on the stove. Zyg was behind her.

'I'm sorry, Sadie,' he said.

'What for?'

'Well, I guess, for telling you this, when you're being so good.'

'Don't tell me then,' she said, brightly.

'I'm not selling,' he said.

Relief. 'Oh is that all?' she said. Thinking, It's too soon. I'll talk him round.

But the following weekend he showed up at the apartment.

'Baba's box,' he said.

'What about it?' said Sadie. She realised too late that she should have denied any knowledge of it. While Zyg was living with her she had kept the things from the box well hidden, in brown paper parcels, at the back of a cupboard, guarded by packets of sanitary towels that she knew he would not move. When he went back to live on the farm she opened up the parcels and had a good look at the contents. Dresses and skirts – good tweed, and fine wool, and dark velvet. She had been a big lady, that posh woman on the transatlantic liner – there was enough material in them to make new outfits, remodel a blouse here, pick apart a skirt there and recut it to sew again. There were shawls both fabric and knitted, and linen – pillowcases and tablecloths with embroidered edges – linen that could be turned into underclothes for Carolynne. There were stockings of thick lisle and Sadie could think of no use for them, but she did not throw them away. She threw nothing away. She reduced the whole box of clothes to pieces of fabric. If anyone from the family ever saw it they would not know that it was from Baba's box. In the spaces between curtain orders she made skirts for herself, a party dress for Carolynne, a waistcoat for John, and shirts. She kept the smallest scraps of cloth, bits of trimming, slivers of silk and lace, all the buttons naturally, but also the hooks and eyes and the snap fasteners. She did not know what she was keeping them for.

A look came over Zyg's face, a shy sort of look, pride and apprehension mixed. 'I was telling Olive about it,' he said. 'And when I looked, it was gone.'

'And why wouldn't it be?' said Sadie. 'How many years has she been dead? Ten? Your mother will have thrown it out. It was all rubbish anyway.'

'It certainly was not,' said Zyg. 'I remember seeing in that box when I was a little boy. I remember it was like a shop, colours and soft things. I just thought of it the other day and I said to Olive, I've got something to show you, and when I went under the bed, nothing.'

'Well, it was there when she died,' said Sadie. 'After that, I wouldn't know. Anyway –' she was going to say something about Olive minding her own business, but she heard the sound of Carolynne's steps on the fire escape and wanted to close the subject before she came in, for fear she might say the wrong thing.

'Hi Dad,' she said. 'What are you here for?'

The shy look came over Zyg's face again, but briefly, chased away by a look of annoyance. 'Now Carrie,' he said. 'Why don't you go and leave us in peace for a little while, while I talk to your mother.'

She went to the bedroom without any argument, rubbing his hair up the wrong way as she passed the back of his chair, so that as he told Sadie what he had come to say, he looked like some sort of large crested bird, a heron, something like that, all neck and nose, and crest, sitting in the best chair as he told her that he wanted a divorce so that he could marry Olive.

When he had gone Sadie went to her kitchen and peeled potatoes with wild strokes that could have cut her but somehow didn't, turned the tap on so hard the water splashed all over her, crashed the saucepan down so hard it rang. She half-heard Carolynne come out of the bedroom and go back in.

The children, she thought. What do they know? She was sure, absolutely stone cold certain, that John knew all about it. Was it possible that Carolynne knew too? And they hadn't warned her, not a hint, not a word. And they didn't mind. However long it had been going on – she hadn't asked, he hadn't said – however long, her children had had the chance to let her in on it.

Olive. Sadie had only ever seen her driving past in a truck, often towing a horse trailer. Just her head, and there was nothing remarkable about it. But John knew her – he was there half the week, he must have seen them together, he must have known for weeks, or months, what was going on, he was watchful, he wasn't stupid. So she couldn't trust him. He preferred his father to her, it wasn't just the farm he went to, it was Zyg. Maybe even John preferred Olive to her. This thought hurt Sadie even more than losing Zyg to this woman. Carolynne had excuses – she was too young to understand what it all meant, she hadn't had the opportunities John had to see what was happening, she wasn't as close to Sadie, she didn't have the same responsibility as a son, and the eldest. Wait till he gets home, said Sadie to herself. But John did not come home that night, nor the next.

It was just after Christmas that news came that Ivy had also died, more, that she had left her house and all her belongings to Sadie.

'Tell John,' said Sadie to her daughter, 'that we are going to England. If he wants to come he needs to say sorry, and if I'm satisfied with what he says, I'll take him.'

But John did not show up, and there was no apology. Sadie and Carolynne went to England without him.

Part 2

NINETEEN

I was eleven. Eleven. She took me away from my dad and my home, and my brother and my aunts and cousins, and my friends and my school and my country.

At the time though I didn't mind. I was happy to come with her to England, not realising it was for good. Strange term, that – for good. In fact it was for bad, and it was for bad for good. It wasn't so much that I missed my dad, I was used to being without him, I had no memory of a time when he actually lived with us; all my life it seemed to me, he had lived on the farm and we had gone to visit. I liked him a lot but I was never sure if he really cared for me as much as I wanted him to. I knew anyway, that John was far more important to him. I was jealous of John, for being older, for being a boy, for being old enough to leave school and go to live on the farm, for being the one everyone loved best. I thought I didn't mind at all that I was leaving *him* and going to England without him. I was going to England without him *again*, because *I* had been to England before, though it was just outside the boundary of my memory, and John had been left behind and he never forgave my mum for that disappointment. *I* went in an aeroplane and *he* didn't. He was about nine years old that first time and I can see now how full of anguish he must have been. I'm lucky I suppose, that he never seemed to blame me for it, only Mum.

I was fond of telling the girls at school that I was half-English (we were all half-something) and I felt pretty important telling them that my mother and I had to go back to England on vital family business, even though I didn't understand what it was. I was excited about going. I didn't know I would miss my dad, and my friends and my cousin Marianne and my home and the farm, and that more than anyone I would miss my brother John. I didn't know it was for ever. *She* says she didn't know either, it was intended to be a short visit to sort out Stepmother's will, but I don't know if I believe her. John certainly doesn't, never did.

We left Canada in February, a cold, cold February, and arrived in England in spring, it seemed to me. White clouds as big as pillows sped across a blue sky, bringing rain for half an hour, maybe, and then the sun would come out again. The journey from Gatwick to North London by train, then on a bus, then another train seemed to take as long as the flight from Ottawa. The sky cleared, the sun went down, the lights came on, it got dark. Out of the train window I saw rows of little brick houses, their back yards, their dustbins and washing lines. Dimly through their steamed up windows people moved about, cooking, or sat down, eating, English people, wholly English. We got off the train and the wind had stopped and it was cold, suddenly as cold as Canada, a frosty night with a moon so bright it dimmed the stars.

Stepmother's house, when we finally got there, was the same as the others I saw, low and joined both sides by houses just the same. Inside it was even colder than outside. Mum turned on all the rings of the gas cooker – I had never seen one before – to warm the room. 'Wait here,' she said. 'Keep your coat on, you'll freeze. I'm going to get us some fish and chips. I won't be long.' Already her voice had changed to something more English. I waited, scared to go into another room in the dark, hungry and cold and nearly dead with tiredness, worrying that this was all some elaborate trick to leave me on my own in a strange country and so be rid of me. I was not at all sure she would come back, but she did, and we ate fish and chips together, and I probably loved her more at that moment, when we were in this thing together, than I had since I was a baby, and certainly more than I ever have since. I swear you don't get fish and chips nowadays like you did then.

Of course, the first people I met, almost before we had finished the last chip, were Ginny Swallow, and her sister Kath. The door knocker was banged practically off its hinges and I could hear someone saying, 'Go easy Kath.' Mum ran to the door as if it was Christmas and I peered out of the kitchen door to see who it was. But it was only two grown up women. One was quite fat, I thought, and had a loud voice, and her clothes were limp and brown. The other was taller, thinner, and had her hair permed and wore a navy blue suit and high heels.

She said, 'Kath came round on the off-chance and I said you couldn't be here yet, and we saw the light through the door.' But we could hardly hear her words because she was laughing, they were all three laughing and I had no idea what they could be laughing at. When at last they noticed me Ginny came and gave me a hug, and Kath gave me a look which meant (I found out later) Another girl. More trouble.

'It's your Auntie Kath,' said Mum. 'And this is your Auntie Ginny.'

They didn't stay long, that first time. When they had gone Mum and I explored the bedrooms and she said we would sleep together on our first night and decide tomorrow in daylight who would have which room. She put the kettle on and made cocoa, just with water because there was no milk of course, and we went to bed, wearing most of our clothes, between sheets that were so cold they felt wet.

If you could see my mother now, skinny and feeble and immobile, with her bad knees and misshapen hands, you wouldn't believe how much energy and determination she once had in her. By the end of the following day – starting before dawn, I should say – fires were lit in all the rooms and the beds were airing, there was food in the cupboards, our things were unpacked and put away in drawers, and Stepmother's things were piled in the front room, waiting to be gone through. All the post was picked up and read and sorted, and the ones that needed a reply were on the table, waiting for her to sit down. No one had heard of jet lag in those days.

Mum and I had never had so much space. She claimed the front bedroom, which had been hers before Maurice was born, and again when he went away during the war, and I had a room of my own, the back bedroom, which shook every time a train went past at the end of the garden. The first night I slept there they kept me awake, but within days I was used to it (I was eleven) and found them comforting, their clanking over the points and the chuffing of their steam. The sooty steam descended all over the washing that Mum pegged out on the line and if I opened the window my bed would be sprinkled with black dust, but I liked hearing them through the night, coal trucks trundling past to the power station, and I would wake up just enough to know that I was in bed and warm, and then go back to sleep, rocked by the noise. Of course at first I didn't know to call them trucks – I called them wagons and people looked at me as if I was a clever baby, clever, but wrong.

In Canada I never had my own room. I slept on a sort of camp bed in the corner of Mum's room, and if Dad came and stayed the night, which was hardly ever, we dragged the bed into John's room. I always hoped he would talk to me in the night and I tried to stay awake until his bedtime but he never did talk, just sighed when he came to bed and saw me there, sitting up on my bed, reading one of his books. He didn't take the book off me, just put the light out without saying anything and got into bed so quietly I could hardly hear the clothes fall to the floor or the bedsprings squeak. Having my own room in England was a big excitement, even though it was furnished in an old-fashioned way, huge heavy furniture, too heavy to move, smelling of polish and mothballs, curtains so thin you could almost see through them, and lace runners and doilies on every surface.

'Don't moan,' said Mum. 'I'll get round to it one of these days. There's other things want doing besides your bedroom you know.' When she said things like that I hardly listened but later, when I was on my own, usually in bed, the sentence would come back to me, I would hear it again like they do in films, and I would realise what it meant. She had no intention of going back home. In fact, she was at home. Home for her and home for me were two different places, a long way apart. The house was hers, her property and her home. Each time I realised it, the ground seemed to fall from under my feet, then I would try to remember the times she had promised me we would go back to Dad and John, and kid myself that she meant it. Only, at last, I gave up asking her, and I gave up hoping.

Inside Stepmother's house the cold retreated once the fires had been lit for several days. I had never known about coal fires before. Mum had to go out a lot, seeing solicitors and people like that, and I sat by the wireless, wrapped in a blanket, listening to Workers' Playtime and Mrs Dale's Diary. In the park there were crocuses, white and purple and gold, flowering in the grass like jewels. My mother took me to the school along the road, the one she had gone to as a child, and left me there. I didn't mind school, it was at least better than being in the house on my own, or even with my mother, going at life like a cavalry charge, but I did mind the feeling I had that I was trapped in a foreign country and that she had kidnapped me and that I would never get to go home again.

One day I came home from school and found a truck outside and a man on the doorstep, knocking patiently. Mum was out, but I had my own door key. He was delivering boxes to us, and the boxes were full of all the things we had packed up before we left home, because, she'd said then, we wouldn't be going back to the apartment above Hobbs the butchers, we would have somewhere better and there was no sense paying rent while we were in England. I believed her. I was eleven. But I began to suspect, as I dragged the boxes off the doorstep into the house, that they had arrived pretty quickly, and that maybe there was nothing left in Canada for me to go back to.

In one of the boxes that the man delivered was stuff I had never seen before. Material of kinds that were unfamiliar, not just cotton or gabardine, but silky stuff, thick stuff, stuff with embroidery and lace. And the biggest box of buttons I had ever seen. What was she going to do with all this? She didn't tell me.

So this was my new life, I began to believe. Not a holiday, not an episode like my previous visit to England, but my new life. John and my dad were far away and had forgotten me and the people I knew now were the old couples in the houses on either side – Mr and Mrs Tilbrook, Mr and Mrs Hare – and Ginny and Kath. I called them auntie, but I never made the mistake of thinking they were a replacement for my real aunts. I had three. Aunt Blanka, who we hardly ever saw and who didn't really count; Aunt Lena of the crippled hands; and my favourite, my lovely Aunt Lisa. Mum seemed to think that I could transfer my Aunt-feelings away from them and to these other people just like that, just as, later on, she seemed to think I could have the sort of feelings for Eric that I had for my dad. She didn't really know much about feelings, my mum.

TWENTY

I was, as I say, eleven. Eleven. Old enough to notice that I was uprooted, displaced, an alien in another country, old enough to miss my home, not old enough to do anything about it. It was not the first time she did this to me, and it wasn't to be the last. She had done it before, when she refused to go back to the farm after the fire. She split our family like an amoeba, and she did it again later when she married Eric (God rot him) and destroyed what little progress I had made with my life. And now, again, when my life was all sorted and settled, again.

I didn't think it through. I am old enough to be a grandmother – I *am* a grandmother, but I didn't have the brains to think it through.

When I moved in with Mum to help her cope, I thought that I could manage to carry on working and that I would still have a life of my own. I let out my flat in the town and took myself and my dear Charlie Fred to live in her horrid, stuffy, overstuffed, overheated chalet-bungalow and began to be a dutiful daughter. It wasn't long before I had to give up Charlie Fred, on account of the fights that went on round the kitchen and in and out of the cat flap, as soon as I was not there to protect him. Bloody Daisy (called after Mum's sister) was just too jealous and territorial and vicious for poor old CF. So off he went to the cat shelter and I cried privately and Mum assured me that he wouldn't mind a bit and I would soon forget him. Sentiments I think I had heard before.

But I still had my job. I left her every morning with, I thought, everything she needed close to hand, my mobile number keyed into the phone by her side in case of emergency, TV remote, magazine, glass of water, medication all within reach, agency carer coming in at midday to check on her and make her some lunch, what could go wrong? Everything. Well no, I exaggerate, she never fell down the stairs or anything dramatic, she just found some new problem every day, so that as fast as I put something in place to solve it, up popped another one. Spilling water all over her as soon as I'd left the house – on purpose, I know it was. Dropping her painkillers on the floor. Ringing me at work to ask how many she was supposed to take. Ringing me at work to say there had been a phone call, no she didn't know who from but someone was coming out now to look at our loft insulation. Ringing me at work to say she couldn't get to the toilet.

'But hasn't the carer been?'

'Who?'

'The lady from the agency. Kelly.'

'It wasn't her. It was the one I don't like. I'm not letting her touch me.' She was rude to all the carers, who after all were only poor women trying to help, she shouted at them to go away and refused all offers of a cup of tea, a ham sandwich, a nice chat. The carer would ring me saying she was worried about her state of mind, she shouldn't be left with access to a bottle of painkillers, surely, and had I thought of having extra visits through the day. But she wouldn't hear of it. 'What for?' she said. 'Do you think I've gone silly? Do you think I can't look after myself?' But then she would ring me at work through the day, crying because of the pain and saying she couldn't turn on the tap to get a glass of water to take painkillers with. As soon as the weather began to turn colder she found a way to get me to come home: she would turn off the heating and the carer would ring me to come home and turn it on again, and I would find her on the couch, Mum, shivering under some inadequate piece of cloth, a coat, a towel, a tablecloth. She claimed it was to save money, no matter that she was a well-off woman and that the money Eric had left her had increased rather than run out, but I know it was a plot. Plots are what she has always been good at.

So I stopped working, I had to. I couldn't go on cancelling meetings at the last minute or asking someone to stand in for me, or being late. I retired, unwillingly.

Unwilling because I liked work, maybe because I had come to it quite late in life, proper, professional work. I loved the competent feeling it gave me, of knowing what I was doing, of doing something that needed to be done, of seeing what I did sometimes be effective, sometimes not, most of all, of being part of an organisation, a useful, working, necessary part of a machine. I was popular at work. I was the one who made them laugh in the office, I kept them going when management was reorganising our service yet again, or making us go paperless, or experimenting with hot-desking. I was one of those who'd been there the longest, umpteen years, I knew what I was doing, I helped everyone, whatever was going on I knew about it, I was part of it. People asked my advice, they sought me out, they really did. I knew the town, I knew the families we worked with and I could tell my colleagues details about them that weren't in any official file.

And my family, I thought, was everyone in the office, more my family than my real one. Janet and Pauline on the front desk were sisters I'd never had, Alan and Naz were brothers, Claudette and Farhana were daughters and the young ones that came and stayed a bit and moved on, earnest and brave and learning the job, they were grandchildren. I don't know why I'm telling you their names, don't bother to remember them, they're old news.

'Come and see us,' they all said at my leaving do. 'We'll miss you. We'll keep your Earl Grey teabags for you.'

'Don't be a stranger,' said Janet. 'Just pop in whenever. We can still go out for lunch on a Friday.'

But no. The first time, the very first time I went back, on a Friday two weeks after I left, Janet was at her desk eating a Marks and Spencer's salad out of a plastic tray, in full view of the public. Not very professional I thought. This wasn't what I had in mind when I set Mum up to spend an hour and a half without me.

'Not going to Nando's?'

'No,' she said. 'I thought I'd save a bit and work through, and try to get finished by five, get off a bit early.'

I went upstairs. Farhana was on the phone and waved to me. Someone I didn't know was sitting at my desk, looking as if he owned it. No one else was around.

'I used to sit at this desk,' I said.

He made a small noise and continued scrolling down his screen, looking up, I could see, previous records of the Foulstone family.

'They moved down here from Yorkshire,' I said. 'Try South Yorks if you need more on them.'

He ignored me. Farhana was still on the phone. I thought I might make a cup of tea for me and for her, but the Earl Grey teabags were not to be found, and anyway I could see that she had a medium Starbucks on her desk already.

I didn't give up straightaway. I did go again, hoping to see Pauline, or Jackie, or Maria, or even Alan, but I felt like a ghost. They looked through me. They looked at their watches and rushed past me. A few weeks later Janet rang me at home and invited me to the Christmas do, and I said I would but when the day came I stayed at home, sulking.

My mother lives in the past these days, pain and the past, that's about all she has, and she tells me stories and most of them I've heard so many times I can remind her of the bits she forgets – though very often I let my mind wander into my own concerns. Most afternoons, when she wakes up from her nap and I take her a cup of tea, she'll ask for the photograph albums and tell me about the people.

The photos have very little to do with me. They belonged to Stepmother, and when we came to England we discovered them in a drawer of the sideboard, some in their packets from the chemist, some lying around loose, some with names and dates written on the back, some without. It was my mum, a person with a passion for organising, who put them into albums, in chronological order, puzzling over sequences and relationships. 'Would you say this is her?' 'Here's someone else with that baby – which one do you think is its mother?' She sat with me at the table, photos spread from one side to the other. 'Look, same dress. Can that be Ramsgate as well?' I was eleven, twelve, bored and bewildered. Obediently I glanced at pictures of my grandfather and my uncle and they meant nothing to me. I would have liked to look at pictures of people in my real family, my dad, my brother and the rest, but we had left without bringing them, and it was years before I got hold of some. (And I brought them here to this house, in an album, but she doesn't care for them. 'Not those, I want the old ones.')

I'm still bored. I know people who are fascinated by their families. They look them up on the internet and go through old census records, just so they can tell you that their great-great-uncle fought in the Crimean War, or some such tale. They would love a collection like this, all tidily stuck in with proper photo corners and neatly captioned in my mother's forward-sloping capitals. *MAURICE IN THE GARDEN. WILFRED SINGLETON WITH SADIE (AGED ABOUT 6)*. There's even a family tree folded and stuck in the back of the first album, based on what she managed to remember, when she had no one left to ask. Today we are looking at Uncle Maurice. She hasn't the fine motor skill any more to turn the pages, so I have to do it.

'This one,' she says, 'they took this one when he was evacuated. Nice people, they taught him some manners, he came back a different person.'

'How long was he there?'

'Just while the bombing was bad – I don't know, two or three years maybe.'

'And you didn't see him?'

'Well, not often. We didn't have a car of course. Even Stepmother's father, he didn't manage to keep his car going. No petrol you see.'

'What about this one?'

'That's when he was back home. Look, school uniform. He passed the scholarship to the grammar school, clever you see, but he wouldn't have got it if he hadn't gone to be evacuated. They settled him down.'

'Well, you're clever too,' I say, thinking of her resourcefulness and independence, and the way she never let emotion get in the way of what she wanted.

'I could have been,' she says. 'I might have it in me, but I've never been taught to bring it out. The school I went to weren't up to much.' And I think, Then why did you send me to the same one?

Today I walk along to the local shop. The stack of cat food gives me a stab of loss. I pick up a pint of milk and a Sun (hoping the woman at the till doesn't think it's for me) but she – she seems nice enough and not a lot younger than me – doesn't even look up. I haven't made eye contact with anyone for days, unless you would like to count my mother.

I walk back, slowly. It's cold, a few snowflakes fall, when I get home my mother will tell me about Canada – Horrible, she'll say. You spent half the year waiting for the snow to melt.

The days drag, the nights have drawn in, it's dark by four o'clock and I close the curtains – great big heavy dark red things like something out of a horror film, made by Mum, naturally, and set off with a huge swagged pelmet. My life, that I made for myself, by myself, although only a matter of weeks in the past, seems so far away and so unrecognisable that I might have died and come back into another time and place.

I had friends, mostly from work, that I would go out with, shopping, or for a day out at weekends. Sometimes I would cook for people or we would go out for a meal. I had neighbours, who would feed Charlie Fred when I was away for a weekend. I had holidays – not on my own, with friends. We would make up a group and go somewhere, a foreign city, or a week in the sun somewhere. If I had an evening in I could read, or watch television, or phone a couple of friends. At weekends there was housework, and shopping for food for the week ahead and usually an evening out, maybe two, to the cinema or theatre. Five days of work – visits to families, visits to prisons, court duty, reports, assessments, meetings with other agencies, emergencies, all the shifting business of young people in trouble with the law, mostly poor kids, mostly not in school for one reason or another, mostly drunk, or high, or low, or just easily led. So, five days of work, and two days of leisure, and though I might moan about work – we all did – I did not want to lose that life.

Think of it, I gave up my flat, my job, my friends. Yes you could say they weren't up to much, my friends, if they haven't kept in touch, but it wasn't their fault, it was mine, or rather, my mother's. She has become more dependent on me, more likely to cry if I say I'm going out, and it has become more and more difficult to get away from her. Anyway, what would I talk about to people these days? Attendance allowances, G.P. appointments, topical ibuprofen. I don't think so.

And then my car. Ever since I had my own money I liked having a smart car. Not a big car, I don't mean that I drove around in a Jag or a Porsche, though I would have liked to. But I liked having something a bit eye-catching, with a bit of what they used to call poke. I had a classic Mini Cooper S, British racing green, and it made me happy. It was special, distinctive, classy. When I first had it I sent a picture of it to my grandson Ewan and he replied with one word. 'Cool.'

But of course Mum couldn't get in or out of it and I was having to get taxis for her hospital appointments, which seemed ridiculous, so Max the Mini had to go. Now I drive a Honda Jazz, like everyone over seventy. I can't even be bothered to give it a name. It's grey, it's almost invisible, as I am. And I'm not over seventy.

Though I look it now. Getting rid of my car – that took with it my last remaining rag of self-esteem. I am getting fat from eating too much and taking no exercise, I'm not bothering to get my hair cut, or put my good clothes on – because who will see them? – and I'm looking tired from not sleeping well – because I don't get tired enough during the day – and yet I am exhausted. I look a wreck.

Mum on the other hand, since she made me spend all my time with her, is looking better. More food, more company, painkillers and anti-inflammatories administered on time, help with dressing, so she always has her nice clothes on, tights and proper shoes, a neat skirt, a pretty blouse that she made herself, years ago, usually lilac with a pussy cat bow, lipstick, sometimes even jewellery. Here's me in elastic-waist trousers and old t-shirts, shuffling about in pair of old socks, hair gone grey from not bothering to get it dyed.

People think, Oh, single woman, no husband, over sixty, she can't have any life worth thinking about, what is it to her if she goes to look after her mother. Nice comfortable house, nothing to worry about, it's not even as if the old lady's demented, give her her meals, make sure she takes her medicine, bit of cleaning, bit of company for her, the rest of the time's your own. If only they were right.

And there are other people who tell me they wish *they* could have looked after *their* mother in her old age. But she was gone too quick, only two weeks after the diagnosis and she was gone, and their voices crack and their faces crumple. I find it difficult to understand. Do they mean it? Did they really want to spend probably their own best years mopping up after an old lady who they left behind long ago? Are they liars or hypocrites, or are there people who don't leave their parents behind them?

What *I* wish is that I could turn my back on her. I don't mean I would leave her here to cope on her own, I would put her in a home to be safe. Putting her in a home is what I dream of but she won't agree to it, and why should she when she's got me. 'Oh,' she says, 'I'm ever so glad I've got you. It's your turn to look after me now.' As if *she* ever did a good job of looking after *me* when she had the chance. She properly fucked up my life, not once, or twice, but four times, and in a big way, not in a simple teenage you're-not-going-out-like-that way. I do not forget and I do not forgive.

TWENTY-ONE

She picks out a school photo and I sit beside her and do my job. 'So which one is you?' and she points with her crooked forefinger.

'Who else?'

She points at the teacher. 'She wasn't a proper teacher. She was just a – what-do-you-call-it? – a stand-in. She had red hair. We used to make her cry so she would blush. You never see anyone blush so hard.'

'Who else do you remember?'

She brings out some names – Doris, Sylvia, Joyce. 'What about this one?' I say. I'm pointing randomly, because I don't care either way and anyway, will I remember what she says?

'Marcie MacNee,' she says.

That's Marcie MacNee? All those times I heard her name, all those years of everyone's lives wondering who, and what and why, but I had never known that she was in this photo, which I've seen a hundred times. I say, 'She got murdered didn't she?'

'Who told you that?'

Can she have forgotten? I heard it all through my childhood. Aunt Lisa saying, 'Watch the ghost of Marcie doesn't come after you,' when we were moving to England. Kay telling me her house was built on the spot where Marcie's body was found. Hearing it discussed by Mum and Ginny and Kath when I was outside the door. Everyone knew. Girls at school, everyone.

'I just know it. Like you do.'

She gets a sharp look on her face. 'Ask no questions and you'll get told no lies. So just you put that – what-do-you-call-it? – picture away and keep your nose out. In fact –' she calls after me, 'you can take that one right out of the book. Go on, take it out.'

So I do, and I put it away – away from her at least, on the fridge door in the kitchen where she never goes, though she still offers to cook our evening meal every day. (What are we having for tea? Would you like sausages? Ooh lovely, would you like me to do it? No it's all right Mum, you stay there and watch Pointless. What do you call it? Pointless. Good name for it, it is ruddy pointless.) And I escape to the kitchen and put the radio on and take my time peeling potatoes while she has a little doze.

The school photograph looks down at me. There are thirty-six girls in the picture, and a teacher. It's summer, the front row is sitting on the grass, there's a tree behind them in full leaf and all their dresses and blouses are short-sleeved. How old are they? Some look older than fourteen, some younger. Innocent as eggs. One or two have a proper bosom, but not my mum. I know she left school at fourteen, this, I reckon is her leaving memento. Sadie Singleton, aged fourteen, just. Marcie is also in the front row and also has no bosom. She sits cross-legged on the grass, white socks, Alice band in her hair and the sleeves of her blouse untidily rolled up. Her expression is a sort of half-smile, a bit wary perhaps, and her dark hair is cut in a fringe unlike most of the others who have it parted and held at one side with a hairgrip. Her features are strong and regular and without the hair she could be a boy.

It's unnerving, how this grubby piece of black and white card contains all these faces, a little powerhouse of stories, all unknown to these girls then, and unknown to me now. Most of them at least. You could say I know my mother's story, or you could say that, maybe, I know nothing.

I went to that school for no more than a term and a half, because I was going up to the senior school, and I can hardly remember anything about it, just a staircase that must have been always in shadow, it was so cold, always. I don't remember though that anyone there was horrible to me in any way, and some of the girls went to

191

the seniors with me and ended up being friends of mine, in a casual sort of way, so I think it was all right there in the juniors. Senior school was altogether another kind of place, and a much worse one.

I had come too late to sit something called the 11-plus, so when it came to leaving the junior school I had to go to something called a secondary mod. I might not have been very clever but I was clever enough to know it wasn't a very good school. My idea had been that English children wore a school uniform, but we didn't, just our ordinary clothes. We were all new, not just me, so I wasn't a novelty any more. They had no need of me. There was novelty enough just being in a school where bells rang every forty minutes, where we had a different teacher for nearly every lesson and we did sewing in a room with real sewing machines. It was too far for me to go home at lunchtime and I had to get used to school dinners.

There was bullying. Big boys pushed and shoved us down the corridors but the big girls were the worst. There was name-calling and spitefulness. There were people who were so bored they would spend a whole dinnertime preventing a first year from going to the dinner room to get something to eat, standing in a ring round her, criticising what she was wearing and pulling the elastic bands out of her hair, and handfuls of hair too. When I told my mum she took me to the shop and they cut my hair off. Nowadays parents would be up the school with a complaint, but not back then. 'Well, you must have done something to them,' she said.

Each little gang had a bit of corridor where they hung about. The ones outside the toilets were the most to be feared, and none of the first years ever dared to go to the toilets after the first week – after having the toilet flushed while you were sitting on it by someone standing on the seat in the next cubicle, after being pushed to and fro between four big girls until you wet your knickers, after someone's hand coming in under the door and pulling one of your shoes off, and then playing catch with it while you ran between them, crying – after all that we waited for a sympathetic, or apathetic, teacher and went in lesson time. ('What is the matter with you girls?')

Why didn't we tell the teachers? We didn't know it was possible. School was vile and scary, but we had no idea of the possibility of it being any different. If big girls punched us for nothing, what would they do to us if we snitched on them? And there was never a sign that a single teacher would be bothered to do anything to help anyway. They came into the classroom, they roared at the boys to sit down and the girls to be quiet, they gave out a set of books, wrote something on the board to be copied down and then sat down with a cup of tea on their desk and read the paper or did the crossword. They never bothered to learn our names until we were about to leave and then they suddenly got all friendly and familiar and we did no work at all. We said they only were nice to us because we would be working in shops and might give them mouldy cheese or soft tomatoes, or some of us might become nurses and be in a position to poison them when they were old and in hospital.

I tried to be good, at first. I tried to learn the things I hadn't learned, and forget the things I had learned that were different. I tried to be nice to the other girls, and smile at them, and lend them pencils and stuff, but I could tell they didn't care for me. They took the mickey out of my accent and pretended I was stuck up – and I wasn't, I just hung back until I could work out what was happening. I guess it made me look a bit slow. I wanted so much to fit in. I tried to talk like them, and dress like them, and like the same things, and I smiled when they laughed at something I said or something I didn't know. I nagged Mum to get us a television, so that I could watch Maverick and The Saint so that I could understand what they were talking about.

My only friend – sort of – was Kay, Kath's daughter. There were two older sisters, Rita and Theresa, a younger one, Valerie, and a little brother, Tony. The two older ones wanted nothing to do with me. They had bras and suspender belts and boyfriends, and Theresa smoked. Valerie was still young enough to be playing chase in the street, and Tony was just a little boy who thought he should be able to do whatever he wanted. Their dad – Uncle Ted to me, bald as a bulb – spoiled him, their mother spoiled him and his Aunt Ginny laughed at every naughty thing he did and called him a scamp and a scallywag and did not see that he was spiteful and whiney and destructive. So on the occasions when I was left at Auntie Kath's – maybe at a weekend, if Mum had to go out – it was Kay I got to know best, as the nearest in age to me. But there was still two years' difference between us and she was running round with a big gang of boys and girls, smoking in the park and snogging boys round the back of the lockup garages.

Sometimes though, at weekends Kay and I would both go to Ginny's and Ginny would get out her big make up case and give us manicures and let us try her eye shadow. Ginny was all right, I thought. She was nice to me. She used to get Corona cherryade in especially for me, because it was my favourite and the three of us would watch the wrestling on her telly, eating custard creams. One day though, she left. Kay told me she had gone back to live with Uncle Bernie.

'Who's he?'

'A man. He's Irish. They live together and then sometimes they split up.'

'Why?' Although I knew, in a dim sort of way, that my dad preferred Olive to my mother, the full implications hadn't sunk in yet. No one I knew had parents who were separated, or if they did, it wasn't talked about. The idea of 'sometimes' splitting up was attractive to me, and gave me hope that we might one day go home.

'He went back to Ireland. He does that sometimes. And anyway, she had to come and look after my Nan while she was poorly.'

And on Sunday afternoons, Kay would come to my house and we listened to Pick of the Pops together, because her dad slept on a Sunday afternoon and she wasn't allowed to turn it up loud. She taught me all about which comics to buy to find out about Cliff, and Bobby Vee, and most important, the Fab Four, the Beatles.

At school if I could, I hung around within sight of Kay, or tried to walk home on the edge of her group. Her group was full of bullies and she was one of them, but knowing her gave me a little protection. At home, she was well down the pecking order but at school she was like her Mum, loud and forthright, quite naughty, often standing outside a classroom door, and she was popular with other girls.

But in that first term Kay was not enough to keep me safe and I hated school. I cried in bed every night and counted the days, hours and minutes until the Christmas holidays.

That was the first Christmas I spent in England and we had our dinner at home, and went to Ginny's in the afternoon, with Kath and her tribe. I liked it. I liked getting little presents – really little, like a pencil or a washcloth (which I was learning to call a flannel) – and I liked the front room with a fire going and all us children sitting on the floor. Christmas in Canada had never been like this for us, not in my memory at least. I think there no one knew how to do it. There was no agreed national way to keep Christmas, or if there was the Jakimowiczes hadn't grasped it. We just had a slightly bigger dinner than usual and the truck didn't come for the milk so it had to keep for the next day. Often there was snow, but the main falls came later, and anyway, in Canada snow was not a recreational opportunity, it was a trouble and a nuisance and made for a lot of wet clothes and a house full of steam as they dried over the stove.

Here in England there was no snow yet, there were little lighted Christmas trees in front windows and special lights in the shopping streets and a feeling of excitement in the air. At school there were suddenly no rules any more, as people were let out of lessons to practise for plays and carol concerts, and we had a party in our classroom on the last day, with crisps and a record player. Christmas morning there were carols on the wireless and Mum made a great fuss of cooking and children rode new bikes and scooters in the street, while I watched them out of the front room window.

We got to Ginny's before they had finished washing up and they had saved pulling the crackers for us and then we crammed into the front room and there were presents under the tree. Joyce and Billy dropped in with their two boys, for a drink and a mince pie, and that's when Kath had the only drink I ever saw her take, a Babycham, throwing it down as if it was medicine.

When Joyce and Billy had gone I wondered what would happen next. I thought they might listen to the Queen's Speech, because Mum told me that Mrs Swallow had been strongly in favour of the royal family, and never failed to have the speech as the highlight of the day. And as she had only been dead a few months I thought that Kath and Ginny might keep the tradition going. I had never heard it, but all the girls at school said it was boring.

'Right then,' said Kath, and Mum and Ginny stopped talking to each other in the middle of a sentence.

'Kath always sings,' said Ginny to me. And so she did, and her girls did too, especially Kay.

'She could go on the stage,' said Ginny. 'I can't sing, I croak like a frog, but that Kay, will you listen to her.' And it seemed to me to be true, she knew all the words, and it was like someone off the radio. Then we all joined in. We sang all sorts. Carols, children's songs, songs that I now know were music hall, pre-war stuff, current songs. We sang Underneath the Arches and Why Do Fools Fall in Love and My Old Man's a Dustman and Bye Bye Love and Peggy Sue and Lily of Laguna. We stopped for turkey and pickle sandwiches, and cake, and then sang till it was late and the neighbours were banging on the wall. Then we sang Goodnight Irene and It's a Long Way to Tipperary and Show Me the Way to Go Home.

Then we all, except Ginny, stumbled out into the drizzle, and Mum put her arm round me as we walked the few doors along to our house.

Then started the coldest winter they'd had for two centuries. So what? I thought, What's a bit of snow and ice? But these Britishers couldn't cope with it. At school the pipes froze and burst during the holiday and we couldn't return after New Year. Didn't they know you had to wrap up your pipes with rags stuffed with wood shavings? What was the problem with walking on an icy path? You had to just go ahead and do it. At least I had two extra weeks off school while they struggled with blowlamps and such to get the water back on, and when we went back people seemed numbed and distracted by the weather. We were allowed to leave earlier – this was to allow the teachers to get home at their normal times, not for our benefit – and the older girls hurried home, too cold in their flimsy outdoor coats to stop and give even the most perfunctory Chinese burn. My coat, though hideously padded, was made by Mum to be warm, and I knew to wear extra socks. I strolled home unmolested. At last the weather changed and the whole world turned into a dripping tap. I had never seen a thaw so fast.

Later – about halfway through the last term of the first year – I gave up being good. I hung around with the bad girls, Linda and Jeannette, and we sat at the back of the class and gave smart answers and wrote on the desks and on each other, and threw flour about in the cookery lesson. It didn't make me happy but it stopped me being so lonely.

At home I was awkward and difficult. I know it now and I suppose I should be sorry for making life hard for my mum, but I still think it was her own fault. I used to hover around doors, listening, in my socks, listening to conversations. Mum had customers all the time in the front room, measuring them for clothes, them standing on a sturdy low table and her going round the hem, then standing back to see that it was straight from all angles. Of course they talked. That way I learnt this or that woman was expecting, that this or that man was never out of the pub, this boy was joining the army, that girl was wanting to stay on at school, that the price of tomatoes was shocking, that Ginny lived with a man without being married to him, that we had no plans to go back to Canada, that Mum and Dad were divorced. Why should I be ashamed of listening? She should have told me.

TWENTY-TWO

The Christmas cards are trickling in.

'There's not many, says Mum fretfully. ' Are you sure you've got them all out?'

The days are gone when you couldn't close a door in Mum's house without sending an avalanche of red and gold pasteboard across the fitted carpet. The elaborate devices to hang cards without sticking pins in your embossed wallpaper have stayed in their boxes for a good few years now, as people die, or realise that Eric has died and there's no longer any point in staying the right side of him. His customers, and Mum's, gone. The yard, the scaffolding, the machines, the plant, the men, the rolls of notes, the dodgy invoices, long gone; and Mum's fancy clientele of footballers' fiancées, with their mood boards and their scrapbooks and their mothers and their best friends, gone too, and all her patterns and samples and photographs up in the loft with her machines and her adjustable dummy, where she can't see them.

'One from Ginny today,' I announce, apparently cheerfully. I've opened it because Mum's poor hands are really not fit even to get into an envelope. Ginny's writing is getting a bit wavery but she still encloses a letter. 'Well dear, I told you that The Old Fella died, so I've been sorting out all that and it's left me with plenty of money. I'm thinking now that I'll give up living here and go into a nice Home, now that I can afford a posh one. Let me know how you are. If you can't write you can ring. All best wishes, Gin. P.S. I think poor old Bess is on her way out, but it will be one less thing to think about.'

'Bess?' says Mum.

'Cat. Ginny always has a cat, she'll miss her, whatever she says.'

'She doesn't seem to miss her husband,' says Mum, 'but then, they weren't married you know.'

I had known. 'Why not?'

'I think he already had a wife. But Nell knows more about it than I do. I'd already gone when he came on the scene.'

In the same post there is a card from Nell, one of the very smallest ones that you buy from charities. Mum tuts. 'She can't be that badly off. No letter inside?'

No there's not, but there's a scrawl on the back saying, Come and visit soon.

'We could have easily missed seeing that,' says Mum.

'You're lucky really,' I say, 'having friends who go back so far.' And when I go into the kitchen and see the school photo, a thought occurs and I take it through to ask her 'Are Ginny and Nell in this picture?'

'Take it away, take it away,' she says. Angry? Flustered? I can't tell.

'No, but were they at school with you?'

'No they weren't, you know they weren't, I didn't know them till the war. Put that away now, I thought you were bringing me a cup of tea.'

'So didn't they know Marcie?'

'Marcie who? What are you on about, you?'

And I leave it because there's no point, but it begins to come back to me, the puzzle, the frisson, the mystery. The real murder, on our doorstep, under our foundations if you were Kath, that kept Kath and Ginny in conversation and speculation for decades, that still has some sort of power over my mother, who long ago gave up talking about it.

You can find anything on the internet. Just the name is enough to get me started. Did you know there's a site that lists unsolved murders? It starts with Colin Roy Campbell of Glenure in 1752 and continues through a shabby and grisly catalogue of lust and greed and insanity, and no doubt someone updates it every month or so with another one. Marcie is in 1944, the only entry for that year:

Nineteen-year-old Marcie MacNee's initial disappearance in the spring of 1944 went unreported by her family who thought she might have run away with a soldier. Her decomposed body was found in December 1944 on waste ground (now a housing estate) near to where she lived. The cause of her death could not be established and no one was ever arrested for her murder.

When you are an only child, especially in those days, when there was no heating in your bedroom, and no television for you to be watching, and your Mum's friends came round of an evening, well, you picked up all sorts of things. Sometimes she would send me to the kitchen to put the kettle on, but I still listened at the door, because I knew they were going to talk about something I wasn't supposed to hear. Marcie was one of those things. Ever since my Aunt Lisa used to try to get me frightened by telling me about the ghost of the murdered girl I had known about it, and hadn't thought too much about it, but now, being on the scene of the crime, and being sent out of the room when the conversation hotted up made me more interested.

'Well, you never liked her,' said Kath.

'No I didn't, and I never said otherwise,' said Mum. 'Just cos you don't like someone doesn't mean you'd go and do em in.'

'I didn't mean that,' said Kath. 'But what if someone might of done it to get back at her because she's had a go at you.'

'Like who?'

But Kath didn't say.

'I wonder where the family went to?' said Ginny.

'How should I know?' said Mum. 'It was her brother that done it, that's why they went away.'

Mum, it seemed to me, wasn't as obsessed with it as they were. They, Ginny and Kath, put up suppositions, they wondered, they asked questions, they what-if'd, and Mum batted the questions away as if she didn't care. They couldn't let go of it.

'Not that again,' Mum once said, and Ginny replied, 'I wish I didn't Sadie, but I just can't stop thinking about it. Kath has nightmares you know, and I wish I did, because at least she gets some sleep, but I'm laying there awake as daylight and whether I want to or not, Marcie just goes round and round in my head. I think if I knew what had happened I could let it go. Or it would let me go.'

Kath said, 'Do you believe in ghosts?' and Mum said, No, she absolutely didn't, and Kath said she thought their house might be haunted by Marcie.

'You should of thought of that,' said Mum, 'before you moved in. You knew where it was.'

'That's easy for you to say,' said Kath. 'But Ted said I was being daft, and what could I do? And we needed the room, them prefabs were so small you could touch both walls if you stretched your arms out.'

'Well you can't have it all ways,' said Mum, which was one of her favourite sayings. I wanted Kath to go on and say about the haunting. I imagined Marcie dressed in white, drifting around on the landing or maybe howling a bit in the garden among Ted's Brussels sprouts.

'I have these nightmares,' said Kath.

'So Ginny tells me,' said Mum. 'But then, you always have had nightmares, even before Marcie went missing. When I first knew you, you told me you had nightmares.'

'That was because of the war,' said Kath. 'I can't help it if I'm sensitive.'

She didn't look what I thought of as sensitive. Kath was a stout plain woman, very different – I thought –

from Ginny. I was quite scared of her because she shouted most of the time – not at me, but at her children and her husband, about the slightest little things. Coats or shoes left on the floor or on the back of a chair, doors left open when they should be shut, lights left on, untidy bedrooms, children coming in with dirty faces, or knees, or torn clothes – this was mainly Valerie and Tony – Uncle Ted being late or sitting down when he should be fetching in coal for the fire. The wireless being too loud, running out of soap powder, or milk, or firewood – all these would make her roar. If we were playing out the front we could hear her – 'Who was the last one in here? Who's left the towel on the floor? Who can't hang their coat up? Who's left this door wide open – was you born in a barn?'

'You should know, Mum,' Kay once answered her back, and got a good slap round the face for it.

Other people have families who phone on Christmas Day, but for some reason – and it must be hereditary – neither Uncle Maurice, nor my daughter Jo can bring themselves to do it.

I'm very fond of my daughter Jo, and if I knew her children no doubt I'd be fond of them too, but I haven't seen any of them for three years and they probably don't remember me. Her husband is in oil. She phones the day before Christmas Eve, just as I'm going to bed.

'When are you going to get Skype loaded up?' she says. I don't tell her that I've got it already, but that I don't want to use it. She would be horrified to see me now, the way I look, and if I see her I might cry.

The children are called to the phone to wish me a happy Christmas, and I take the phone through to Mum so that they can all wish her a happy Christmas too, and then Jo comes back on to wish Mum a happy Christmas, and then she wishes me a happy Christmas, and we each say something about the weather in our respective countries, and then I wish her a happy Christmas, and then she wishes me a happy Christmas again, and then it's all over.

In spite of all those wishes, our Christmas is no happier then any other day. I get up, I get Mum up, we have breakfast together, then she sits in front of the telly while I do other things until I can't think of any more to do and then I go in and sit with her while the dinner cooks. In honour of Christmas we are eating at lunch time, and having what passes with us for a slap-up feast, which means two sorts of potatoes, and pudding. We do not have crackers and paper hats, thank god. She remembers, and I do too, the days with Eric, when drinking started at breakfast time, Christmas dinner went on till five o'clock in the afternoon, drinking went on till well past midnight. Friends and acquaintances called at the house at any hour and many of them stayed till they staggered off in the early hours, puking in the front garden hedge as likely as not. Eric loved it, I never knew what Mum thought about it. I hated it, and one of the good things about leaving home was that I never had to see that sort of Christmas any more.

I say that Mum lives in the past but I do as well now. It's catching. When Mum dies I will be on my own. Don't be silly, people say – was there ever such an irritating comment? – you have a daughter and a brother, and grandchildren.

I don't bother to argue. Something about our family compels us to live as far away from each other as the planet allows. So yes, I have a daughter – in Brazil, along with her husband and children, and yes I have a brother – in Canada, and a cousin – even further away in Canada, and an aunt somewhere over there too. And even an uncle – but he's in Australia and I believe there is a cousin or two in that direction, unless they have decided to reside in Dubai, or Singapore, or Paraguay, or Uranus. It's all right for Christmas cards with exotic stamps, but it isn't what I would regard as human contact. I have fantasies about – when Mum has gone – joining a commune. I've done without close company, a man, sex, for many a year. As I say, my work colleagues were my family. But you need someone to say good morning to. For the time being, I have to make do with Mum, and her memories, which trigger mine.

I never went back to Mum's house until Eric had died and been safely cremated. By then they had moved to their retirement home – this detached chalet bungalow near the Forest. Not that Eric ever quite retired. He drove most days down to the yard to oversee and bully and pay off, and shift odd items of material that had ended up there. But Mum sold the shop and the bridal wear business and – with a tidy pile of satin offcuts, lace scraps, buttons and bows – continued to design and sew her pictures and sell them in fancy craft shops through Essex and beyond.

Until Eric died I saw Mum maybe once a year, maybe twice. Strange, awkward, hostile meetings they were, me and Mum, that had to be arranged through Ginny. It was never me that initiated the meetings. I actually think it was Ginny who took it upon herself to organise them, not Mum who asked for them. I never let Mum know where I lived. A park, a café, a library, was where we met, somewhere I could take Jo to meet her nana without having her in my home. We stayed out of the phone book, we never even registered to vote; though we never married I used Roger's name and his name, luckily, was Smith. It was all so we would be hard to find, if Eric tried, but maybe it was all a waste of time. He was probably not even bothered, once he'd got rid of me.

Jo had her Smith grandparents, she had no need of Mum. She played, or read, or swam in the leisure centre, or sat at a café table and coloured in a colouring book, and took very little notice of the woman with expensively cut hair and slightly too much jewellery, who always asked if I had heard from John and I said No, usually, which was true, usually. Then she would ask about my studies and, later, my job, question Jo about her school and fail to listen to her solemn answers, and then tell me some news about Ginny, or Kath, or Nell, which I already knew, of course, from Ginny.

Ginny came to see me two or three times a year, driving herself in her little Fiat 500. She brought presents for Jo, duty free cigarettes for Rog and me if she'd recently been abroad, and news. I knew when she went to see Nell, and how the children were growing, and what they looked like and what they were doing, and how Heather was adopted and – even more dramatic – had been a foundling, dumped on the steps of the police station in a town called Retford, a town not famous for anything. Heather was growing up a bit wild, maybe because she was adopted, maybe because Nell and Hamish couldn't seem to discipline her. Heather and her brother Duncan, said Ginny, did not get on.

I knew what Kath's children were doing, leaving home, doing well (Rita), having children themselves (Kay), getting into trouble (Tony), getting married (Val) and divorced (Val again). I knew that Ted died, and later, that Kath was seeming not herself, and quite quickly, died herself.

That's only time I remember going to see Ginny, instead of her coming to see me. Of course by this time I had the use of a car, Jo was old enough to come home to an empty house after school, I was a woman with a proper job, I was nearly thirty-five and no longer a frightened girl reliant on Ginny for protection. Just as well because the Ginny I found was a shock. At the moment when she opened the door to me and stood back to let me in, I wasn't even sure if she knew who I was. She smelled of whisky, though it wasn't even midday.

She had put her make up on, that was clear, but it was all smudged with crying, her face was swollen and her hair was wild like brambles. Bernie wasn't there. I didn't ask but she told me he had gone to Ireland unexpectedly and had left straight after the funeral. That's right, I thought, put any amount of distance between him and someone who needs him.

But once we were sitting in her little kitchen and she was putting spoonfuls of instant coffee into her flowery mugs, she spoke like herself.

'Sorry I look such a sight,' she said. 'I'll pull myself together, Carrie, you know that. I've just had a rough night.'

'I'm sorry I couldn't get to the funeral,' I said. 'They wouldn't let me off work. It has to be a relative before you can take a day off that isn't booked a month in advance.'

'You could have pretended to be sick,' she said.

'I suppose.'

'No,' she said. 'You did right. Your Mum came, did you know? Came with Nell, that was good of them.'

'Did it go all right?'

'Could have been worse,' she said. 'I don't think there's a right way of doing funerals. I don't like cremations either, but apparently it was what Kath wanted. Val and Rita did all the organising.'

'All the family there?'

'Yes, for a wonder,' she said. 'Tony. Very upset. Theresa – I wasn't expecting her but Val had been in touch and she managed to get down on her own. Kay of course. Malcolm missed it, but he's another of these men who can't stand people being in a state. He turned up later.'

'Whose house did you have it at?'

'Kay's. It was nearest, and not bad for space. I gather Rita and Theresa had words, but I couldn't tell you what it was all about, I wasn't really able to pay attention.'

'Poor Ginny,' I said. It was the first time I had ever seen her look her age.

'Poor Kath,' she said. 'Younger than me you know. Well, she'll have no more nightmares now.'

It felt such a final thing to say that we both sat in silence for a while, then she pushed my cup of coffee towards me and opened the biscuit tin. I really wanted a biscuit, but it didn't feel right, so I pretended I hadn't seen them.

I didn't stay long. She had people to see, she had to repair the damage done to her make up, and she more or less told me to leave, in a direct, nice, Ginny way. She thanked me for coming, hugged me, sent her love to Jo and Roger, promised to come and see us soon. Which she did.

TWENTY-THREE

Stepmother had been a dressmaker. Apparently, according to Auntie Ginny, she'd never had a day's illness in her life, and then one day was found stark dead, still holding old Mrs Pickering's skirt that she was taking in a few inches, Mrs P having lost so much weight. Mrs P would soon be dead too, I gathered. My life was full of death. My Baba, my step-grandmother, Mrs Pickering – and Auntie Ginny told us as soon as we arrived that her mother was dying too. I began to worry that my dad would die before I could see him again. I got letters sometimes, from him, and John also put a little message on the bottom, and Olive sent best wishes and hoped to see me soon. I knew Olive of course, but no one told me she was going to marry my dad, and it was only when a wedding photo arrived, addressed to me, that I knew for sure that my parents were divorced and I had a stepmother too, just as Mum had had.

Stepmother had used the front room for business. It was all there, the sewing machine and piles of paper patterns, some dating from before the war, scissors and pinking shears, needles and cotton thread of every colour, pins and thimbles, and boxes and boxes of pieces of material, offcuts from all the garments she'd ever made. My mother set to work from where Stepmother left off. She started by finishing garments that were left there, unfinished, and giving them back to their owners, free of charge, so that the owners – except Mrs Pickering who had died by then – were grateful and impressed and came to her the next time they wanted something altered or made. It took a while though, to build up business, but she had plans, my mum, and she didn't mind things being a bit slack for a while.

She was intent on building up a good business. Altering hemlines and mending pockets was not going to pay the bills, and even curtains, though she would do them if asked, were not interesting enough for her. She realised that nobody was going to carry on having their clothes made when there was ready-made stuff on every High Street that cost far less. But people would still do it for weddings. From the evidence of her own wedding photograph, and others that I'd seen, people – ordinary people I mean – wore their ordinary clothes to get married in, but times were changing. All the girls and boys born at the end of the war – that we didn't call baby boomers then – were getting pregnant and getting married. The pregnant ones needed a suit for the registry office that didn't make too much of their bump, and the smug un-pregnant ones splashed out on veils and lace and a posse of bridesmaids in nylon net and velvet rosebuds.

She changed her name. Only for business purposes. She couldn't go on pretending to be Ivy Singleton, and 'I can't go into it called Sadie Jakimowicz,' she said. 'People will think I'm Jewish.'

So she called herself Sarah, which was actually the name on her birth certificate, and thought about Jackson as a surname, then decided against it because it was rough and common sounding, so that wouldn't do, and she made up this surname: Jacklin. (A few years later I told her that there was a real famous person, a golfer, with the same name. I did it to upset her, but she was thrilled that it turned out to be a real name. These days, in occasional confused moments, she believes that they are somehow related.) So she became Sarah Jacklin Bridal Wear, famed along the A1010 from Edmonton to Enfield Wash. That's me being nasty and I shouldn't. She was good at it and her fame did spread, by the mouths of satisfied clients, and when she moved further round the North Circular customers would come from as far as Chelmsford and Southend and even from south of the river. I have to admire her for what she did, but I do it grudgingly, inwardly and silently. It was me that had to move over to make room for her success.

And. It was all right for her to change her name, but I wasn't allowed to. I always had trouble with my name. For a start it was too long and when I began school it took me ages to learn how to spell it, but at least in Canada I was not the only one with a foreign name. Well there was the odd Polish name here in England too, even in my school, but I hated being called Carolynne, as if my parents couldn't decide which name to call me and just tacked two together. For a time when I started at secondary school I used to write Carol Jackson on my school books, but I didn't like that either and besides, the other Carol in my class was a big dull heavy girl that I didn't want to be confused with, and I didn't want her to think I was copying her in some sinister way, or else that I wanted to be her best friend. Besides, the teachers were forever not giving me back my books, and I was too scared to ask for them. In the end I shortened my name to Carrie, which was what my dad had often called me, but Mum refused to use it. We used to have hour-long arguments because she'd called me by my full name when asking if I'd like tea or cocoa before bed. Even now, the odd Carolynne comes out of her mouth when she thinks she can get away with it.

She loved the mere process of sewing. She did it all day and then, in the evenings, with a little sigh of satisfaction, she sat down in the back room with a cup of instant coffee and the wireless on and spent the evening on what she called My Own Sewing. Back in Canada – in a previous life it seemed to me – she made me a cushion. I've still got it, it came in the boxes from home, with my books and dolls and summer clothes. Cushions in any case were not as ubiquitous as they are nowadays, and no one I knew had a cushion of their own – in Canada I used to bring my friends home to show it to them. It was quite simple, a cream background, with an appliquéd tree on one side, not done with just one lollipop shaped piece of green, oh no, this was built up with different materials, leaves of different greens and browns, and – it was an apple tree – the apples were buttons, red buttons, spherical, and arranged just so naturally you'd think she knew what an apple tree actually looked like, instead of copying a picture from a magazine. Hers was so much better than the magazine one that she said she was going to send in a photo of it, to show them, but we had no camera, so she couldn't.

Now, in England, with a whole new supply of scraps and buttons, she set off on sewing pictures. Probably there's a fancy term for what she was doing but she didn't know it, just made it up as she went along. Some of them were just made of buttons, nothing else – like one of the sea, all done in pearl shirt buttons, different shades of white, mostly, with some blue and turquoise ones, but although she had a collection of buttons dating back to the previous century, the supply couldn't keep up with her, so she turned to making pictures with bits of material, sewn on to canvas – she didn't believe in glue – and the buttons sewn on as little features, I suppose.

I took no interest in all of this, it seemed to me something old-ladyish and beneath my notice, but actually she was very talented and they were little works of art, in their way. She displayed them in her front room where she measured people for their clothes, and of course some people were caught by something they saw, or thought it would make a nice present for someone, and it was a little sideline for her. I am sorry now that there are no pictures of her early work, no record at all, and yet they probably still exist – fifty years is not that long for something beautiful to survive. They *were* beautiful, it's not just my childish memory I'm sure, other people thought so too. She even took commissions occasionally. I remember that she gave a piece to Kath once, for a birthday maybe – I wonder what happened to it. It was a landscape, fields and far off trees, and a road going through it that she did with a piece of grey tweed. And I know that Ginny once asked her to do one for Nell, of flowers in a garden, that would be a late one, after we moved away, and I wonder if Nell has still got it.

You have to realise I'm looking back from a great distance. A length of time unimaginable to me as I was when I was eleven, twelve, thirteen. If you had told me that I would one day forgive my mother I would not have believed you, I would have screamed at you and slammed some doors and shouted that I would never forgive her, not if I lived a million years. And I would have been right.

If you had told me that I would one day live with her and look after her in her old age I would probably have put my head in the gas oven as people could in those days. But here we are.

So every day she was there in the front room, meeting the people, making decisions for them (oh yes she did), arranging fittings, cutting, sewing on the machine, hand-finishing – all those bits of guipure lace and satin-covered buttons – more fittings, then the tissue paper and the big boxes. I had never been a bridesmaid and couldn't remember the only wedding I had ever been to – my Aunt Lena's – but any glamour pretty soon went out of the idea of a fancy wedding. Just as well because I never had one. I didn't mind helping her if both she and I were in the mood. Sometimes at a weekend, or on a wet day in the holidays, when I was moping about looking for something to do, she would let me into the room and I would tidy her reels of thread or pick up all the bits from the carpet or make some boxes out of the flat pieces of cardboard they came as. And she would tell me about the people who were going to wear these dresses, and make me laugh.

'Mother of the bride,' she said. 'Wants chocolate satin dress and jacket, coffee lace, apricot lapels and trim, and she's having cream accessories. Well I didn't say it, but she'll be like a walking gateau.'

Stepmother was soon forgotten, or maybe Mum became her – I wouldn't know, I never knew the woman. One time Mum took me to see her grave. She was buried with my grandad.

'Daisy sorted out the funeral,' said Mum to Kath, who was with us, 'It was good of her, seeing as she never had nothing to do with Stepmother.'

'What about the headstone?' said Kath. 'Her name's not on it.'

'That's up to Maurice,' said Mum. 'Daisy's done her bit. And me, I've had all the sorting out to do. Maurice can see to the headstone. She's not *my* mother.'

She looked around her at the gravestones, pale grey under a pale grey sky. 'This is where I met your father,' she said to me.

I looked around me too, at the weeds beginning to grow and the faded flowers, mostly plastic, that littered the pebbly grave-beds. I couldn't imagine what she meant, and I didn't want to ask her, so I never did.

TWENTY-FOUR

The idea of visiting Nell sticks in her head. Before she gave up driving, about eight years ago and not a moment too soon, it seems that she went there two or three times a year. Since then they've only spoken, less and less often, on the phone. She doesn't say but I can hear her thinking, that it's about time I took her to visit her friend.

I don't know Nell. When we came to England they were in Lincolnshire, and when Nell, widowed, moved closer, I was gone and living somewhere else. I know she came to Mum's wedding, maybe her husband and children came too but I don't remember them. I was there, I was dressed up suitably, and I didn't draw attention to how I was feeling, but I wasn't having any part of it. I didn't dare to have a tantrum to spoil it but for the whole of the day I skulked in the background, eating prawn vol au vents.

Nell's daughter lives with her now, as I do with Mum, but of course I don't know her. When I ring her to arrange to visit she sounds – I don't know – young for her age, uncertain, unconfident. But pleased.

'Tell me about Nell,' I say to Mum. 'Have we got a photo of her?'

Of course I've seen it before. Nell as a teenager was like a modern catwalk model – long legs, flat chest, impassive face. The only other picture is of her with her husband, wedding carnations in buttonholes, looking ordinary, not a model any more.

'Did you go?'

'How could I? I was in Canada by then. She didn't get married till she was about twenty-seven.'

'But you kept up with her, you didn't lose contact?'

'Oh, you could always depend on Nell to write. Ginny's letters were better, she would tell you all the gossip, you see, but you could wait months before you heard from her. But if you wrote to Nell she would write straight back, even if she only said there was no news. And Kath never wrote at all, only a card at Christmas, and that never got to us till January.'

Nell's husband in the photo looks happy, as she does. 'What was he like?'

'Well, he's no oil painting as you can see.'

True, his hair is thinning already, he has more teeth than chin and Nell is at least two inches the taller. 'He has nice eyes,' I say. 'Were they happy?'

'Oh I think so. I never heard her say a bad word about him. Very clever man.' Mum says this about anyone who has ever passed an exam.

'Wasn't he a doctor?'

'Looked after all those people who came back from the war the worse for wear. Head injuries, mental problems, things like that. People that couldn't just get back to their normal life, that couldn't get over what they'd seen, that sort of thing.'

'And he died.'

'Fell off a cliff. Only in his sixties. No age at all. She blamed herself you know. She said if she'd been with him he wouldn't have gone on that walk. Stayed behind you see, she was looking after Duncan's children and the police didn't know where she was. Talked about it every time I ever saw her, what a good man he was and why did she let him go without her.'

She goes on some more but I'm not really paying attention, until she shivers. 'Are you cold Mum?' I add the gas fire to the thick heat in the room and leave her to the TV. No doubt Pointless will be on soon.

When we go to Nell's, on a mild damp day with no risk of snow to make her fretful, Mum sits beside me in the car, whistling softly through her teeth the way she used to do when she was sewing. It's a sign of contentment, like a cat purring.

Where they live is tiny; it's what they call a maisonette, though I can't see the difference between that and a ground floor flat. Tiny front garden, full of pots, apparently empty of plants, and when Heather opens the door, a dark little hall, no room to hang up our coats, never mind swing a cat.

Nell is almost tearful. 'You should have come sooner,' she says. 'I thought I was going to die without seeing you again.'

'She had a nasty turn before Christmas,' says Heather. 'But she's not going to die, are you Mother?'

'Well I'm better than I was,' she says, 'but not *better*.'

'I should say,' says Mum briskly, 'that you're looking in the pink. And I must say, you haven't lost weight, ill or not.'

I'm – impressed is the word – by how fat she is, soft and fat, struggling out of her chair not because of her joints, like Mum, but because of her own weight and the force of gravity. Heather is as thin as her mother is fat, her hair is as white as it is long, she drifts about like a wraith. I myself have made a bit of an effort.

'Did you hear from Ginny?'

'Not lately,' says Mum. 'Did you?'

'She rang,' says Nell. 'Terribly chesty, she can hardly breathe.'

'Always smoked,' says Mum. 'I talked to her over Christmas. Smoked. Her and Bernie, Kath and Ted. That's what did it.'

They don't need me. I look around the room, unable to take in all the *stuff* that's in it. Walls covered in paintings, drawings, some old in fancy frames, some in clip frames; and photos, of Hamish – I recognise him – and of several different children at several different ages, and of another man at different ages, on a beach, on a boat, with and without one or several of the children. The son, I surmise, and his family. No wife.

On every surface – windowsill, mantelpiece, top of cupboards, television, squeezed in front of the many books on bookshelves – vases of dried grass, house plants, ornaments of pottery and wood, and on a small table an ancient dusty computer struggling to be seen under a pile of papers, magazines, letters, who knows what else.

Heather moves a pile of newspapers off the small settee so that Mum can sit down. If I sit beside her, as I'm supposed to do, where will Heather sit? She moves unhurriedly, vague, but calm. She offers tea, and I offer to help. In the kitchen she slowly gathers her hair into a bunch and skewers it with some kind of clasp to keep it out of her way.

'How is your mother keeping?' she says.

I tell her about the arthritis.

'That must be awful for her,' she says. 'Didn't she sew? I mean she was very good at it, my mother says. How dreadful to be unable to do anything, after a lifetime of making things.'

'Well yes,' I say. 'But that's life isn't it? It'll happen to all of us.'

'I know,' she says sadly. 'My mother can't garden any more. Not that we have much space to garden in, but she's so unsteady now that I couldn't let her go outside without me being there.'

'I saw the pots.'

'Oh yes. Full of bulbs. Come again in the spring and there'll be a fine show. Then we have another set of pots that I fill with summer bedding. It's not the sort of gardening she approves of but it's the best we can do these days.'

'I don't know another sort of gardening,' I say, which is true. I've avoided anything to do with gardens all my life.

'What she'd like to do,' says Heather, 'is to grow plants from seed and plant them in the ground, not in pots. But we make the best of it.'

'She used to have a garden then? I think maybe Ginny told me about it.'

'She had a lovely garden. She put everything into it, her whole life. Where we lived it became quite famous, you know, just around the village, people used to come to the house and ask to see it. A lot of fruit too. We used to sell it when I was small but then my dad decided it wasn't quite the thing for us to be selling stuff at the garden gate. He never liked to stick his head above the parapet, very conformist, my dad, quite timid sometimes.'

'He was Scottish wasn't he?'

'There's a clue in our names,' she says. 'And quite strait-laced. He didn't cope very well with our teenage years. Me and Duncan, we pushed him quite far, especially me. But it's funny, he didn't get angry, just sort of sad, and patient, and my mother just used to sigh and go back to her garden, and me and Dunc just went on getting drunk and staying out late and riding round in stolen cars.'

I laughed. 'You seem such a nice girl.'

She laughed too. 'Weren't you?'

'Hideous. Though I had the excuse of a stepfather. But we all get through it in the end.'

'Most of us do. I hung about with the worst people though. You think village kids are harmless but they're the worst. At least in Lincolnshire they are.'

'And everywhere else.'

'I was lucky,' she says. 'Have you seen how they drive in Lincolnshire? I could have been killed on the back of some souped up motorbike, I could have got pregnant, I could have been poisoned by any number of substances. But I was lucky. I didn't deserve it, but perhaps my parents did.'

She seems completely at ease with me, not shy at all, ready – eager even – to reveal herself. Maybe, like me, she doesn't get out much. But it turns out that she still has a job, though mornings only, as a technician in the art department of the local sixth form college.

'Did you train in art then?'

'Long long ago,' she says. 'I don't have room to do any since mother came to live here. Only a bit of drawing now and again. But that's all right, I've never made my living from my own work, I've always had to teach or something else to get money, my own stuff is just a hobby, that's all.'

She provides vegetable soup and little triangular cheese sandwiches for lunch. We can't all eat in the living room, for lack of chairs, so Heather and I have ours standing up in the kitchen. We can hear our mothers' voices in full flow, interrupting, mishearing, misunderstanding, then laughing, getting back on track, but we can't make out what they're talking about. What can they find to say about their narrowing lives?

I tell Heather about giving up work and about being lonely and fed up. She asks me about Jo and my grandchildren and I find I have told her about Roger and how we stayed together till Jo left home and then all of a sudden there seemed to be nothing any more to keep us together.

'It wasn't him, it was me.'

'Not two sides?'

'No, he would have jogged on for ever I think. It was me. I was restless, I couldn't settle, I did a bit more training, I changed my job, all that sort of thing, and it only made me more restless. Then – oh something happened, I won't go into all that – and we split up.'

What happened – what I'm not going to go into with Heather – was that Eric died suddenly and I fell apart. And Roger couldn't cope, and I found someone who I thought could.

But it doesn't matter. She's off telling me about her childhood.

'I was an outsider. All of us were, up there in Lincolnshire.'

'How come?'

'All odd. Dad, he's the doctor at the nut house, Mother, well she's shy, a bit awkward with people, we've got no family, Dad's family are in Stirling, we see them once a year. People couldn't place us so we had no place. Only Duncan, he seemed to find a place for himself, football and cricket, all that, but the rest of us were ignored. Politely. As if they were scared of us. I was the worst, I'm the adopted abandoned child – oh yes, everybody knew all about it – and what's more, *foreign*.'

'How, foreign?'

'Black. I know I'm not black enough to be noticed in a city, but in Lincolnshire, sixty years ago – well, you didn't have to be very black to stand out.'

She has very dark eyes and her skin is more yellow than any other colour, but when her hair – still crinkly – was dark, then, yes, I can see she would have been noticeable in the 1950s, in a rural setting.

'Racist remarks then?'

'Not so much that. A lot of people were very polite, even children were told not to mention it. But that was the trouble really, it was like something only I could see, like the emperor's new clothes in reverse, nobody could see but me that I was different from all the rest. Even my parents didn't mention it. As if it might not be true if they could keep quiet about it.'

'You didn't stay there then? When you grew up?'

'I went abroad. I went everywhere.' She smiles at me, looking straight at me, challenging me, I think, to see the person she once was when she was adventurous and free, challenging me too not to feel sorry for her.

But how can I not feel sorry for her, when I feel so sorry for myself.

'And then you came back?'

She tells me then about her father's death, how her mother went to live with Duncan and his family, how Duncan then divorced that wife and found another one, and Nell had nowhere to live.

'Her house, the one she lived in with my dad, well, that was tied to the hospital. She had to move out. She had some savings but she put them into Dunc's house, so they could build an extension for her to live in. It wasn't even finished before they split up and sold the whole lot. She did very badly out of it.'

'Sounds like Duncan behaved very badly.'

'He did. And his wife. Maggie. Of course we don't see her any more.'

'Children?'

She tells me about Duncan's many children, some now grown up with children of their own. I don't ask if she has ever wanted children, but I tell her more about Jo and my own two far away grandchildren. I feel more myself than I have for months.

She makes more tea, neatly and carefully, loose leaf tea and a china teapot with a woolly cosy, and we go back in to the old ladies. They are talking about all the people they have known who have died. I wonder, does this make them feel better, as survivors, or worse, knowing it's yet to come. I wonder, how does it make *me* feel?

'Tell me about Ginny,' I say to Nell, to get them off the subject of death. 'What about her and Bernie?'

'What about it?'

'When did they meet? Mum doesn't know, she was abroad at the time.'

'Oh,' says Nell, 'I'm not sure. After the war definitely, but I think they met and then lost touch and then met again. Her mum and dad never really came to terms with it. She didn't let me meet him, hardly ever, in fact he kept out of the way, they didn't go out much together, only to the pub.'

'In case his wife saw them?'

'Oh his wife was back in Ireland, and his children. Sometimes, when he had the money, he used to go back over and see them.' Of course I know all this.

'Ginny didn't mind?'

'Oh she did. But what could she do? Sometimes she left him, but she always went back.'

'What was he like though?' says Heather. 'You did meet him?'

'Oh, only once or twice. Handsome I must say. Your dad' – nodding at Heather – 'didn't approve.'

'I thought Dad was a boyfriend of Ginny's,' says Heather, 'before he married you.'

'Oh we were all mixed up then, weren't we Sadie.'

Mum nods, looking lively, looking happy. Nell is becoming quite skittish.

'You probably don't know,' she says to me, mock confidential, 'I could have gone out with your dad.'

'Why didn't you?'

'Oh I had a boyfriend. Gus – remember?'

'I remember Gus,' says Mum. 'Kath was always after him.'

'Good grief,' says Heather. 'It sounds like some TV soap. Interlocking triangles.'

'I wasn't in any triangle,' says Mum firmly. 'Your father was the only one I went out with.'

'Tell me about my dad.' I can't stop myself from saying this.

Nell shifts herself till she seems to become part of the upholstery of the chair she's squeezed into. 'You know how we met him?'

'No I don't think so.' I'm glancing at Mum but so far she doesn't seem to mind.

'We were off to the pictures weren't we.'

'I had to meet you up the High Road.'

'But you had to pick up your dad's boots from the menders, remember.'

'That's right, that was typical of Stepmother, making me go to the pictures with a pair of boots under my arm. Well, I'm taking a short cut through the cemetery, it was getting dark –'

'We were on double summertime but it still got dark –'

'And I see him there, crying, sitting on a gravestone. And I know he's a soldier and I know he's Canadian, from his uniform, we knew all the uniforms. And I stopped and said, What's the matter?'

'And what was the matter?'

'Something or other, he'd had some news from home.'

'His friend died,' says Nell. 'He'd had a letter and he was just upset and far from home.'

'So I says to him, You can come to the pictures with us if you like, my friend's waiting for me at the gates, so he tagged along didn't he –'

'And then he asked me to go dancing the next week,' says Nell.

'And did you?'

'We both did. Kath and Ginny were supposed to come to but they didn't have any money.'

'They never did, did they.'

Mum wags her finger at Nell, actually wags her finger like someone singing a comic song, as if Nell's a naughty girl and not a fat old lady, and turns to me. 'You don't know what this one was up to.'

'Tell me all the bad things my mother did,' says Heather.

'Well, we go dancing – me, Nell and your dad.'

'And your dad – he told us his name was Jack, didn't he –'

'I believed that till we went to the town hall to get the wedding licence.'

'It was just what people called him,' I say.

'Well I know that,' says Mum, 'but I thought it was his name. When we got to his family, every time I called him Jack I got the dirty look from his mother.'

I remember my terrifying Polish grandmother and I can believe that.

'Anyway,' says Mum, 'he's dancing with me and he's dancing with Nell and he's not a very good dancer' – I can imagine that – 'and then all of a sudden, Nell's gone I don't know where and he's gone, talking to some Polish airmen, chattering away in this language, that was the first I knew of him being Polish –'

'And where was Nell?'

'Oh,' she says, 'I was talking to some French sailors.'

'Nell came from the Channel Islands, see,' says Mum. 'Any time she sniffed out a Frenchman she went off with him.'

'Not like that,' cries Nell. 'It was just to talk.'

'Jabbering away in French,' says Mum. 'Parley-voo. Well, eventually, your dad turns up again and says, Where's Nell, and I say I have to be going, the last bus will be along soon, so we go off looking for her and there she is sitting on a Frenchman's knee and swigging brandy from a bottle.'

'Mother, I'm shocked,' says Heather delightedly. 'Did my father know about this bad behaviour?'

Nell giggles. 'There are lots of things your father never knew about.'

'So anyway, she's got my cloakroom ticket and I need to get my coat and I'm arguing with her, and Jack's offering to see her home and she's gabbling away in French.' I can imagine Mum getting huffy and cross. 'So Jack walks me to the bus stop and sees me home, and after that, we were together.'

'But you told him,' cries Nell. 'You told him I had a boyfriend.'

'You did. You had Gus.'

'Well yes.' Nell simpers a bit, maybe comparing Gus to my dad, and not to my dad's advantage.

'Come on then, tell about Gus.' Heather and I are pretending to each other that we are doing this for our mothers benefit, but – I don't know about her – for a change I'm quite enjoying it. Their stories are more lively this afternoon, still nostalgic, less melancholy.

'Kath was after him,' says Mum. 'Remember they moved into the house next door and she thought she would get her hands on him.'

'He was a sweet boy,' says Nell gently. 'He asked me to marry him but we were too young. And then he went and got killed in France.'

'Poor Nell,' says Mum, as if she isn't there. 'She had such a rotten time. Her brother was killed too.'

'And my father,' says Nell, 'he died in the war, and my mother a few years after.'

'We don't have many relatives,' says Heather. 'It's a good thing Dunc has generated a few replacements.'

Then they start talking about that blessed bike ride. I've heard this before and from the look on Heather's face I suspect she has too.

'Come and look at this,' she says to me.

In Nell's bedroom – pill boxes lined up on the dressing table, smell of talcum powder, bed raised up at the pillow end – Heather points to something on the wall. It's Mum's fabric picture, and I have to say, it's a bit of a disappointment to me. Smaller than I remember, and the colours are clashing and the design – the cottage gate and hollyhocks – is taken straight from a biscuit tin lid.

I look sideways at Heather. She's artistic, so what must she think of it?

'Hm,' I say.

'Look at the stitches,' she says. 'So neat. Absolutely beautiful.'

'You don't think it's a bit – sentimental?'

'Of course it is,' she says. 'But who cares. Look at the work that went into it. And my mother really likes it, really really likes it. I'm going to show your mother we've still got it.'

Mum is at first uncomprehending, doesn't recognise her own work. Probably she, like me, remembers it differently. But she pulls herself round, is grateful for the fact that Nell has kept it all this time, sets off on a story about a shop calling her to ask for more to sell. 'They'd sold out, in one weekend, I wouldn't have believed it, but there, six gone, just like that.'

It's been a really good visit. Heather and I like each other, we have common ground, she is only an hour away, and we could become proper friends. I carry the tray back into the kitchen for her, and ask if she's ever heard of Marcie MacNee.

'I don't recall that name,' she says, 'but then, Mother doesn't talk much about that time in her life. Your mum being here, that's kind of unlocked her memories.'

'Better maybe,' I say, 'not to live so much in the past.'

'She broods,' says Heather. 'She doesn't say it out loud but she goes over it, all those losses, and sometimes I find her crying, and she's got very bitter.'

I tell her about Marcie, not the full three hour exposition, obviously, just the bare facts.

'Ooh,' she says, smiling. 'A mystery. I'll let you know if she ever says anything about it.' But I know she won't ask outright. We exchange email addresses anyway.

'Will you come again Sadie? Will you bring her Carrie?' Nell is looking tired and I know how she feels, I am ready to drop with the unaccustomed effort of being polite and sociable. Mum is as perky as ever.

'Of course. If it's all right.'

'Please come,' says Heather. 'Don't leave it too long.'

Nell struggles out of her chair and she and Mum hug and kiss, in danger of toppling over. Heather and I smile at each other. If we were men we might shake hands, or if we were different women we might kiss, but as it is, we smile. Warmly though.

TWENTY-FIVE

Down the road, on the corner near the station, in a house all covered with soot, another old lady died. Mrs Horns.

'I see Eric's back,' said Ginny to my mum, and it was not long before I saw Eric, standing outside the house on the corner, in his suit, directing a couple of men who were shifting a wardrobe or a piano out of his mother's house. He always wore a suit, a dark one, and a white shirt and a colourful tie, and his shoes were always polished up to a bright black shine, but when you looked they didn't match, one of them was specially made to be misshapen, to accommodate his foot which had got smashed up in the war. He walked with a limp.

Eric Horns started hanging around my mum. He called at our house, he took her to the pub and to the pictures, leaving me at home on my own or sometimes round at Kath's. He took her for rides in Epping Forest at weekends. He invited her to dinner-dances and introduced her to people he did business with. She took to having a shampoo and set every Saturday morning at the hairdressers, instead of doing it herself on a Friday night. I wasn't sure what all this meant. The signs seemed to tell me that she liked him but that made no sense to me. He was little, almost fat, he had bad teeth and talked about money all the time, money and how he had got the better of people. She had known him, of course, ever since she was born, but I didn't see why that meant she had to like him.

Ginny advised Mum not to marry him – I know because I was listening – but Mum seemed to think people had it in for him because they were jealous of the money he had made, and she held out against believing that he had a nasty side. 'He's always been a gentleman to me,' she said.

'You know he's been married before?'

'So what?'

'She divorced him.'

'I know. He's told me all about that. And I don't think, actually, that you can talk, Ginny Swallow. At least Eric's not married now, not like someone I could mention.'

'That's different.' Ginny did not sound put out. 'Just so long as you know, Sadie, it was his wife that sued for divorce, and you know why.'

'He's told me.'

'Cruelty. Did he tell you?'

'That's what she said. He let her do it, he's a gentleman. She'd got a fancy man you know, that's what it was all about really. He's told me.'

I agreed with Ginny. That's what Eric was, cruel. He liked hurting. He kicked cats and dogs, he flicked the ears of small children, he had a gun and used to go shooting things, rats and rabbits, just for the fun of killing. His favourite memory was that once when he was in the army he tied two cats together and hung them over a washing line, alive, clawing and biting each other, and spitting and yowling. 'What happened then?' I said and he said, 'Don't know. Left em to it.'

'Nell told me he was a horrible little boy,' said Ginny. 'Nailing frogs to fences and things like that.'

'All boys do things like that,' said Mum. 'He wouldn't do it now, he's a grown man. How would Nell know about it anyway, she didn't come here till later.'

'Gus told her.'

'Oh Gus,' said Mum. 'She'd believe anything he said. Am I supposed to take notice of stuff that if it happened, happened twenty-five years ago or more?'

But she didn't know, because it wasn't her hair he pulled when she was out of the room, it wasn't her toes he trod on with his big orthopaedic shoe.

Until we moved to Ilford I spent my evenings and weekends with my best friend Jeannette. In the summer we hung around the chip shop, the bus shelter, the swings. In the winter we did the same but when it was too dark and cold we tried to find an indoor venue. Someone's house was best. Not usually mine, because Mum wasn't very welcoming, and if Eric was there Jeannette hung back at the door and then found an excuse to go home. And Jeannette's was not much better because she had a number of younger sisters who shared her bedroom. Linda was a good person to be friendly with in the winter. Her mum and dad were out quite a bit and they had central heating so her bedroom was warm, and she had a transistor radio that we could take up there and listen to Radio London. But she was possessive about Jeannette and there was sometimes a bit of an atmosphere if one of us talked about something we had done together without her.

Mostly we talked about boys, and sometimes we talked about sex. Jeannette and I knew next to nothing. Jeannette said her mum couldn't even know where babies came from or she wouldn't keep on having them. Linda had a book about how babies came about and we looked at it, but hardly dared discuss it for fear of showing how ignorant we each were. After a short while one of us would put it aside, sighing in a bored sort of way, and move on to Linda's stack of Seventeen magazines.

Our other friend was Pamela, but she was hardly ever even allowed out, and once the street lights came on she had to run home. As time went on that made it harder to be friends with her. On Saturdays we liked to go round the shops, looking at the clothes and shoes, and hanging about the record stores where the boys congregated. We had no money. We would have liked to have Saturday jobs – we talked a lot about that too – but they were all given to the girls from the grammar schools, because sec mod girls were thought not to be able to add up, and would always give wrong change, besides not knowing how to be polite to customers. Even Woolworths didn't want us.

I was almost ready to leave school and I was planning to go to secretarial college. I had a vision of myself working in London, living in a bedsit, or sharing a flat with other girls. We would all be fashionable and go to lots of parties, and young men would call for us in sports cars and take us for drives in the country at weekends. My hair would be long and glossy and I would flick my head and it would swing round and settle perfectly back in place. I would work at a desk with a phone and a typewriter, and sit on a swivel chair with my legs crossed, so that people would notice my slim ankles – that would be when they miraculously became slim – and a young executive would fall for me, and we might get stuck in the lift together, or maybe he would be too shy to speak, but then he would move into the flat upstairs to mine, or maybe – you can tell I got through a lot of women's magazine stories. That was because we had a lot of women's magazines at home, on account of Mum needing to know the fashions.

Then one day Mum told she was going to marry Eric.

'I'm not coming,' I said.

'Don't be stupid,' she said. Persuasion was not one of her talents.

'She'll be there,' said Eric, and he was right, I was. They took no notice of my wishes, just assumed I'd be there, and when the wedding day dawned, there I was, dressed in a yellow dress and jacket that fitted perfectly and made my face look like a dirty sheet. Ginny was there of course, without Bernie, and Kath was there, with Ted (there for the beer) and Valerie and Tony. Apart from them, it was all Eric's business friends and their wives. Big old men with braces and loud laughs, wives with sparkling necklaces round chickeny throats, clutching their handbags while they threw back their Dubonnet and lemonade. Mum, I recognised though I would not have admitted it, looked far more classy than anyone else.

Eric's friends. Or contacts. I tried to avoid them but of course I got to know some of them. Harsh people, who thought that because they had had a bit of luck and drove a car and were buying their own house, they were entitled to look down on anyone who lived in a council house, or was poor, or clever, or good. This is what I know now. At the time though I accepted their view of themselves and believed that Mum had gone up in the world and wondered why I didn't like them. They often tried to be nice to me, they gave me presents and offered to take me to dinner dances, and the women gave me advice about not putting nail varnish on bitten nails, and on the advantages of a good haircut.

Mostly they lived in Ilford, and that was where we were going to live too. Ilford, where you could work at the juke box factory or not. I did not. Secretarial college was not to be mentioned. Eric was kind enough to give me a job at the scaffolding yard, where I sat in a freezing hut and counted the poles and boards when they went out and came back in. There was no swivel chair, no opportunity to toss my hair alluringly, no lift, no handsome young executives. Probably – I know now – there wouldn't have been any of these if I had got my way and been an agency temp, but. There was a phone, which would ring, and people whose names I didn't catch – usually just first names – had that been Dick, or Derek? Or the names of firms – A.J here – not going to get it back today – and they'd ring off. 1471? – not in those days. Caller ID? – years into the future. Excuse me, I'd be bleating into a phone that was purring its ring tone back at me. And I'd have to tell Eric that an unknown someone was going to be a late return and he would pinch me on the arm, or kick me on the ankle. I had little bruises – and some big ones – all over me, but no one ever knew.

Mum carried on being Sarah Jacklin Bridal Wear. Eric got her a shop. She had a shop window, two people to do the basic sewing, someone to manage the orders and the payments, and a daft, pretty girl whose job it was to hover around customers being sickeningly enthusiastic. Her name was Ann, she called herself Antonia and loved weddings so much that there was never a chance that her good taste would put anyone off spending their money. Mum and a staff of four, plus the cleaner. Not me, you notice, she wouldn't employ me.

'I can add up, you know,' I said to her, often. 'I'm not stupid. I could do that work as well as Brenda can. And you wouldn't have to pay me as much.'

'You get what you pay for,' she said. 'Before I'd employ you, my girl, you'd have to wash that muck off of your eyes and get a proper haircut.' At that time, at fifteen, I combined a shaggy hairdo with eye make-up that was more dramatic than pretty, but which I couldn't bring myself to give up or modify. How many hours had that taken me, to master eyeliner, eye shadow, mascara, without poking my own eyes out or getting it all down my face. I liked really pale lipstick too. They hadn't invented Goths then, but I would have been one if I could.

'Keep Death Off the Roads,' Eric called me, frequently, thinking he was clever. I took it as a compliment.

'What about Ann then?' I said. 'I could do her job.'

Mum did not even bother to reply.

I blamed her. Once again, she had forced me to go away from Jeanette and the other few friends I had, from Ginny and the little streets and shops that I was getting used to. I had left school so there was no way of making any new friends, and I missed my old ones more than I would have thought possible. Evenings I spent in my room, to keep away from Eric. Weekends the same. I thought of running away but didn't know how to. I cried a lot, and wrote letters to my dad which I never sent, asking him to come and get me.

How many times in my life has my mother destroyed my peace? When I was eleven, that was the big one, but not the first one. Because it was her, I know, not my dad, who decided that our family would live in two separate places. She thought it wouldn't matter to me that I could never go to my friends' birthday parties because on Saturdays we were at the farm, and she thought it wouldn't matter to me that I would only see my dad for a few hours a week, and then when he was working. He sometimes called in to see us, but she never invited him.

At last, when I turned seventeen, and realised that I was the only person who could change the way things were, I met Roger.

TWENTY-SIX

John has phoned, which is nice, though rare. He lets Mum have a long chat. She tells him about how many pills she takes, about what she had for her lunch, about Daisy's gluey ear. She mentions the weather a few times, asks after Chris and the children and grandchildren, and begins again on the bloody cat's ailments. It's me that has to put the drops in by the way.

At last I get to speak to my brother.

'I'm selling up,' he says. 'Got a buyer, got a price, me and Chris are going off in the RV, do some travelling, look for a place we might like to settle down.'

'So,' I say after a small pause, 'I'll never see the farm again.'

'Sis,' he says, 'you haven't seen it in more than forty years. You never came when you had the chance. Unless you're here before the middle of April you've had it. We're out of here.'

It affects me more than I imagined it could. Always, it has been in my mind. It was the place where I come from, and a place I was going to go to again. When I had enough money, when Jo had left home, when I had a good job, when I could take three weeks all together, when I'd saved a bit more, when I'd retired. It has been a future target, and it has been a future target for so long that all the futures have come and gone and been forgotten. I know it's been said before, but where do our lives go?

I did go back to Canada once, paid for by Eric, just after they got married. I imagine that they wanted me out of the way for a bit, but I didn't care. I was just happy to go. I was delirious. I was fifteen, I had just left school without an exam certificate to my name – not just me, nobody had one – and I had no prospects except what Eric was prepared to offer, but I was going to see my dad, and my brother, and my aunts, and my cousin

Marianne, and the farm. Olive as well of course, but I wasn't excited about that.

Oh, they came, a whole gang of them, to meet me at the airport, John driving a big car, and they whisked me home, across to the island, the late afternoon sun lying on the lake like a golden fire, and on the land like a blessing, and I remembered the road, and the trees and the houses and the gates, and everything, until we got to the farm, and then I remembered nothing at all. Or, I did remember, but what I recalled was not there.

There were the gates, not the old broken, grey wood ones – new, smart, white five-barred ones, with those curved pieces of wood sticking up at the ends. The old track was tarmacked and smooth and the fields each side contained horses behind wire fences that were not bent down.

'Where's our house,' I said, because what I could see was a new house, timber framed with brick in-fill, two complete storeys and a smooth unpatched roof.

'The old house is behind,' said John. He swung the car to a stop. 'We turned it into a bunkhouse.'

There was no evidence of cows, and no chickens in the yard. In fact the yard was a car park, with some tubs of plants at the house door. The smell was of horse.

I realised then that the notices I had seen on our way along the road, saying things like, Livery Stables, Riding Lessons, Pony-Trekking Holidays, Rescue Sanctuary for sick horses, all with a logo of three Js, and three horseshoes, were us. We were Horses.

'What's JJJ?'

'It's me,' said John. 'Or, if you look at it another way, it's me, Dad and Olive, we're all Jakimowiczes.'

'So am I,' I said.

He was quite nice, as brothers go, and he might have understood what I meant. He said, 'Well, of course you're one of us. But you don't live here do you.'

We piled into the house, John, me, Dad, Aunt Lisa and Marianne – and Olive and Lena were there waiting, and the kitchen was all clean and new and didn't smell of soot and cheese but of disinfectant and baking and something I later realised had been new plaster. And later in the evening John's girlfriend showed up – Chris, she was called, nineteen with the sort of shiny straight hair I wanted – and they went out.

I had left school and I longed to be part of the life of John and Chris – though their life was horses – but instead I was part of the life of Marianne, who was only thirteen.

I had missed Marianne. We had sent letters to each other, affectionate ones, always ending with the hope that I would be able to visit soon. The real Marianne was not someone I recognised. Maybe the tragedy had scarred her, maybe living with Aunt Lena, and looking after her, and her grandfather, made her strange, I don't know. It was like being friends with an old woman. She looked at me oddly, as if I was wearing the wrong things. She said things like, 'now mind you wrap up warm.' She went to church and promised to take me there in the same sort of way as John and Chris promised to take me to the ice cream parlour, like it was a treat. Marianne's church happened more often. She was shocked that I spoke harshly of Eric. She lived with her mother, my Aunt Lena, and her grandfather, Paul's father that is, in a house about a mile away. When I went there, which I did most days, as everyone else was too busy to pay much attention to me, I was scared. The tragedy, which Marianne could not remember but knew all about and recounted to me in obsessive detail, still hung over them. It had, they said, daily, caused the death of Paul's mother. Granpa had dealt with it by turning into the sort of recluse who never speaks about it, to anyone, and he spent his days, and part of his nights, walking compulsively round the lake, round the island, through the woods, along to the ferry, back again. Then he put his foot into an animal trap, one of his own, which he had set to catch beaver, and at the time I was there was laid up with it, like a bear in a cage.

Aunt Lena was a sort of saint, everyone said. They talked about her endlessly. 'She could have done anything,' said my dad. 'She was the one with all the brains.' She's still got her brains, I thought to myself, what does she do with them?

'Thank goodness she was left with Marianne,' said Olive. 'It gave her something to live for. And the love and the care she's put into that little girl – it will never be repaid you know.' I didn't understand what she meant. One thing you could say for my mum, she never expected thanks for just being my mother.

'I can never be as good as Lena,' said Lisa. So that's why you don't try, I thought.

Marianne fussed round her mother, doing all the things that she couldn't do because her hands were set into shiny scarred claws. She sat with them hidden under an apron – what was the apron for, I wondered, if she was never going to go into the kitchen. She spoke to me as if she was the pope and I was there for a religious experience – though as far as I understood, she never went to church. That was another thing Marianne did for her. Well, I'd never been to church either, never been inside one in my life, so when Marianne took me I had nothing to compare it with. It certainly wasn't like Westminster Abbey, which I'd seen on the telly when Princess Alexandra got married. It was a little wooden building, more like a church hall – I'd been in them, to youth clubs and so on – with some wooden chairs and an ordinary table at the front. They did a bit of singing, but I didn't know the words, and a bit of praying, at which I looked down at my feet so they wouldn't see I was keeping my eyes open – it was a superstition with us at school assembly, that if you shut your eyes to pray, and didn't really mean it, then the opposite would come true. I think it was Pamela's idea.

Then there was a long speech, which I didn't listen to – no, I did try to listen but it didn't start from anywhere that I recognised so I was lost in unfamiliar words, and puzzled by the urgent tone of it all. At school religion, by which I mean morning assembly, was a dull, predictable, undemanding and slightly comforting interlude before we got to all the boredom and suppressed hostility of the classroom. Here, the man – vicar? priest? how should I know? – was pressing us, pushing us towards something I didn't know about and it was all desperate and if we didn't do what he said we would go to hell, and worse, the whole world would go to hell. I don't know if that's what he said, but that's what it felt like, so I chose not to listen.

Marianne was evidently some sort of pet amongst the congregation. After the service they came round, offering her baskets of apples and tins of biscuits, and a complete pie of some sort, and asking after Lena as if she was on her death bed. They shook my hand, and asked me how I was, and how my mother was, hoping I could give them some juicy bad news about her and I was acute enough not to tell them that she'd just got married, though I think they knew anyway. They knew what she was like. She was a woman who had abandoned her little boy, and her husband and run away from a life that she had freely chosen, back to something soft and easy. Even, I gathered, some suggested the fire might not have started if there had been enough people around to do the work properly. It was only to be expected that she would top it off by marrying again. Dad was innocent in all of that, he had been the hardworking one who had done his best to hold the family together, and looked after his mother as well, so it was fine for him to get married again.

The new buildings and the horses were not the only things that had changed since I'd gone away. Our family had become part of the community. It was on account of Olive of course, she was a local, everyone had known her since she was born, and after they got over the shock of her marrying a divorced Polack, the only thing to do was to incorporate Dad, and John, and the rest of the family, into the community of normal people. John was a kind of hero. He was twenty-one at this time and seemed older. Everyone told me how wonderful it was that he had been able to turn round the farm into a going concern. Of course they knew that it could not have been done without Olive and her money but it had been John, it appeared, who had had the ideas, the *vision*, the get-up-and-go, to make it happen. Even Olive said as much.

Marianne was in love with him. She said things to me like, There's nothing wrong with cousins marrying, is there? and, I don't think John and Chris will stay together, do you? I didn't know the answer, or how to reply to her, but I didn't need to. John and Chris got married a couple of years later and stayed that way. Marianne hung around for a while, but as soon as her mother died – young, and suddenly – she took herself off westward and never came back.

Olive was in some ways like Mum. Short and slight and fair, and a steely businesswoman. But I suppose it was the differences that were more important. She loved animals – horses especially of course – and being outdoors in all weathers. She believed in having fun, which to her meant trekking and camp fires and watching the sun come up over the lake. My dad was a different person from the one I had known, he smiled, he talked, he took an interest in my life. He was pleased to see me. This was quite a novelty for me. Naturally, it was difficult for me, as I chattered on about my small English concerns, to avoid including Mum in my talk, but every time I did, it seemed to me, Dad and Olive and even John, went deaf. Their eyes flicked away and they concentrated hard on some other bit of what I was saying and redirected my thoughts. I realised that Mum was written out of that particular history.

Lisa, though, had different ideas about Mum. She must have admired her, in the same way as I admired Chris. Mum had arrived on the farm, foreign, pretty, exotic, and Lisa experienced a breath of difference, and a glimpse of possibility. Not that she had done much with it as far as I could see. She was married but had no children and mostly lived apart from her husband. No one talked about him. She worked on the mainland but lived mostly at the farm. I shared her bedroom while I was there and she talked into the night as if she was a teenager like me, instead of a woman in her thirties. She even asked me about Marcie.

'So, did they ever find out who killed that girl?'

I liked talking about Marcie. I had listened to enough whispers and guesses to be fairly confident that I knew all the likely ways Marcie could have died. The problem was only which one was the true one.

In the two weeks I was there Lisa and I took it to pieces.

'What does your mother think about it?'

'Oh Mum doesn't want to talk about it. But –'

'She suspects someone.'

'She's certain. It's the one she comes round to again and again. The others – the other women, her friends – they say someone and the next week they say someone else, but Mum always sticks to the same one.'

'Who is that?'

'Her brother. Marcie's brother I mean, not Mum's brother, he was only a boy when it happened.'

I was allowed to stay in the room when they accused Marcie's brother. Kath said she knew they had fights but he wasn't a bad boy, just got upset when he couldn't speak, so used his fists. He and Marcie were fond of each other really. Mum would say he might not have meant to do it, sometimes boys that age didn't know their own strength.

'He would have owned up,' said Ginny. 'He would have let his auntie know, he couldn't keep it from her. And if he didn't mean it, it would only have been manslaughter.'

'So why did they flit?' Mum would say. 'That looks suspicious, wouldn't you say?'

'So,' said Lisa. 'Not proved either way. He's a Maybe. Who else is in the frame?'

'Someone called Mr Page. Somehow connected to someone called Nell. She was a friend of all of them. But they all say he was too old, and Ginny says he was a nice old man, he wouldn't do something like that.'

I was paraphrasing. What she actually said – once when Mum was out of the room – was, 'If it was a dirty old man job I don't know why we're looking at poor old Mr Page when there's a much dirtier old man nearer home.' And Kath nodded her head as if the last word had been said on that particular item. I didn't know who she meant.

'OK,' said Lisa, 'let's leave him out of it. So?'

'Someone called Gus,' I said. 'He was Nell's boyfriend I think. But Kath wondered about him.'

I had to listen at the door for this one.

'He was frustrated,' said Kath. 'He told me, remember, Sadie, I told you. Nell wouldn't let him touch her. He couldn't stand it, he told me. And there he was, going off to get killed.'

But Mum wasn't having any of it. 'I knew Gus from a baby,' she said. 'He's four weeks younger than me, that's all. I grew up with him. He never had a bad bone in his body. He would never do a thing like that.'

'Well,' said Kath, 'you say that now but I don't remember you being that upset when he got killed. Never shed a tear, is what I remember.'

'I had other things to worry about,' said Mum. 'If you remember.'

'Was he there though?' said Lisa. 'If he wasn't in the vicinity at the time he couldn't have done it. If he was away in the army.'

I remembered Ginny saying, 'They were all home, weren't they, just before they went back into France. There was nothing for them to do, the army just kept giving them bits of leave till it was time to go.'

'So who else was in the army?' she said, and suddenly I didn't want to talk about it any more, in the dark, because the faces that came to me, and the names, were two that I knew. Eric was one, and the other was my dad.

'Come on Carrie, who else?' And luckily I remembered Billy Swallow, and the single occasion Mum mentioned his name, and how Kath and Ginny went quiet, and then Kath cried and said Sadie wasn't being fair, and Ginny proved to her that Billy might have been a bit wild but he had never harmed a fly, and look at him now with Joyce and the kiddies, he was soft as lights.

'Jeepers,' said Lisa. 'It's a tough thing, having your brother suspected.'

'I need to go to sleep now,' I said.

Going to sleep, and even Lisa sleeping on the mainland for a couple of nights, couldn't stop me thinking when I got into bed the next night.

Eric. They had stopped accusing him since Mum said she was going to marry him but I remembered all the times they said he was that sort of person.

'How could he though?' said Mum. 'He was laid up with his foot, if you remember.'

'That didn't happen till D-Day,' said Kath. 'Do you remember, he never even got as far as the ship, this big heavy weight – a jack or something – fell on his foot, and he couldn't go.'

'What a shame for him,' said Ginny. 'But Kath's right. He was around the place when Marcie disappeared.'

I lay looking at the grey square of window and heard the mosquitoes whining to get through the mesh. Eric could be a murderer and he was my step-dad. I hated him and Mum said I was wrong to hate him, but if he was a murderer I was right.

And. If it was him then it couldn't have been my dad. Not that I ever believed that it could have been, not for a second. They didn't know him like I did. He was a gentle, bewildered soul. Even Mum said, me listening outside the door, 'Zyg wouldn't have the gumption to do something like that. Anyway, he was with me. You don't know what you're saying, Kath Swallow and I think you need to think again.'

And Kath said she was sorry.

'You know Carrie,' my dad said to me. 'You could come over here and live with us.'

It was two days before I was due to fly back to England. The setting sun was shining through the windows and I was sitting with Dad and Olive at the kitchen table. All the time I had been in England I had been thinking of the farm as it was before the fire. I had lain in bed and brought up my memories like a book, the brown, puddingy smell of the cows and the dreamy dim light of the milking shed. Running in the fields with John, whacking poison ivy with sticks, making daisy chains with Marianne, climbing on the broken fences, throwing scraps for the hens.

All that was gone. I hadn't wanted it to be true at first, but in two weeks I had got used to the farm as it now was, I had stopped missing the old ramshackle place. John was grown up, and even I felt that I was older. My perspective had changed, everything had changed. My dad though still himself was like a different person, broad, smiley, well liked, as if he had grown up too.

'Stay here,' said Olive. 'Don't go home. We'll miss you.' I wasn't sure whether she meant it, and the idea seemed so big and wonderful to me that it could not possibly happen. It was like someone saying casually but seriously, You could marry George Harrison.

'I've got to go back,' I said, thinking of my return ticket. I honestly believed that if you had a ticket you had to use it. I suppose, looking back now, that they respected what they thought was my wish to be back with Mum, and my friends.

'You know,' said Dad, 'there's always a home for you here.'

I could not look at him for fear of crying. 'I've got to go home,' I said again, hoping they would tell me I had to stay.

'That's all right,' said Olive. 'You'll come back again. We'll see you soon.'

I went home to England, and Mum had moved out to Ilford to live with Eric, and I had to go and live with them. I carry in my head from that day to this the picture of my dad sitting at that table with the sun behind him. His shirt was open at the neck, and I could see the white flesh below the collar that never caught the sun. I never went back to Canada, and I never saw my dad again.

TWENTY-SEVEN

Roger gave me a cigarette as we stood sheltering from the rain. He put two in his mouth, lit them both with a match and passed one to me. It was a Player's Navy Cut untipped and I usually smoked Number 6. The rain lashed down, lit, weirdly, by a setting sun that made it seem like gold, melted into drops. We stood side by side, looking out, and a cloud went in front of the sun and the rain turned silver and then grey. I tried not to show that I was getting little threads of tobacco in my mouth, and wondered what to say. Then the rain stopped and we went on our way, me towards home, him somewhere else, without exchanging a word, not a single word.

The next time I saw him was months later, on the top deck of a bus, foggy with smoke. I saw him but didn't sit down next to him for fear of being forward. But he must have seen me looking in my bag for a cig – though actually I was looking for my purse – and he reached across the aisle and put a lit one into my hand. I said, 'Thank you,' and smiled, but he was looking out of the window. I had to get off before he did, so I couldn't tell where he might live.

I used up weeks of my life getting on that same bus, and hanging about on that same street. Sometimes I thought I saw him and then it turned out to be someone else, and that would make me wonder if I really recalled what he looked like, and I panicked that when I saw him again I wouldn't recognise him. Maybe I had already seen him and let him pass by. And then I went to a dance. I went with a girl I knew only slightly, a tiny, cheeky girl whose name I forget. I was wearing a red shift dress like a long t-shirt, and a long string of gold coloured beads, and I wasn't expecting to have a nice time. As we approached the door, to show our tickets and have our hands stamped I saw him, in a doorway again, with two other boys, leaning, smoking. He looked straight at me this time and I saw his eyes were a very bright brown, like conkers, and it was too late – my friend pushed me forward and I was inside. I didn't think he was coming in to the dance – all three of them were wearing jeans, and would not have got past the doorman.

I had an awful time. There were no windows so I couldn't look for him. They wouldn't allow pass-outs so I couldn't casually go out for a fag – we could smoke inside in those days anyway. I couldn't leave the dance altogether because I had to wait for the end to go home with Denise – that was her name, see how it comes back to me. I had to dance with people, I had to dance looking at the door in case he was coming in after all. I was unable to make proper conversation and no one wanted to dance with me twice, or buy me a drink, or stay and talk to me. But – at last – it worked out all right. Denise met a friend, I pretended that I had a headache and would go home on my own, it was only around nine when I went out of the door, and he was still there. On his own, leaning, silent, waiting for me. He never said, in all the following years he never admitted it, but I knew then and I know now that he was waiting for me.

So that was how I started going out with Roger. We led a quiet life. He worked as a glazier, driving the van sometimes, replacing broken windows day in day out, mostly in factories and schools. Weekday evenings we went for walks, or sat with his parents and his brothers in their hot, busy front room. Roger would tell us about a new thing called double glazing.

'Houses will be quiet,' he said. 'You won't hear the traffic. No draughts either.'

'Like being in an aquarium,' said his mother. She was always a bit off-centre. 'Everyone tucked away being silent. I don't know if it would suit me.'

Weekends we would go to the pictures or sometimes a folk club (which were all the rage at that time) and go back to my house for a session on the settee after Mum and Eric were home from the pub and safely in bed. Two or three hours we lay there, his yellow-stained finger inside me and my hand down his trousers, breathing into each others ears and neck, whispering, and at last I would go to bed, dazed and buzzing, and he would stumble off to walk home, smoking.

Then one night I heard a noise. Roger was in position to see him first, he must have tensed, something anyway made me open my eyes and twist my head round. Eric stood in the doorway, in pyjamas and silk dressing gown, a cigarette in his mouth, unlit. Rogers's hand slid out.

'Don't let me stop you,' said Eric, casually. 'You carry on, old son, don't mind me.'

I tried to pull my skirt down and my tights and knickers up but should have done them one at a time. I scrambled up, bundled like an armful of dirty washing, and Roger fumbled to do up his trousers. Eric did not move.

'I'll be off then,' said Roger to me.

'Do that, old son,' said Eric, apparently pleasant. 'I don't suppose I'll find you here again.'

When I got to my room I wedged a chair under the door handle and spent the night, some of it, wondering if Eric cared enough to get some of his boys to beat Roger up. I was expecting, next morning, to be interrogated about who he was and where did he live, and I was ready to lie and inflate the number of his brothers and add ten years to their ages and several stone to their weights. Eventually I could stay in bed no longer – it was a Sunday – and I got up. It was a soft blue summer day and the house seemed empty. I was at the kitchen sink putting water in the kettle when I heard him coming, limping up behind me. I thought I was ready but he said nothing at all. I could feel his breath on the back of my neck and I was scared suddenly, and screamed even before he put his teeth onto my bare shoulder and bit down, hard. His hand was on my other shoulder, holding me there. He said nothing of course, his mouth being full of my flesh, and I said nothing, only screamed.

At last he let go.

'I'll tell Mum,' I said.

'Feel free,' he said. He was still close behind me and I could feel, I'm sure I could, his erection against my bum. I still had the kettle in my hand and I suddenly knew that I could swing it round and bash him on the head with it, but I didn't dare. I wish I had. So many times over so many years I've replayed that moment and added a vision of Eric stunned or dead on the kitchen floor. How I wish.

The bruises lasted for weeks, and the disgusting little puncture marks where his bottom incisors had been, but I didn't care because by the time it healed up I was long gone.

TWENTY-EIGHT

Mondays I change the beds. Thursday evenings I remember to put the bin out for collection, general rubbish one week, recycling the next. Tuesdays I pick up Mum's magazine from the newsagent. Saturdays I send an email to Jo, Fridays I clean the bathroom. The tasks come round so quickly, yet the time in between passes so slowly. The routine housework and the trivial jobs I used to do in the spaces between work and having a social life now make up my whole life.

Most weeks now Ginny rings. First I talk to her, about how she is, what she's done, whether she's seen Val, things like that. But Mum is always impatient to have her turn, waving at me imperiously to hand the phone to her. One day she phones while Mum is asleep so I can have a longer conversation. I ask her about Marcie. 'You used to talk a lot about her. Do you still think about her?'

'Carrie,' she says – she's one of those people who use your name every sentence, 'Carrie, I think about her every day. Do you know, I hardly knew the girl except to say hello to, but it feels like she's overshadowed my whole life. People think Carrie,' – she's also one of those people who can keep on talking indefinitely – 'that murder – I don't mean death, death's natural – but murder now, that's not natural and yet people use it for entertainment. Just you look at the telly – murders every night, and in the papers and on the news, there's nothing people like better than a murder, even sometimes in comedies, and it's not right Carrie, but it's only when you know about a real one that you realise, you realise it's something real.' She laughs suddenly, which makes her cough and wheeze. 'Take no notice of me, love, I just get on my high horse and I can't get off.'

'But who do you think did it?'

'Now Carrie, don't ask. You don't want to know what I think. That's the trouble you see, too many people to get hurt, and you might think you wouldn't be, but you would Carrie.'

'If you mean Eric -'

'No I don't mean Eric,' she says. 'I mean, he might have had something to do with it, he might have been the one that got her pregnant, but any of them might have been -'

'She was pregnant?'

'Didn't you know that? Oh yes she was, certainly -'

'How did you know?'

'Through Nell.'

'Nell knew? Marcie told her?'

'Well I don't know about that exactly. Look, I'm sorry Carrie, I can't tell you any more, too many people, you know? Is your mother awake yet?'

And that's it. Later though, I phone Heather with the new bit of information.

'Oh my,' she says, 'it's all coming out of the woodwork now.'

'Did you know?'

'No, not at all. Mother never talks about Marcie, never, it's just not on her list of subjects, but I'll tell you something she has told me, and more than once, so I'm sure it's true. Her mother, my grandmother – she died before I was born – she used to do abortions.'

'No!'

'Yes. She was a back street abortionist. In Guernsey and then again when they came to England. And Mother says she was very good at it, she gave up when she started getting ill though.'

It was Ginny who saved me when I ran away. It was her doorstep – the one she shared with Bernie – I was sitting on when she came home from work on Monday. In the house the phone was ringing.

'It's Mum,' I said. 'Don't tell her I'm here.' But it wasn't, it was one of Ginny's friends.

Ginny assumed at first I must be pregnant, as had happened to two of her nieces.

'No, I'm not,' I said. 'I've never –'

'What then?' she said. 'What sort of trouble.' And I told her about Eric and his punches and kicks, and showed her my shoulder, though I couldn't see it myself.

'I think it needs something on that,' she said. 'It's gone through the skin. ' And she painted it with some yellow liquid that she kept for Bernie when he cut his hands or grazed his knees while building.

Bernie came in while she was doing it. I don't think I had ever spoken to him before, though I recognised him, so I must have seen him some time in the past. People had always said how good-looking he was, but to me, a man in his forties, getting stocky, with short hair and hairy hands, was a long way from what I found attractive. But he was nice to me, and I could tell he was shocked at what Eric had done.

'Honestly?' he said. 'You're honestly telling me that this – this *person* – has done this? Does he think he's a fucking vampire or something?'

'Don't swear Bern,' said Ginny. 'I don't want her thinking we're as bad as he is.'

I wrote a letter to Roger, to tell him where I was, and the next weekend he came over and we went for a long walk, where about every quarter of a mile we had to stop and hold on to each other, and sometimes I had a little cry. We were like Maria and Tony out of West Side Story.

And gradually it all got sorted out. I got a job in an office, just by telling them I had worked in an office before, and Ginny dealt with Mum – how I never knew, and after a year or so I moved out of Ginny's and in with Roger, over to Willesden, where Eric would never go, and Jo was born and my real, grown up life began.

The next time Ginny phones it's to invite herself to come and see us. Val will bring her, Val her niece, Kath's youngest daughter. Mum and I have a conversation to remind ourselves what happened to them all.

'Rita, of course, she's done very well for herself.'

'Of course.'

'Not on the telly any more, too old I expect, but still on the wireless sometimes, according to Gin.'

'Radio, Mum. No one calls it the wireless any more.'

'I'll call it what I like, Miss Know-All.'

'Well what about the others? I mean, I know about Kay, but what about the others?'

I never saw Kay after she got married, when she was only sixteen. Of course she was pregnant and there was no wedding to speak of. She disappeared out of my life and I thought nothing of it. When her children were born Mum passed the news on to me but I wasn't interested. She is dead now.

'Well,' says Mum, 'Kay died.'

'I know. What about the others? Is Val married? What does she do?'

'Married? No, not any more. I think she's had a couple of husbands. She does a lot for Ginny, I know that, she doesn't know what she'd do without her.'

'Does she have a job then?'

'Oh she must do. Drinks a bit, Gin says, so she must have to earn some money you see. But good-hearted I believe.'

They arrive on a sunny day in early spring, a blustery wind tossing the daffodils in all the gardens.

Val is the size and shape I remember her mother being, but her style is more Ginny than Kath. She has a deep tan, a large friendly smile and does not find it necessary to dress in black to minimise the size of her bosom. She helps her aunt out of the car but once upright, Ginny walks without help into the house.

She looks poorly though – Mum and I agree on this when they have gone – and needs to sit down, wheezing, after walking only as far as a chair in the front room. She is, always has been of course, the oldest of the group of them, and she looks it, as skinny as Mum and even more wrinkled, but smiling, really happy to see us, warm and cheerful.

'So what brings you here?' Mum, not as welcoming as she might be. I know though, that she is so pleased to see a friend that she daren't show it, for fear of showing too much.

Val says, 'We thought we'd have a day out, didn't we. And Auntie says to me, It's a long time since I saw Sadie, so we've had a little run out this way.' Which is not strictly true as it was all arranged in advance.

I'm busy taking coats and making tea and by the time I get settled in the room Mum and Ginny are well into conversation and there's nothing I need to do except chat idly to Val.

Val helps me with the washing up, notices Mum's school photo, magneted to the fridge.

'What's this?'

I point out Mum, her friend Sylvie who she lost touch with, the red-haired teacher, and Marcie. 'Do you know about Marcie?'

'Do I? I should say so. Don't forget we lived on top of the murder site. My sisters used to tell me it was haunted, that house, I think my mother really believed it too.'

'Nightmares.'

'Not half. We all slept through it, we were so used to it, but my dad never got used to it, he used to say he'd rather work nights, he got a better sleep in the day without her screaming and clutching at him.'

'But no one ever was arrested for it.'

'No. And too late now, whoever it was must be dead by now, or nearly. What would be the point?'

'Does Ginny still talk about it?'

'Sometimes. But the thing is, she's settled it in her mind what happened and now she doesn't go on about it so much. She's sort of come to terms with it.'

'She took her time.'

Val nods seriously. 'It was a big thing. Not that she was fond of Marcie, I think my mum was more friendly with her, but it was just the not knowing. Didn't your mum feel bothered about it?'

'I don't think so. She always said she knew who did it, and it was Marcie's brother, and so she didn't want to talk about it any more. I tell you what though, if I bring it up now she gets into a bit of a state.'

'I'll tell you what Ginny thinks,' says Val. 'But I'm not sure I agree. She thinks Marcie died of natural causes.'

'What? Just lay down and died? Nobody does that.'

'It seems to make her feel better. It's the idea, to her, that there was always someone there, waiting at the same bus stop -'

'– drinking in the same pub -'

'– that's right, serving you your fish and chips. And they'd done this thing and no one knew, and you were suspecting someone else, and they didn't know you were suspecting them so they couldn't say anything –'

'– or they did know they were suspected and it was ruining their life.'

'So I think she feels better saying, natural causes. She even used to say it to my mum when she was ill.'

'Your mum – it bothered her then, did it?'

'I think it killed her. Yes I know that's on the dramatic side, but I do. I know she smoked and that won't have helped – I'm going to give up myself one of these days – and I know she had quite a hard life with not being happy with my dad, and he died quite young and all of us children were troublesome, except me. You know, two of my sisters had to get married because they were pregnant, and my oldest sister more or less didn't have anything to do with the family once she was grown up, and Tony was always a little bugger and he just went from bad to worse so even when she was ill she was always down the police station for him, or going to court with him –'

'All that and nightmares too.'

'And I think the nightmares were on account of Marcie, and that house. And yet, after Dad died, she wouldn't leave it. She could have got a flat instead, there was only me and Tony left at home, Auntie Gin would have sorted it out for her, but she wouldn't, she stayed there, on top of the place that gave her nightmares.'

'My mum says your mum had nightmares well before Marcie –'

'I think that's true. She was the sort of person who could only let out things like that when she was asleep. But it can't have helped, can it.'

I remember plain Auntie Kath, in her old brown coat, stretched across her chest with buttons pulling apart. She was never a happy person, as I recall. Shouting mostly, unless she was moaning.

'You know,' I say, 'Heather – you know, Nell's daughter. We saw her at Christmas. She looks after her mother all the time, in this tiny house, and I believe she's actually happy to do it. Like, she really loves her mother. Do you think you could have done that? If your mother was still alive?'

Val thinks before she speaks. 'I'd like to think I could. But none of us ever really got on well with her. And actually, none of us ever had to think about it did we? With her dying before she got to a real great age. Rita wouldn't have, that I know, she'd have paid someone else to do it. Kay might have done. It would have made her feel wanted I suppose. It might have been good for her. But I don't know if I could have done it.'

'No,' I say, 'I don't think I can either. It's making me resentful. I don't enjoy anything about it, not her company, not her conversation, not the feeling of being useful. I'm not good at doing it. And I've become a whole other person, and I don't like myself.'

'Can't you get out sometimes?'

'I probably could. It has become an effort. It's another thing I hate myself for, not making any effort at all.'

Val gives my shoulders a squeeze. 'Chin up, mate,' she says. 'I'm at the end of a phone, any evening. I don't mind if you have a moan.'

TWENTY-NINE

'Mum, I need to talk to you.'

'What is it now?' When she speaks to me like that I wonder why I'm even asking her permission for what I'm hoping to do.

'Jo has asked me to go and visit them.'

'So? What's that got to do with me?'

'Well, if I go, we'd have to find a way of looking after you.'

'Don't be ridiculous,' she says. 'What makes you think I need looking after? I'll be perfectly all right on my own.'

I go out of the room. I feel like a teenager all over again. I stand looking out of the kitchen window, breathing, addressing the cherry tree under my breath. 'So I do nothing for you, is that it? You can get your own shopping can you? You can use a tin opener can you? You can do up your own buttons then. Put your shoes on then, let's see you do it. Fill the kettle, go on. Would you remember to take your pain-killers? Can you work the remote control? Can you change a bed? Load a dishwasher? Brush your hair? *Get dressed* even? Can you even wipe your own bum? *I do it all*, do you hear me? *You are helpless.* God knows Mum, I don't *want* to be a twenty-four hours a day nurse and home help, I do it because I have to, and don't think that I do it out of gratitude for what you did for me. Because I don't. Because what did you do? You ruined my life, not once, not twice but *four* times. Four. So just this once, just notice what I do to help you and don't give me this shit about being perfectly capable, *Because you are not. Get used to it.* Because I am going. I am going to spend three weeks on the other side of the Atlantic, with my daughter and my grandchildren, because she has asked me to. You, on the other hand, are going into a *home*. And if you are lucky, when I come back, and in my own good time, I will come and get you, and if you say one thing – *one thing* – that implies they look after you better than I do, then you will stay there. Understand?'

The cherry tree understands clearly. It sends down a scatter of pale pink petals to let me know. And I understand too, this is how I feel, and I feel no guilt at all. I am going. Come September I will be on a plane, she will be tucked up snug in a twilight home, doing community singing and therapeutic sitting-down exercise. I won't bring up the subject again just yet. I'll let it settle. What I will do though, is email Jo to say Yes, and start looking at flights.

I realise as I'm logging on that the feeling I've been having for months now is the feeling I had towards the end of my time with Roger. Trapped. Stuck. Invisible. It's the time I didn't want to tell Heather about. What actually happened is difficult to explain.

Eric died as the country was marking the fiftieth anniversary of D-Day, which was somehow appropriate, as he had managed to miss it. Ginny told me ('Don't tell your Mum.') that she was certain he had dropped the jack, or whatever it was, purposely on his foot, so as to get out of the invasion force.

'Wouldn't that hurt?' I said.

'Like hell,' said Ginny. 'But it wouldn't kill you.'

Why was I so scared of Eric? There were things I never told Ginny, or Roger, but they were things that were so silly and trivial that I was ashamed to admit how much they unnerved me. The way he looked at me, from my face to my feet and back again, not in a sexually threatening way, but with deep dislike in his expression. The way he treated me at work, making me wear an overall like a cleaner, shapeless, maroon, too long. The way my shoes disappeared from the hall and reappeared outside the back door, damp.

I wasn't allowed to have private conversations with my mum. Eric took me to work in the car, and often brought me home again. Because he knew I liked listening to Radio One, he tuned it to Radio Three. If Mum and I were ever in the same room, he was there too. It took me a while to realise what he was doing, and I must say that I blamed Mum as much as him, but maybe she couldn't help it. If he went to the pub, she went with him; if she said she was tired, or wanted to watch TV, he stayed at home too, silent, fidgeting, until she gave up and would say, 'Oh go on then. Just a quick one.' And they would go out and leave me.

I had no money. The arrangement was that if I needed anything I had only to ask. Make up, shampoo, tights, sanitary towels, cigarettes, I had only to ask and it would appear. New clothes were bought by going with Eric and Mum to the shops.

Naturally I stole. If ever there was loose change, petty cash, money in a jar to pay the milkman or the papers, I would try my best to pocket it. He knew, of course he knew. He let me know he knew and I waited for him to get his revenge, and the waiting was even worse than the revenge was.

I was allowed out though. When they went on holiday I was left alone for a week or ten days. If they were going to the pub, which they did several nights a week, though Fridays and Saturdays were the big drinking nights, he would give me some money for chips and say I could go and meet my friends. As if I had any. But I did take the money, and I did go out, and mooch around the streets, not spending much, because I knew I had to hang on to any money I had, in case I needed it. As, in fact, I did.

But Eric's death seemed to unlock strange feelings in me, of wanting to go back in time, or back to Canada, of wanting things to be different.

I remember waking up early in the mornings and lying in bed ages before I had to get up for work, watching the curtains change colour as the sky lightened. Roger was beside me, asleep. He had turned over on to his back and I could hear his catarrh rattling and smell his sour smell of tobacco. I knew I smelled the same.

'I'm going to give up smoking,' I said to him later that day.

He smiled. 'Bet you don't.'

'We both could.'

'I will one day,' he said. 'I can do it, when I want to.'

'I want you to,' I said.

But he wouldn't join me. I gave up. It was something I could do to change the way my life was. I applied for a new job too, and got it. I started playing badminton two evenings a week. I started to sleep alone. Partly, it was true, that Roger's tobacco smell was uncomfortable to go to bed with, and partly it was to see if I could. And yes, I could.

I didn't mean to meet someone else, I wasn't looking for another person, I was actually looking for no person at all, but I went for a drink with a man called Dennis from the badminton club. He was about fifteen years older than me, and married, and I hadn't thought of him in any way other than as someone whose smashes were completely unreturnable. But one summer evening it was still light when we came out and there was talk of going to the pub and sitting in the garden. Dennis offered me a lift, but we must have misheard the pub the others were going to, because when we got there, they were not to be seen.

He was a good listener, Dennis. He didn't bother telling me about his troubles if he had any, he didn't give me any advice, or pass any opinion. He just sat there in the driving seat, in the car park of the wrong pub, while I told him about my awful life, and gave me

262

tissues when I sniffed, and somehow, when the car park was empty and dark, I found I was having sex with him on the back seat. I imagine now that he didn't hear a word I said, just sat there waiting for the moment to pounce.

That was it, that was the extent of it, and I never let on to Rog that it had happened, but it was the beginning of the end. The runaway train gathered speed and hurtled round corners and became like a cartoon train, wheels leaving the tracks, people screaming out of the windows, steam billowing till it filled the sky. It's hard to remember now, how it happened that I was living on my own, with a new job, in a new place, nearer to my mum. What was I thinking of, to move back within striking distance? Did I think she would be a comfort to me?

THIRTY

This could be their last meeting, all three of them together. Nell is ill, Ginny is ill. They look it. Ginny is going into a nursing home, she says it will be like prison, ha ha, and this is her last chance to get out and have a drink. Anything could happen to any one of them, any day. We all know this.

They meet at our house, Mum's house, it being about equidistant from both Nell and Ginny. The occasion is Nell's birthday. Her ninetieth. Mum has already had hers, Ginny will be ninety-two in October. And yet they were young once.

It has been good for me, to have something to arrange. I've cleaned the house, made food, had my hair cut and dyed – I see in Val's expression that she notices the difference.

'Happy birthday Nell.'

'It was Gus' birthday too,' Nell says to me. 'We were born on the same day, and when we found out we said, We're twins! Both at the same time. Can you believe it?'

Silly old lady, I think, and I arrange my features appropriately.

The French windows are open, our small garden is looking quite tidy and even pretty, thanks to a few afternoons from a gardener, who has hacked off a lot of trailing stuff, and cut the grass until it has learned to behave itself. An afternoon at the garden centre with Mum's bank card has produced some pots of brightly coloured flowers and hanging baskets over the front door, ready to drop earwigs on anyone standing on the doorstep.

'I could cry,' says Ginny when she arrives and hugs Nell.

Nell in fact is crying, and then so is Ginny. Mum looks on, not taking part in this emotional stuff.

'It's been too long,' says Ginny, and Nell dabs her eyes and blows her nose and Mum says, 'For goodness' sake sit down, Ginny Swallow.'

Two thin ladies and one fat one sit inside, cups of tea and walking sticks within reach, talking as if it's their last chance, no settling in, no polite pleasantries with these three. One thin lady and two overweight ones sit outside, close enough to jump up if need be, far enough away to have our own conversation and leave them to theirs. The sun shines on the garden and on us.

Heather and Val have been introduced and are reserving judgement on each other, I can see that. Very different styles, Heather all floaty scarves and wooden beads, Val just back from Turkey, suntanned and flashing a reckless amount of chubby thigh.

'You've been invited to Brazil then?' says Heather to me.

'I'm going. It's booked. Mum's going into White Lodge while I'm away. We've been to look at it and it was very nice – as it ought to be for that price.'

'So she's all right with it?'

'On condition that it's not for ever, yes. She might even enjoy herself, though I wouldn't say that to her face.'

'Auntie Ginny's sorted,' says Val. 'She's done it all herself, phoned up different homes, called a taxi, been to look at them, made a decision. I offered to help, but she wouldn't have it, she likes to be independent. You've got to admire her.'

We pause, wondering, I guess, should we ask Heather about her plans for her mother. And decide not to ask, but anyway she answers.

'I'm hoping I can keep Mum at home for now,' she says. For now meaning till she dies, I suppose. 'She would go into a home if I asked her to, if it was for my sake, but I know she'd miss me. Besides which, of course, there's the question of the cost.'

'You feel needed,' I say. 'I just feel taken advantage of. And your mum loves you, you can tell just by being with both of you.'

'Your mum,' says Val, meaning mine, 'she's more out of the same box as mine was. Give you a clip round the ear sooner than a kiss or a hug. But I tell you what Carrie, I didn't really get on with my mum, but when she died I was miserable, and I still miss her. Amazing isn't it.'

'Hard to believe, honestly, that I'll miss mine,' I say, and Heather looks shocked, and slightly pitying. We are quiet, thinking I suppose about mothers, and being old, and getting old, and wondering who will look after us when we get to ninety. In the quiet I can hear the three old ladies.

'Well, Kath let it ruin her life,' I hear Mum say, and I know they are talking about Marcie. We three stay quiet, listening.

'I swear,' says Ginny's voice, 'this is the last time I'm ever going to mention her. I'm going to say my piece and then I'll have done, Sadie, if I ever start again, just remind me I said that.'

'Ha!' says Mum.

'I think,' says Nell, 'it was staying there, on the same street even, that made you unable to forget. Sadie and I, we moved away, and that helped us, we weren't reminded every day.'

'Well,' says Ginny, 'I don't know what Kath would have done if I hadn't stayed. And once she'd gone, it didn't seem worth moving. And I wasn't on the same street all the time. Some of the time, years sometimes, I was with Bernie in his house.'

'Not far away though,' says Nell. 'All the people around you as well, who knew all about it, still talking about it. Where I was no one had ever heard of it. Even Hamish didn't know about it.'

'And you never told him?'

'I did, once, a little. But he really wasn't interested.'

'I bet,' says Ginny, 'I bet Nell, you never mentioned about your mum.'

'What about her?' says my mum.

'My theory,' says Ginny, 'this is what I was going to tell you, I've got it straight in my mind and whether I'm right Nell, or whether I'm wrong, I shall go to my grave believing this, and I hope neither of you is going to be offended, Sadie, because if you are I shall just ask Val to take me home, but I'm going to get it off my chest, and see if I can breathe again.'

Val and Heather and I look at each other.

'Nobody interrupt me,' she says. 'You can have your say after.

'Now, Marcie was no better than she ought to be, as they used to say. Ain't that right? And so she goes and gets in the family way, but there's no one going to own up and say it was him and shall he marry her, because they all know that it could have been someone else. Could have been our Billy, could have been Gus, could have been Eric –'

'Couldn't have been Eric,' says Mum. 'I know for a fact it couldn't have been Eric.'

'I'm not saying it was, Sadie,' says Ginny, 'only, it could have been.'

'I know it for a fact,' says Mum. 'Eric couldn't, do you know what I mean. He might have wanted to, but he *couldn't*.'

Does she mean what I think she's trying to say? Eric was impotent? Really? It's like being on the scene of a car crash, slow motion, we three should do something to stop it, but we listen, fascinated, paralysed.

'Do you mean,' says Nell, kindly (but with an undertow of glee, I think), 'that he couldn't, *medically*?'

'That *is* what I mean,' says Mum, and there's a pause, I guess while they all put this new piece of information under their belts, and wonder where the story was up to.

'Right,' says Ginny, 'to continue. What can Marcie do when she's up the duff? That auntie of hers would kill her, or at least turn her out of the house, so she can't even tell her. She has to tell someone, so she tells your Dad, Sadie.'

Nell, I think it's Nell, makes a little sound, then says 'Wilf?' loudly.

'Why would she do that?' says Mum. 'What's my dad got to do with it?'

'Well, you know what he was like. He liked the girls, you must know that.'

Nell speaks. 'If we're going to let all the secrets out,' she says, 'I might as well tell you Sadie, your dad was what they would nowadays call an abuser. He used to chase me all round the house when Ivy was out. Gin will tell you, I had to go to her to find somewhere else to live, it was so bad.'

'How bad?'

'Now Sadie,' says Ginny, 'it wasn't as if he was a rapist –'

'He could have been,' says Nell. She's getting quite angry, I can hear it in her voice, wobbling. Heather's looking anxious. 'He *didn't* rape me, but he would have if I hadn't run away. He was capable of it, I know he was.'

A bit of my mind wonders what my face is doing. The rest of my mind is shouting, This is my grandad they are talking about. This is who they were talking about all those times I listened at the door after I was supposed to have gone to bed. The dirty old man was my grandad. I say nothing. Val looks as if it's no surprise to her, what they are saying. Heather looks embarrassed.

'Well,' says Ginny, trying to get her show back on the road. 'A girl who was in trouble, Wilf would be able to tell em what to do, having had experience, you might say, and what to do was to go and see Nell's Mum, because she knows what to do, and she can get rid of babies.'

'You never said that before,' says Mum. 'All the times you talked about it, you and me and Kath, you never brought Nell's Mum into it before. Why's that then?'

'Tell her, Ginny,' says Nell. 'Everyone else is getting their dirty washing hung out, it's only fair.'

'I was going to,' says Ginny. 'I got pregnant myself, see, and Nell's Mum sorted me out. But I never wanted to let Kath know, and I certainly wasn't going to let Bernie know, so I never said, not to anyone. But Nell, you knew of course.'

'Whose was it?' says Mum.

'Bernie's of course. But he'd gone back to Ireland, he didn't know, and he never got to know either.'

'You never even told him?'

'Not a word. And I'm glad I never told him. He would have been angry, and then he would have been sorry, and then he would have been angry again, and I don't know which would have been worse.'

'I never told Hamish what my mother did,' says Nell. 'He was a dear man, but he wouldn't have understood.'

'And I expect there were things you never told Jack,' says Ginny. 'Or Eric.

'So, Marcie gets rid of the baby, with help from Nell's mother. But something goes wrong. So just think, Sadie, think how awful that was for poor Marcie, bleeding to death, and couldn't tell anyone. Or maybe she did tell someone, like her auntie. Or maybe she struggled round to your mum, Nell, to ask what to do. Or maybe she just lay down in the ditch and died. That's what I think.'

'But,' says Nell. She sounds reluctant to spoil this murder story with no murder, but I imagine she doesn't want the blame to fall on her mother either. 'What I've often wondered – and I expect you have too – why wasn't Marcie's body found for all those months? You can't believe it was there all the time, right near the hedge, and the path just the other side. Someone would have seen something or –'

'Smelt something,' says Mum.

'Well that's true,' says Ginny. 'And don't think I haven't thought of it. I think her body must have been somewhere else. Maybe in an air raid shelter – remember, we didn't use them the last year or so of the war, the raids hardly happened did they – and then I think someone found her, what was left of her, poor thing, and didn't want her in their garden, in their shelter, and got someone to move her.'

In the garden, Heather, Val and I try not to imagine it, fail, and shudder.

'And what I think,' says Ginny, 'and you won't like this Sadie, but I've been putting two and two together for so long and this is what I think – do you remember when Kath and me were taking you home, when the baby started coming and we met your dad at the gate?'

'No,' says Mum.

'Well, I grant you, your mind was probably elsewhere, but I remember, and Kath always remembered this as well, that we met your dad and he was in a peculiar state, very funny indeed, not his usual self. It was like he had been drinking.'

'He didn't drink. Never drank.' says Mum, a bit huffy.

'I know. We thought it was funny at the time, but it was Boxing Day wasn't it, he could have had a tot somewhere, so we thought no more about it. But if he's just been asked to help move a body, well, he's going to be in a bit of a two and eight isn't he? A bit twitchy?'

'I don't know about that,' says Mum, and then, as a concession to Ginny. 'I must say, Gin, you've put a bit of thought into it, over the years. I wouldn't be surprised if you're right.'

'Poor Marcie,' says Nell.

'Not nice,' agrees Ginny, 'but better than being murdered don't you think?'

'I don't believe a word of it myself,' says Val in a whisper, and I have to say that I don't either.

'It's like that Jeremy Kyle,' I hear Mum say, and after a small pause, Ginny snaps, 'No it is not. It is nothing like that awful man, you will not say I am a bit like him, Sadie Singleton, or whatever your name is.'

I move a little, as if I might go into the room and break up the fight, or distract them, but Val shakes her head at me.

'Jeremy Kyle,' says Ginny, more calmly, 'is a parasite. This is different. We aren't going to blame anybody, or make anyone cry, or give them lie-detector tests. We are going to feel better after this, not worse.'

'You do watch it then,' says Mum.

Ginny goes on. 'Because we have to think of Marcie. Think what it was like, dying.'

'So young,' says Nell.

'And alone,' says Ginny. 'It might have been different, I've thought about this a lot, if we'd been different.'

'How do you mean?' says Mum. 'If you mean I should have been friends with her you've got another think coming. She bullied me.'

'Yes we know, we've heard all that. She pulled your hair. Why did she?'

'She was just like that. She had a nasty nature.'

'I bet people called her names didn't they. I bet people said things about her brother.'

'*I* don't know,' says Mum, huffy.

'Kath would have been friends with her you know, if it wasn't for you Sadie. Kath would talk to anyone, but you told her she couldn't be your friend if she talked to Marcie.'

'For goodness sake, if you're going to bring up things from when we were children –'

'Like pulling your hair at school? You started it Sadie.'

'This is silly,' says Mum. 'I don't know why we're talking about this. This is supposed to be Nell's birthday party.'

'And you said,' says Nell, 'that this wasn't about blaming anybody.'

They go quiet. Then Ginny says, 'Sorry. I get a bit carried away.'

'You always did,' says Mum.

'Do you know,' I say to Heather and Val,' I know it's a bit early in the day but I think it's time to open a bottle. Take their minds off it.'

'And ours,' says Val. She is nearly crying.

The old ladies are silent as I slide past them towards the kitchen.

We have a proper lunch, sitting round the table all six of us. I'm not much of a hostess these days, or cook, but I have made a real effort for this. Proper places, polished glasses, little posy of flowers in the middle, nice small bits of chicken in the casserole so not too chewy for their poor old teeth. They go quiet while eating, concentrating on being polite; even Mum seems suddenly socially awkward even though it's her house and her table we're all sitting at. But Heather and Val, now they have got used to each other, keep up the chat, about relatives and how many grandchildren everyone has (Nell is top of this league table, thanks to Duncan's serial marriages) and have begun on the hospital appointment sweepstake as I clear the plates and bring in Nell's birthday cake and a bottle of Prosecco. I haven't put candles on the cake – it seems tactless somehow – and I cut small pieces (to save some for

272

later) and put them on Mum's prettiest china. Val opens the bottle and decides that Prosecco is harmless in driving terms – 'No one ever got drunk on this.' – and pours some for everyone.

Ginny raises her glass. 'To absent friends.' And adds, 'Bernie especially.' He's been dead less than a year, I remember.

'And Kath,' says Mum.

Nell says, 'Hamish' and Heather says, 'Daddy' at the same time.

And the silence that falls is a busy one, full of people dead and gone, or just absent, and five out of the six of us get teary-eyed behind our vari-focals.

Late in the afternoon clouds darken and thicken. Heather and Val and I are still sitting in the garden, wondering about putting the kettle on for yet another round of tea when the first thunder starts. We go inside, disturbing the old ladies from their afternoon shut-eye, crowding the room, changing its atmosphere as we move chairs and handbags and step over feet. By the time I bring the tea in it is so dark that I have to switch a light on. Big drops of rain hit the window like drumbeats.

'Five o'clock,' says Ginny. 'I tell you what, Carrie, it's been a lovely day, and if you had a bottle of sherry about the place, that would just top it off nicely.'

'Auntie,' says Val, as if she's shocked, as you might be if a child asked for sweets or ice cream before being offered them. And I think of all the cherryade and custard creams that Ginny gave to me, and all the kindness and advice and rescue, and I think that a crateful of sherry would not be enough to repay her.

Nell and Heather pass on the sherry, but Val calculates that a small one won't hurt, and Mum and I join in too, no matter that it will cause her joints to flare up, and that I will fall asleep as soon as the guests have gone, fail to clear up, and be grumpy all tomorrow. The time is now, I think to myself.

'It's like this,' Nell is saying. 'The snowdrops come up and you just love to see them, and then they go over and the daffodils come out, all cheerful, and they go over, and the bluebells in the woods come out and go over, and so on all through the summer, flowers open and die, roses and daisies and whatever else and then the winter comes again and there's no flowers to be seen, and that's where we are, no flowers even to look forward to.'

'Just Christmas,' says Ginny. 'Just a bit of holly all stiff and prickly,' and she laughs, and so does Mum, and Nell looks out at the garden where the petunias in pots are being battered by rain, and the bushes are being tormented by wind.

'You have to look on the bright side,' says Mum. Little Mary Sunshine. I don't think.

'We didn't do so bad,' says Ginny.

'We got ourselves this far,' says Mum. 'That's something.'

'It's quite a lot,' says Ginny, 'when you think how poor we all started out.'

'Everyone is richer now,' says Nell. 'Look at us. We count as poor these days, but we have a nice little house, and enough food, and when you think where we used to live.'

'Well, we worked for it,' says Mum. 'Or if not, our husbands did. Bernie included,' she adds graciously to Ginny.

I look at Heather and Val. Are they listening? Are they wondering as I am, Have we done as much with our lives, in terms of added value? Oh I wish, I wish – where did it all go?

'Oh but girls,' says Sadie, my mum, 'do you remember that bike ride?'

The rain stops beating on the windows, the wind stops blowing, it's early summer, the three of them ride on bikes of gold, with strong legs and straight backs, squabbling and laughing and never tiring. And Kath is with them, loud and clumsy, singing, her clear voice floats back to them, and there they are on a wartime morning, with their own teeth and working eyesight, ready. Ready for all that love will do to them, and all that life will do, and death. Ready for making the choices that don't even seem like choices, that will turn their lives this way, or that, and ready to find themselves helpless in the face of choices made for them, by circumstances.

They ride without effort, goddesses, their legs pump them up hills, easily. They swoop down hills, Freya, Persephone, Brigit, Maia, scattering daisies and apple blossom and birdsong, careless and confident and looking straight and blind, with their young eyes, into the future, whatever the future holds for them, and even Marcie is still alive, even Gus, and tomorrow morning they will wake up and their knees will not ache and they will breathe without thinking, as if they will do it for ever, and their futures will unroll like the road, day by day by day, and even with all the days that pass, they won't forget this one. It will always be there, contained within their little lives, this feeling, this day.

ABOUT THE AUTHOR

Susan Day has been making up stories since before she could do joined up writing, but it took a while before she become brave enough to let other people read them. *The Roads They Travelled* is her second book.

Sue was brought up in Enfield, has lived in Colchester, Leicester and Paisley and settled in Sheffield. She has a husband, three children and a garden.

Also from Leaping Boy Publications

THE CHILD WHO FELL FROM THE SKY
Stephan Chadwick

Untold secrets of a post-war childhood.

A true story of a child born in war-torn London soon after the Second World War whose early memories are of the care and security given to him by his grandmother and a guardian angel who watches over him. At six he finds out a devastating secret that changes his life. He withdraws into his own world, searching for understanding and meaning. Isolated from his family and children of his own age he turns to his angel for love and guidance but even she cannot save him from what is to come.

'This is an extraordinary, raw, and powerful book.'
James Willis, *Friends in Low Places*

Books by Lucinda Neall

ABOUT OUR BOYS

A Practical Guide to Bringing the Best out in Boys

This book looks at what motivates and de-motivates boys and how to help them navigate the journey to manhood. Written at the request of parents and youth workers who had read Lucinda Neall's book for teachers, it is packed with practical examples from everyday life.

'A really accessible, practical and useful handbook.'
Sue Palmer, *Toxic Childhood*

HOW TO TALK TO TEENAGERS

If you have teenagers in your life – at home, at work, or in your neighbourhood – this book may stop you tearing your hair out! It will give you insights into how teenagers tick, and strategies to get their co-operation.

➢ Explains how teenagers see the world
➢ Packed with examples from day-to-to life
➢ Focuses on what to say to get them on board
➢ Includes 'maintaining boundaries' and 'avoiding conflict'
➢ Gives tips on how to stop the nagging and shouting
➢ Encourages adults to see the positive in teenagers
➢ Concise chapter summaries for easy reference

'Has captured the art of dealing with teenagers in a fantastic, easy to use guide.'
John Keyes, Social Inclusion Manager
Arsenal Football Club

Books by Helen MccGwire

The TOM AND JAKE Series

Six charmingly written and illustrated little books about Tom and Jake, two little boys who live with their family and animals in an old farm-house in Devon. The stories are based on the experiences of the author's five children during the 1960s, whilst living in the countryside.

Tom and Jake

More About Tom and Jake

Tom and Jake & The Bantams

Tom in the Woods

Tom and Jake & Emily

Tom and Jake & The Storm

Ideal for reading to children, and for revisiting a 1960s childhood.

www.leapingboy.com

Lightning Source UK Ltd.
Milton Keynes UK
UKOW03f0131140217
294342UK00002B/15/P